THE KILLING
OF
ANNA
KARENINA

Richard Freeborn

Dynasty
Press

Dynasty Press Ltd.
36 Ravensdon Street
London SE11 4AR
www.dynastypress.co.uk

First published by Dynasty Press Ltd.

ISBN: 978-0-956803-89-4

Text designed by Shore Books and Design
Blackborough End, Norfolk PE32 1SF

1

This was no Russian landscape.

This was England.

A blue-green stretch of river water. Slabs of sunlight. Butterflies like dry snowflakes blowing horizontally into his eyes.

And then his momentum increasing down the steep narrow lane.

He was going faster, faster.

Suddenly he saw something. In the corner of his eye.

He felt himself lifted into an exultant new dimension of speed that scattered blues and greens in all directions. The bicycle's front wheel spun upwards and hurled him violently forwards in a little earth-bound parabola – lightly, wantonly, effortlessly, in a beautiful moment of ecstasy, as only a Russian prince could experience it.

Then the ground punched him rudely in the mouth, split his lip and a pain shot up his left side. He slithered some way through thick grass on his left arm and came to rest on his back looking up at the curving branches of a willow.

At once he did what he had learned to do as a young officer in the last war against the Turks. He ran his uninjured right hand over the parts of his body he could reach in order to isolate the pain. His left arm was bleeding, of course, and his shirtsleeve was ripped. He tasted blood, his fingertips were wet with it, but the really sharp and scarcely endurable pain for the moment came from his left side where he had hit the ground hardest.

A cracked rib? He couldn't be sure.

He lay where he was and waited.

He waited for the new pain to subside or the pain of his old war wound to return as it often did, but it didn't, so he lay still for a few moments. Closing his eyes, it struck him as particularly odd that some kind of metallic insect was close by, until he realised it was his watch ticking in his waistcoat pocket. Relieved to find it undamaged, he pulled it out and snapped open the lid. Three-thirty.

Mid-afternoon. Right. He raised himself. The pain thrust him back instantly as if it had slapped him. For some moments he could scarcely breathe. Then he forced himself almost upright again onto his right elbow. He was lying beside a river. All he could see through a line of reeds were birds continually swooping over the water's surface and half-a-dozen cows standing in tree shade by the far bank.

Tranquil, English, poetic, rural. Wordsworth's "sylvan Wye" bathed in the heat of a summer afternoon. What an irony that he should have pedalled all day to reach it, only to fall off his Rudge Explorer at the last moment! But that was a fact: his bicycle lay on its side, bent and unusable, except that his leather-bound water bottle was still sticking out of the bag strapped to the luggage rack. It was close enough to be reached. He inched painfully towards it, unscrewed the cap and took several sips.

The liquid tasted delicious. Laced with a little brandy, the water had a reviving, uplifting freshness despite being lukewarm. He replaced the bottle and drew himself slowly back into the shade of the willow. At that point he must have fainted.

He only remembered sliding back against the trunk of the willow before everything changed, "melted into air, into thin air, and like the baseless fabric..." Of what? Of what sort of baseless fabric? Oh, he couldn't remember! Shakespeare again! He was continuously remembering lines from Shakespeare and then forgetting them! Instead, he was running towards the Turkish lines. To left and right of him, in slow-motion unreeling of a spool of memory, men one by one either fell slowly or slowly raised their arms in mortal agony, their cries as weird and shrill as the grimacing shadows through which he ran. Then as if floating, not flying, the butterfly bullets came at them from the Turkish redoubts with the very slow motion of snowflakes idling their way through clear summer air. Somewhere a scream broke through the rush of air and flashes of sunlight. He knew he had been hit. He awoke suddenly to an awareness of sweat pouring out of his hair and running into his eyes.

Insects buzzed, water rippled, leaves rustled. Less distinct, hardly audible, perhaps imagined, were voices or cattle lowing. Otherwise a universal hush seemed to engulf the whole of nature.

Then it was all destroyed like a stone thrown through a windowpane. The shrill noise of a train whistle suddenly cracked the silence to pieces.

What startled him about it was not so much the sound as the added awareness of being where he was and seeing for the first time the blood running down his left forearm.

He at once did what he should have done earlier. Tearing away the already torn shirtsleeve, he quickly devised a kind of tourniquet bandage by drawing the cloth tightly round the wound with the aid of his teeth. That effort as well as the sharp pain in his left ribcage convinced him he ought to stay where he was for the time being. He must give himself time to recover, he told himself. In any case, the low hanging willow branches provided shade and concealment while a gap in the nearby reeds gave a good view of the river.

He was content to fantasise that here, right in front of him, was the poetic essence he had been searching for, the essence, that is to say, of England at its most bucolic and beautiful. As for the train whistle, it was consoling to think that civilisation could only be a short distance away. His bicycle being broken, he would have to go back to London as soon as possible. In the meantime, he allowed himself the luxury of watching the vista of river water sparkle in the sunshine.

It was so long what he had wanted to experience, the ultimate insight into what English poetry celebrated, the true pantheistic meaning of Wordsworth's poem about Tintern Abbey and the "sylvan Wye". True, it *was* sylvan, tree-lined, that is to say, shady along its banks, sun-flecked in the un-shaded midstream and a metaphor for life itself in its slow, endless flow. Until, that is, a movement near the far bank attracted his attention. A white figure looking exactly like a ghost was standing in shallow water, its whiteness accentuated by the deep shade of the overhanging trees. To see a ghost on a hot summer afternoon was certainly surprising, but he was fond of reading English literature and there were all manner of ghosts scattered around English literature. He was quite content to believe he was seeing a ghost here on the banks of Wordsworth's "sylvan Wye".

Even English ghosts, though, were unlikely to wear full-length white cotton pants and a white shirt. Nor would they be launching a rowing boat. This was exactly what this ghost was doing.

Black-canopied, oar-less, the boat came slowly floating out of the jade depths of the trees. For a moment, startlingly, it seemed trapped like a fly in a magnifying glass in the full glare of sunshine falling on that area of open water.

At that very moment the train whistle sounded again. Simultaneously the prolonged wailing of its echo seemed to be interrupted by a gunshot. There was no doubt about the gunshot, nor about the sound of a locomotive going at full speed. The chatter of train wheels punched gradually decreasing holes in the stillness. By that time the white figure had come out into the sunlight. It seemed about to scramble aboard the boat when there was a sudden cry of agony more piercing than the train whistle. A certain amount of hopping about in the water followed.

He had been shot! The figure in white had been shot!

It was the only possible conclusion. A Russian prince, used to Turkish gunfire, could only assume that the practically simultaneous sound of a train whistle, a gunshot and a piercing scream was no coincidence. He naturally raised himself to see more, but all he could see was the boat floating out into the river's flow, still close to the far bank and apparently empty.

A boat launched without oars would most likely be empty, of course, especially if the likely occupant had just been shot. On the other hand, its black canopy seemed to match another blackness. There *was* someone lying in it. Someone dressed in black. He drew himself almost upright despite the pain.

Yes, peering above the reeds he saw quite clearly there was a figure dressed in black in the boat with a heavily veiled face propped up against a headboard. The sight was sombre and funereal in the brightness of the afternoon. The idea that it might be a corpse going downstream on a sort of waterborne catafalque was so appalling it came as a real relief to find the impression contradicted almost immediately. A modest fluttering of the tassels fringing the canopy seemed to be copied by a matching flicker in the blackness of the shaded interior. A hand emerged. Thin fingers stood out against the side of the boat.

This looked like an appeal for help, except that it soon turned into an elegant gesture. Something was thrown in a ritual fashion on to the river's surface. The prince saw it was a red rose. Gliding onwards, the black boat went gently downstream quite close to the far bank and the red rose floated behind it on the sunlit surface of the river water with the glistening brightness of a drop of fresh blood.

Suddenly, to the prince's astonishment, the figure in white reappeared, clearly dressed in long white pants and white shirt. He had evidently *not* been shot! He did not even seem to be seriously injured, because he was walking swiftly along the far bank beside the boat, evidently holding a rope or some kind of line to guide it. What is more, even more astonishing in the circumstances, the prince thought he heard words being called out he could understand – calls of encouragement, that is to say, instructions about what to do next. He could *understand* the words. They were in Russian, in a language a Russian prince would not have dreamed of hearing on the banks of Wordsworth's "sylvan Wye"! Amazed, he sank back into a sitting position against the trunk of the willow. Soon, though, all calls were out of earshot, just as the black boat was out of sight. The former quiet descended.

What had he just seen and heard?

Dreamy images floated in front of him with the coloration and inconsequence of butterflies passing in and out of beams of sunlight. Then English poetry came to his aid once more. He was reminded of Shakespeare. The stately progress of the boat downriver brought to mind the lines describing Cleopatra's barge –

"The barge she sat in, like a burnished throne,
Burned on the water" –

The boat he had seen had indeed seemed to burn blackly on the water! No funereal catafalque, he was sure of that now. His imagination had run away with him. No, it was a black boat burning on the water, in itself, of course, a source of awe and wonder, at which surrounding nature and the very air itself had gone to gape, as Shakespeare had described it so vividly, and made *"a gap in nature"*.

Yes, he had seen *"a gap in nature"*!

A return of the breathtaking ache in his left side brought him sharply back to reality. No, if he could glimpse that rose on the water once again, he would know he hadn't been dreaming. So he began climbing to his feet.

At that moment he heard a jingling noise close by. Something was approaching. He flopped back against the tree.

2

'Ah! I saw your legs sticking out. So you're hurt?'

A man was looking at him through the willow fronds. Moist hazel eyes blinked and sandy eyebrows were raised anxiously in pink, clean-shaven, chubby features. An open collarless shirt, baggy shorts, bare knees and thick stockings contrasted with a middle-aged, well-bred voice and a military style peaked cap worn straight across the forehead. Just behind him stood a pony and trap.

'Yes, I see what may have happened. You've hurt your mouth. And your arm. I say, I haven't, er, have I? I'm most terribly sorry if I've… you know… Have I?' The questioning could only produce a quandary of puzzlement and gratitude that was immediately succeeded by a change of tone when the speaker noticed the twisted bicycle frame. 'Ah, yes, of course, of course, a nasty accident! I see now – your bicycle! Too bad, too bad!' He seemed relieved to acknowledge that it was an accident. Simple understanding of the reason soon followed. 'You're a stranger to these parts, I imagine. You didn't know how steep that lane was? I'm right, aren't I?'

'Yes, I fell.'

'Oh, dear! Oh, dear! Are you, er?' The bloodstained makeshift bandage was referred to. 'Nothing untoward, I hope?'

'Pardon?'

'Badly hurt or broken, I mean?'

'I don't think so. A bad, er... my rib, I think... I'll be all right... in one moment.'

'I thought it might have been... something worse. You may have heard a gunshot?'

'Oh, I did, yes!'

The hazel eyes gave one frowning glance and then blinked hastily in what appeared to be embarrassment at not observing the proper etiquette, gunshot or no gunshot.

'Let me introduce myself. My name's Holmcroft, Oswald Holmcroft. Glad to meet you.'

A hand was offered out of politeness. A Russian prince would probably have disdained it in other circumstances. Now, though, it was a welcome aid in the effort of standing upright. What Oswald Holmcroft saw as he helped the stranger to his feet were deep-blue eyes, dark hair clinging in strands to damp temples, a straight nose in a handsome, manly face notable for long, pallid cheeks either side of a firm, frankly arrogant mouth.

'I can see you're...'

There was a pause as he probably noticed that the torn shirtsleeve used as a tourniquet and bandage served merely to enhance the irreproachable upper-class good taste of white linen waistcoat and linen trousers of a quality entirely suited to the owner of a Rudge Explorer. Oswald Holmcroft went on briskly: 'Yes, well, I can see your poor bicycle is, well, yes... I ought to explain I was shooting rabbits, you see. There are a couple there.' He made a swift gesture towards the trap and then, to prove his readiness to be a Good Samaritan, added: 'You'll need medical help. Can you, er, get up there, do you think?'

He indicated the fairly high step needed to get into the trap. To his surprise, he received a quite different response.

'Did you see it?'

'What?'

'I saw a boat... a black boat... Did you see it?'

'A black boat? No. I can't say I did.' Quite justifiably the subject was changed. 'I can see you've had a shock. Coming down that lane, so overgrown now. It used to be the way down to the old ford, you know. Here, let me help you up into my trap. Do you think you can manage it?' The wilful overplaying of the Good Samaritan role seemed deliberately evasive. 'There's a good chap, let me...'

The offer was waved aside. Natural arrogance led to a clenching of princely teeth and a determination to climb into the trap unaided. A handhold was reached. At the same time contact was made with the barrel of a sporting rifle. The metal was still suspiciously warm, either from the sun's heat or recent use. A couple of dead rabbits lay beside it. Also on the floor of the trap was a long hooked object resembling a Bishop's crozier. This had to be stepped over, causing the trap to jerk forward. The pony swished its tail somewhat indignantly.

Both movements, especially the swishing of the tail, occurred virtually simultaneously and were more likely the result of Oswald Holmcroft lifting the twisted Rudge Explorer into a sort of luggage net attached to the back of the trap. He almost immediately sprang up into the trap and seated himself beside the prince. As he seized the reins, he asked blithely what the initials stood for – *D R?*

The initials *D R* stamped on the leather bag strapped to the bicycle's luggage rack had been noticed, the prince realised. Shame, not to say sheer reticence, always made him reluctant to reveal his full name for the simple reason that it naturally invited a title and the title could hardly pass as normal in any but the most sophisticated of English venues.

'So sorry. Forgetting my manners...' The *D*, he admitted, stood for Dmitry.

'Perhaps it would be a good thing if we introduced each other formally,' said Oswald Holmcroft. 'As I've told you, my name's Oswald. Good to meet you, Dmitry.' He held out his hand for a handshake and they shook hands. 'My old trap won't jar you, I hope. It's got nice soft springs. Off we go!' A light smack from the reins set them in motion to a jingling of harness bells. 'And the "R"?'

'Ros-tov. Prince Dmitry Nikolaevich Ros-tov. The last syllable is accented.'

'Good heavens!'

The surprise on hearing the name was so great the trap almost jerked to a halt. Oswald Holmcroft instantly apologised for distressing his companion but then quickly set the pony going again at a gentle walk.

'*Prince Rostov*! What a very extraordinary thing!'

'Why?'

'Well, *Prince Rostov*, I suppose you must be here for our soiree?'

Our soiree? What on earth could that mean? The prince was used to sudden deference and indeed perhaps momentary confusion when people heard the title. Talk of a soiree was completely unexpected. He explained he had been on a bicycling holiday for the past week because his wife had had to return to Russia to look after a sick mother.

'I was at a loose end' (he emphasised the phrase in demonstration of the kind of apologetic, throwaway ease that he felt a true freeborn Englishman would make in explaining what he was doing there) 'at a loose end, you see, I decided I would enjoy a holiday looking for...' He licked his lips, tasted blood and added a little awkwardly that he was a great admirer of English poetry, feeling that his companion was unlikely to share his enthusiasm and might even regard it as eccentric. 'Wordsworth, for example,' he explained. 'I was looking for Tintern... for his "sylvan Wye".'

'Well, it's here! Right beside us! A bicycling tour! Well, well.' Oswald Holmcroft was now quite practical. 'Tell you what, I'll take you off to see our new quack. This isn't too jarring, I hope?'

'Tishe iedesh, tishe budesh!' the prince murmured to himself, glad that the riverside track, largely overgrown with thick grass, offered a gentle, hissing bed for the wheels to pass through and did not jerk him about too much. He held his left forearm cradled across his chest, breathing in softly through lightly clenched teeth.

'I shouldn't really call him a quack, he's too young,' Oswald Holmcroft said. 'But I'm sure he can patch you up.' An uneasy pause followed. He added, as if speaking to the back of the pony: 'I thought I detected an accent. There's a compatriot of yours here, by the way. You *are* Russian, I suppose?'

'I am. Who is... this, er... compatriot?'

'We know him as "Crow", Mr Kingston. I've never discovered his real name. You see, we have a little community here. Or we like to think it's a community. Half a dozen of us, followers of your great writer Leo Tolstoy. We try to live according to the principles of Tolstoyanism. So we have needed someone to sort of initiate us and keep us informed, and Crow does just that. He translates. He also does some composing. But your name – Rostov – it made me wonder if you were related?'

'Related?'

'Not to old Crow, I mean. No, no. To your great Count Leo. You're a prince, he's a count. I know it may seem a long shot and I'm no respecter of titles myself, but it just seemed to me...'

The prince interrupted him to say he was not directly related. 'My grandfather was Prince Nikolay and my father was named after him.'

'Ah, yes, of course. No, it seemed to me so appropriate – you being here, a Russian prince, I mean, just when we're having our soiree.'

At first it was one of those remarks spoken in an effort to appear affable but of no real consequence. On second thoughts, the prince realised how much in the way of inner speculation it could conceal. At the time he was naturally more concerned about the jabbing pain of his injury, although fully alerted to the strange little awkwardnesses and diffidences, the shadings, as it were, in Oswald Holmcroft's manner. He reckoned he was a pleasant enough man in a stolid English way, but his insistence on prolonging his boyhood by sporting schoolboy bare knees, short trousers and so on suggested immaturity. His boots, for example, were especially odd. A real schoolboy would probably have spurned them. There was also the discrepancy of professing such a pacifist creed as

Tolstoyanism while having a gun and shooting rabbits – *if*, of course, that was all the gun had been used for.

He heard a distant rumbling. 'What was that?' he suddenly cried.

The sound so upset him he was shaken by a fit of shivering. His teeth started chattering uncontrollably.

Without a word, a kind of waterproof cape was fished out from beneath the seat. Oswald Holmcroft had obviously expected a storm.

'Very likely thunder,' he said. The gesture of handing the cape was so considerate the prince could barely thank him through the rat-tat-tat of his teeth.

'Delayed sh-sh-shock,' he explained. He tried to say that something similar had happened when he had been badly wounded in the Turkish war. The thunder had sounded like artillery.

'Think nothing of it,' his companion said.

Huddled under the cape, the prince now clenched his teeth even tighter to suppress the shivers and hide them. He forced himself to pay close attention to the slowly passing scenery.

It surprised him how everything had changed. No black boat to be seen, no red rose on the water, no cows in the shade. The far riverbank had become steep and thickly wooded. Deep shade at the water's edge and what appeared to be inlets were almost like inverted reflections of tall turrets rising above the treetops at the summit. Oswald Holmcroft again came to his aid.

'See up there, above the trees. It's the Irminghams' place. Lord and Lady Irmingham. Stadleigh Court.'

Irmingham? The name rang no bells, except that Stadleigh was recognisable and had the strange effect of dispelling his shivers. He remembered seeing the name on the map and asked whether it was connected with a railway.

'Quite right. Yes, absolutely correct. We do have a railway nearby. Stadleigh Halt is about a mile downriver. The railway comes down from Ross-on-Wye. It's not for you, if I may say so. You'll need to rest up a bit before going anywhere by train.'

The last remark was true even if it sounded like a rebuke. The prince's native pride was threatened by what it implied. He murmured quietly that he never liked giving in to anything. Especially not to pain.

'No one likes giving in to pain, prince, that is absolutely correct,' said Oswald Holmcroft. 'But sometimes you have to, you know. It can get too much.'

This left the prince puzzled.

'It can go on and on,' the other added.

'Oh, of course.'

'For generations. I mean it – for generations.' The reins were flicked gently and the pony responded with a modest increase in pace.

The prince said nothing.

'There comes a time when the sense of loss becomes as malignant as a disease, I can tell you. I know a bit about illness and injury. When I realised you were having an attack of the shivers, I knew exactly how you felt. There's not a lot you can do about a cracked rib. Bind it up and hope for the pain to go away is the usual treatment. And plenty of rest.'

The trap bowled along.

'I get attacks like that. They don't last long. Some rest, some tea and having our young doctor look at you, that'll do the trick. I shall be glad of some tea myself. If we get thunder, there'll be rain. I think I can smell it in the air.'

They went past a wooden bridge wide enough for a horse but hardly for a vehicle.

'That's our footbridge to the Court,' it was explained in an offhand way. 'Everything follows the river here – the railway, the lane…and of course the river also dictates who owns what.'

The prince was about to ask more about who owned what when their route suddenly wound away from the river between low hedges and turned abruptly into what appeared to be a group of houses, farm buildings and a small stone church with a short spire. All surprise, let alone inquiries, vanished the moment the other remarked: 'You speak very good English, prince, if I may be permitted to say so.'

'Thank you. I was partly educated here. Oxford. I am perhaps more English than the English. After twenty years I think I can claim…'

He acknowledged to himself instantly what nonsense this was. The idea of being more English than the English was so preposterous it made him blush with shame. Oswald Holmcroft leaned close and asked *sotto voce*: 'Better? The shivers?'

'Yes... yes.'

Then still *sotto voce*: 'All this used to belong to us, I have to tell you. Irmingham, the present owner's father, bought the Court from my father. We, the Holmcrofts, are more native to Stadleigh Court than its present occupants.'

It was as if the prince's claim to be more English than the English had simply been parried in the way it deserved. In short, Oswald Holmcroft was asserting a prior right to both his Englishness and this domain, without a trace of envy. He drew the trap calmly to a halt as he spoke and sprang down to the ground, all his resonant manner once more restored.

'Here we are! Oh, by the way, there's something you should know. Lady Helen Swanning is sure to want to meet you. Shall I introduce you as a prince?'

'Thank you, no.' The prince told him that Dmitry Rostov would do. After two decades spent in England it still amused him to note the sorts of uneasy protocol caused by the title.

'Oh, come, I mean...'

They had stopped in front of the only thatched cottage in a line of small, tight-packed two-storey brick houses. Fronted though they were by small gardens and hedges, these brick houses appeared wilfully untidy, with peeling paintwork, missing roof tiles and neglected guttering. They seemed implanted here, like alien growths in the rural scene. The prince could not help feeling that they represented their own kind of "gap in nature". But the idea took an instant pratfall the moment Oswald Holcroft helped him to the ground.

'Oh!' he found himself exclaiming.

Bloodstained and unkempt as he was, he was caught completely off-guard by the young woman he saw standing in front of him. She looked impossibly exotic in such surroundings, so striking was her Italianate beauty, and far too young, far too young, for someone called Lady Helen Swanning, who should have been much older, the prince felt, and far less beautiful! Against a background of such conventional decorative features as a pergola, hollyhocks, roses and an apple tree, she struck him as having a startling and wildly improbable resemblance to Rosetti's *Monna Vanna*. Her abundant copper-red hair and beautiful features made luminous by the shade of a wide-brimmed straw hat, especially as the pergola had the effect of a frame, seemed to give her the appearance of gazing from a pre-Raphaelite portrait. Her eyes were a deep blue, though the shadow of the brim darkened them slightly, but their crystal whites shone brightly in the warmth of a welcoming smile that lit up her entire face. However statuesque she might appear standing on the brick pathway in a simple blue dress without any ornament, she seemed quite self-confidently ready to downplay her youth and beauty in the interests of hospitality.

'Lady Helen, may I introduce a visitor and new patient for our doctor, a Prince Dmitry...'

'Rostov. Dmitry Rostov,' the prince managed to stammer, trying painfully to bow.

'*Prince* Dmitry Rostov.'

Oswald Holmcroft sneaked in the title almost triumphantly and then, as if it qualified him to speak on the prince's behalf, explained briefly that he had been on a bicycling holiday and had 'come a cropper' down by the old ford.

'Oh, good heavens, that's such an out-of-the-way place now! I haven't been there for ages! So nice to meet you, prince. I can see you're in need of our doctor.'

She immediately turned towards the house and called out the name 'James!' in a ringing voice. When she then asked in the same tone of voice if he'd rather wait for the doctor or follow her to the house, he was so overwhelmed that the shivering resumed slightly – more in awe and excitement than in anything like pain. He knew how easily he could be affected by the touch of a woman's hand on his arm in a dance, for instance, and her hand was already on his arm. She continued smiling, literally as if she had expected that reaction, and began leading him carefully up the garden path.

'My dear prince, it is such a privilege! We are delighted to help! Dear Oswald may have told you...'

But whatever he may have told him remained unsaid because at that moment she changed her mind and once more called out the name James.

'James!' she repeated, 'James!'

He apologised for being a nuisance.

'Oh, what nonsense! You're nothing of the kind. We'll be delighted if you can stay for our soiree. Dear Oswald may have told you about it.'

3

They went up the garden path and entered the narrow hallway of her cottage. A tall young man in shirtsleeves dashed out of a side room. He tripped over several pairs of boots lined up by the skirting, apologised and immediately tried putting them back in place.

'Dear, dear James, please! Our Dr Parkinson,' said Lady Helen rather airily, as if she were talking about a clumsy dog, 'so keen. But a tremendous asset to us. I'm sure he'll be able to help. His consulting-room is just there.'

Propelled forward and given the description of a Russian prince, the new arrival could do no more than let himself be offered up as a new exhibit. The bloodstained bandage proved as scarlet as the young doctor's scarlet cheeks. He glanced at the injuries and waved him into the room from which he had just rushed. Lady Helen said she was sure everything would be all right.

'Such a shock, a bicycling accident,' she added on parting. 'James'll look after you.'

The door to the consulting-room was closed. James himself immediately started apologising: '*So* clumsy of me! She called, you see, and...'

'I know what you mean.' The prince finished the sentence for him. 'Lady Helen is a woman of commanding beauty.'

'Commanding,' he agreed. Brief glances of conspiratorial

understanding were exchanged. 'She does love to keep all those boots there for patients. They're for when the weather's bad. Good works, that sort of thing.'

The prince could guess what he meant, even if it sounded odd. The doctor's tone then changed as he ordered his new patient to sit down: 'Willya nae tell me what caused this.'

A straight-backed wooden chair was pushed forward as he spoke. The sharp gesture was sudden and somewhat awkward as if matching the plainly false Scottish accent. The prince did not question the reason for what seemed at best a professional mannerism rather similar to Lady Helen's remarkable, if showy, Monna Vanna beauty. He concentrated on sitting down and described as best he could what had happened.

'So it's anoother accident due to bye-cycling, is it? An' a sad sight y'are, if I may say. So I'll need to make a wee preparation. Just bide your time a wee while.'

A busy, taciturn washing followed, evidently designed to impress. It no doubt drew attention away from the consulting-room's contents – or the lack of them. The prince let his eye roam over a table, an old microscope, a shelf of medical texts and a few bottles containing variously tinted liquids, but could hardly fail to notice a large unframed wall chart of the human anatomy depicting the skeleton and various body parts picked out in lurid blues, yellows and reds. No doubt it frightened the life out of impressionable villagers.

Averting his eyes from its alarming presence, he glanced towards the window and through net curtains saw Oliver Holmcroft busy at that moment collecting the broken bicycle from the back of the trap. As for Dr James Parkinson, with his back bent over his ablutions, he appeared slender and boyish in his shirtsleeves with his curly fair hair rising above the collar at the nape of his neck.

'So I must ask you, sir, if you'll allow me to remove your waistcoat and shirt,' he said, drying his hands with a towel.

These items were removed and the examination began. It was done efficiently, with a firm and gentle touch. The difference between this treatment and the harsh treatment the prince had received at the field-station after being wounded in the war against the Turks was striking. It may have occurred two decades previously but he had been reminded of it by the accident. He complimented the young doctor on being so considerate and the latter gave him a querying look.

'So you're also one of 'em, sir?'

'One of 'em?'

'I think they're called Russophiles.' The Scottish accent was a little less noticeable and a faint sparkle could be discerned in the doctor's eyes. 'They're all over the place here.'

The prince was utterly bewildered and said so. The doctor reverted to broad Scots: 'Weel, all I can tellya is ye fell off your bye-cycle, did all this hurt to your poor arm, but nae a fracture, which is a blessing, an' I've washed and dressed the wound as best I can, but it's your rib-cage, tha's wheer I'm not sure. You've maybe cracked your rib an' maybe it's just a nastie bruise, d'ya ken what I mean? So I'll gie ye a wee length o' bandage and bind it up. Mind, it'll hurt, but it'll be for the best.'

'I assume,' said the prince as the doctor paused, 'you're from Scotland, from Edinburgh perhaps...'

Whether this was a query or an observation became irrelevant when there was a tap on the door and a young maidservant came in carrying the prince's suitcase.

'Oh, yes, thank you, Jane.' She was directed to open it and extract a fresh shirt. A playful smile stretched the doctor's lips. The fresh shirt was extracted, Jane left the room and the bandaging proceeded. 'I always put on a Scottish accent,' Dr James Parkinson announced casually. 'People down here in the south don't believe you're a doctor unless you have a Scottish accent. I was trained at Birmingham, you see. If you say you qualified at Birmingham people wonder why you weren't good enough to qualify at Cambridge. You are not a native Sassenach, sir, are you?'

The prince would never have dreamed of assuming a foreign accent. His whole aim over the last twenty years had been to be more English than the English. He compromised by saying somewhat neutrally: 'I confess I have an accent. I am not native. I am Russian.'

'For the soiree?'

'No. What is this soiree?'

'I am not entirely sure what it is. I'm too new here, you see. But if anyone turns up, it is assumed it is for the soiree. That's all I can tell you. Being Russian yourself, sir, and what they call a Russophile – well, sir, I imagine you're a Russophile, being Russian...' a princely nod greeted the logic '...you'll most likely want to stay for the soiree. In any case, as your doctor, I am giving you medical orders to rest for at least three days and the soiree is in three days' time. Does that satisfy you, sir?' A despairing gesture followed. He stood up and began tidying away his things. 'Mind you, if it satisfies you, it certainly doesn't satisfy me. I mean, look at what I'm expected to work with. No proper equipment, shortages of materials. That bandage was the last one I had.'

The prince said he would gladly pay for it, of course, just as he would pay for the treatment. The bandage was painfully tight and he would be happy for the doctor to remove it. The offer was ignored. Instead there was a lot of busy activity over emptying the bowl that had been used for washing and replacing iodine bottles in a cabinet that was then carefully locked.

'Beggars cannot be choosers,' was Dr James Parkinson's eventual response as he looped a sling round the prince's neck to support the left arm. 'You may pay me, sir, if you wish. Personally, I would prefer it if all medical help were free.'

'Free! Surely, if you have to buy bandages and I can afford to pay, then I should.' The prince's free right hand slammed down two sovereigns on the table.

'If you can pay, well and good. But I have a mission. I want to work in the tropics, possibly Africa or South America.'

He had been persuaded, he said, to come to this remote spot in Herefordshire by one of his teachers who knew Lord Irmingham. It would be good training for him and he could earn a little money to fund his missionary plans. He explained what he meant as he helped his patient on with the clean shirt and the linen waistcoat.

'The whole idea...' he shook his head over what he was saying '...the whole idea of a community has come from Lord Irmingham. I admire the spirit of charitable self-help, co-operation, friendship and so on. It's what I should like to help create somewhere in the tropics. Mind you, it's far too paternalistic! And there's no need for excess, sir! I am not going to be impressed by your filthy lucre!' He picked up the coins, clinked them together and then thrust one of them back at the prince. 'It's the parasites at the Court, they're the problem.'

'Parasites?'

'Ay, parasites!' The remaining coin was spun up in the air and then pocketed. His light-brown eyes subjected the prince to a long, unblinking, serious inspection. 'The Irminghams, sir, bought this estate about forty years ago, so I'm told. They pulled down the original manor house on the other side of the river and built Stadleigh Court. Import of Russian timber, export of steel pins, that's how they made their money.'

The prince acknowledged he knew a little about the import of timber but nothing about steel pins.

'Well, then, you'll see how the Russian connection started. Lord Irmingham is an idealist. He has read the things your writer Tolstoy teaches – you know, non-opposition to evil by violence, vegetarianism, making your own clothes and so on – and he believes it all. He's convinced everyone should do the same. So he entertains people who are likely to be persuaded – which is the object of the soiree, as I understand it. Of course, it's all very fine if you can afford it, if you're a Rothschild or a Carnegie, but Lord Irmingham's no Carnegie and he can't afford it. At least that's how I see it. I haven't been here long enough to find out more. What I do know is he's got two children, his son Gerald and the other is the Lady Helen you've just met.'

The mention of Lady Helen made him blink rapidly and glance out of the window.

'She lives here, does she?' the prince asked.

'Oh, yes, this is her house. It's a lot bigger than it looks. It was her idea that I should have a consulting-room here. The old doctor had one near the church. Where I lodge.'

'She's an extraordinarily beautiful woman, isn't she?'

Enough confidence had been established between the two men for Lady Helen Swanning's beauty to be appreciated without the prince fearing he might encroach on the young doctor's feelings.

'Oh, aye, I'm not calling her a parasite,' was the immediate whispered answer. 'It's true, she *is* beautiful. And she takes it all very seriously. She is commanding, as you said. Are you feeling comfortable now, sir?'

'Yes, yes. What does she take very seriously?'

'The Tolstoy thing, sir.' He said she was learning Russian under the guidance of Mr Kingston. 'A serious-minded, very beautiful woman, that's who Lady Helen is.' Whatever the young Dr James Parkinson's feelings were, he successfully concealed them at that moment under a professional manner stripped of its Scots accent. 'I must advise rest, sir. For at least a few days. As for where you can stay... Ah, Jane, what is it?"

The maidservant had reappeared. She announced, standing in the doorway in a black frock with a white apron, her hands to her sides and the chin of her small oval face pointed tentatively towards them, that tea was ready in the sitting room and her mistress hoped to see them.

'Are you up to it?' the young doctor asked. His one raised eyebrow seemed to refer as much to the emotional challenge of the occasion as to the physical effort required for it. The prince nodded. Jane led the way into the sitting room.

It was a spacious room for such a cottage and obviously part of an extension to the original structure. Armchairs and a sofa in flower-printed covers were the main furnishings distributed on a red-patterned Indian carpet. A fan-shaped brass screen stood in the fireplace and harness brasses gleamed on the wooden mantelpiece. The fragrance of red and yellow roses in vases competed with a lingering smell of wood ash.

'Repaired?' asked Oswald Holmcroft, rising from the sofa where he had been sitting beside Lady Helen. 'How are you feeling, prince?'

'Much better, thank you. I am very grateful to Dr Parkinson.'

Lady Helen had tea things and a silver teapot on a little table in front of her. She at once gave orders for everyone to be seated. Oswald Holmcroft for some reason took this to mean a seat by the fireplace, some distance away from the sofa. The doctor and the prince were directed to sit in armchairs immediately facing the little table.

'Tea with milk, prince, or would you prefer it with lemon and sugar in your Russian manner? We have both, so it's no trouble.' Lady Helen instructed Jane to hand round a plate of cucumber sandwiches and some cake. 'My, isn't it growing dark!'

The dramatic darkening of the room in the last few moments was followed by the loud noise of heavy raindrops audible through the open window. Then came a clap of thunder. The window was drawn shut at once, which had the effect of creating a momentary awkward silence filled with the sound of tea being poured out and tongs used to place sugar lumps in a teacup and a glass topped with slices of lemon.

'There,' said Lady Helen.

Twenty-four, the prince thought, watching her. Such Monna Vanna beauty, dramatised by the sudden darkening, could not make her any older. He could not escape the sense that she ought to be presiding over a solemn society tea party of well-dressed London ladies rather than meting out sugar lumps and lemon slices here in Herefordshire.

'Prince,' she said, 'I think you are going to have to stay here, aren't you? I mean, you can hardly travel with such injuries. And it looks as if we're in for a storm. Where do you live?'

He said he lived in London. A house in Portland Place.

'Then it's out of the question. You cannot possibly go to London tonight. I think James will agree.'

The doctor agreed.

'Right, then that's settled. We have a spare bedroom and blankets and pillows. Or if you'd prefer, there is the inn, but it would mean going out again and with your injuries...'

'No, no.' The spare bedroom would be perfect, he assured her and added that he was very grateful.

'In any case, prince, you will need time to recover from the shock of your accident. And of course something will have to be done with your bicycle. Oswald, do you think the forge could do something?'

Oswald was certain the local forge could mend the frame.

'So, you see, it's much better if you stay here.' She raised her teacup and drank while the prince swallowed a mouthful of hot sweet lemon tea. Putting down her teacup in its saucer with a faint bell-like chime of bone china against bone china, she went on: 'It's really very fortunate you've arrived like this. You see, you're in time for the soiree.'

'Please tell me what this soiree is.'

'Oswald's told you, hasn't he, about our little social experiment here? We're trying to have a little community. We do so admire your great writer Count Tolstoy. But our community's not yet properly Tolstoyan, so I won't call it that. It's father's idea, but a compatriot of yours, Mr Kingston, is the keenest of all and it's such a pity he is not here to meet you. He has had to go over to the Court. We try to be as self-sufficient as we can. I made this dress of mine, for instance. Oswald's had a shot at making his boots.' The boots, hardly elegant, protruded rather like outsize leather slippers from the ends of Oswald's large stocking-clad legs. He grinned at his own handiwork. 'And we make our own bread, our own soap, our own ink, oh, a host of things! It's rather fun really. But of course we *do* have to buy lots of things from outside. So it's really just a game we're playing. Is the tea sweet enough for you? That's something we have to get from outside, you see. Oh, and I should add that we're very keen to have people from outside as well – visitors, you know. My father runs social occasions over at the Court. He likes to convert his guests to his way of thinking. Yes, dear, what do you want?'

She had spoken easily, rarely blinking her magnificent dark-blue eyes and hardly reinforcing her words with any gestures, but at that instant Jane suddenly re-entered the room almost at a run. Looking flustered, she announced that the doctor was needed urgently at the Court.

'Oh, dear, oh, dear!' cried Lady Helen. 'But in such rain it seems such a pity!'

Dr Parkinson's own reaction was a robust shrug of the shoulders and a quick downing of his cup of tea. He offered his apologies and quickly left the room. A carriage had arrived from the Court, it seemed, so he would be in the dry for the journey. Meanwhile, the rain sounded as loud as a sea at high tide. Munching a sandwich, the prince looked through the window at a back garden of shrubbery, damp lawn and distant glistening greenhouse.

Once the doctor had left the atmosphere changed. Lady Helen became quite intimate.

'Prince,' she said, 'Oswald tells me you are Prince Nikolay's grandson.'

'I am.'

'You see, the Tolstoyan connection is very intriguing to us. Are you closely related, if I may ask? I know it may seem that I am prying, but I have a reason for asking.'

The prince instantly tried to satisfy her. No, he was not, strictly speaking, related to Count Leo Tolstoy but knew him, of course, and the family at Yasnaya Polyana. They were all kindred, so to speak.

'What about the Karenins?' she suddenly asked.

The question was so unexpected he could scarcely believe it was being asked in all seriousness. He tested the question's possible intent by asking who she meant.

'Do you mean Anna Arkadyevna?'

'Well, no, prince, I really didn't mean to...' Her reaction was puzzling. It was as if she had been taken by surprise and appeared ready to change the subject. 'You see, I said just now how fortunate it is that you're here at this particular moment. There is the soiree, of course, but I was thinking about another possibility.'

She exchanged glances with Oswald Holmcroft. He did not seem to reciprocate and merely clasped his hands together.

'No, well, perhaps we can talk about that a little later,' she said. 'More tea?'

The prince thanked her and politely refused. He could tell that something was being deliberately hidden from him, so he took the opportunity to ask whether there was any explanation for what he had seen that afternoon.

'A black boat? A black figure inside it?' Lady Helen glanced again at Oswald Holmcroft. 'And you say a red rose... That's quite odd.'

As a matter of fact, it didn't sound at all odd. He was about to apologise for mentioning it when Oswald Holmcroft intervened with an even odder sort of contradiction: 'Yes, well, in a way, I suppose, it was...' His large hands were unclasped and slapped down on his bare knees '...it was, er, connected.'

'Connected?'

'With what we've just been talking about, Lady Helen. What the prince saw was probably connected with the, er... with what we've just been talking about.'

These hesitancies annoyed the prince. He said he thought he saw someone being shot but he did not mention that he had seen the same figure shortly afterwards walking along the riverbank and speaking words he could understand. The looks on his listeners' faces showed obvious disbelief.

'Oh, but not being shot!' said Lady Helen. 'Oswald, didn't you say...'

'Yes, I'd been shooting rabbits. I was very careful to...' At which point he may have remembered how he had reacted to the sight of the prince's wound, for he quickly added: 'I kept everything under control, I can assure you, Lady Helen.' It was hard to tell in the dusk whether he was embarrassed or not. 'The boat you saw, prince, very likely belonged to the Court. The behaviour of people from the Court can be very strange.'

'And of course if, *if* somebody has been shot by accident, that would explain why James has had to go over there so urgently,' was what Lady Helen supposed, but Oswald Holmcroft poured cold water on this possibility: 'I doubt very much whether anyone has been shot, I really do, Lady Helen.'

She let silence diminish any shade of rebuke in this remark before raising her chin and saying: 'Did you know, Prince, that Oswald is our local historian? He is also well-known for his work on Cromwell.'

'Forgive me, no.'

'Oh, yes. His work on Cromwell is in all the libraries.'

'Then in that case I will have to...'

'I doubt very much,' Oswald Holmcroft interrupted, 'whether you actually saw anyone being shot.'

The prince did not feel it right to contradict this and smiled faintly. There was a pause. All three suddenly realised the rain had stopped.

'Good heavens, it's time I was going,' said Oswald Holmcroft.

He made his farewells at this point rather too promptly, saying he was so grateful for the cup of tea and what a pleasure it had been to meet the prince.

'He lives with his mother,' Lady Helen explained when he had left. 'And she always gets worried if he's late. He's a dear person. You must read his book on Cromwell. I can lend you a copy, if you like.'

He thanked her and said he would like that very much. The prince could not help feeling that among the secrets being kept from him the hardest to fathom was exactly what the boyish historian of Cromwell felt towards Lady Helen. He could hardly have felt nothing at all. She was far too intelligent and commanding to be ignored and far too beautiful, surely, for mere friendship; but as soon as they were alone he realised she was more truly feminine and domestic than she had seemed at first. She noticed him smother a yawn.

'Oh, prince, you must be tired. I shouldn't go on chattering like this. Just wait and I'll...'

Her immediate concern was to ensure the spare bedroom was comfortable. She attended to this in person with Jane's help. After a brief interval, the prince was summoned to follow her upstairs and was grateful to find myself shown into a low ceiling-ed bedroom containing a high metal bed with brass knobs at each corner. He had to admit he was feeling extremely tired. Cucumber sandwiches, cake and sweet tea had been most satisfying, but he had to prevail on her hospitality for one further favour – a sheet of paper, if she would be good enough to let him have one.

'Paper, prince?'

'I would like to send a telegram.'

'Of course, you must let your people know what's happened. Your wife will be anxious.'

'No, no.'

He noticed how she turned away immediately, perhaps hiding her embarrassment, and foraged in the top drawer of a bedside cabinet. He explained that his wife had gone back to Russia to see her mother, who had not been well, and he was a kind of grass widower. Lady Helen had gathered enough already about his short bicycling holiday for there to be no need to say more about it, except to add almost by way of apology how fond he was of English poetry: 'It's a little hobby of mine. When I have the chance, I travel to places I have seen mentioned in famous poems. I was looking for Wordsworth's "sylvan Wye". That's really why I'm here and so indebted to you. I must not prevail on your hospitality a moment longer than necessary. No, I am sending for my man. What address shall I give?'

She was disconcerted. 'Ah... Yes...' Frowning, she added: 'It had better be Stadleigh Court. I'll take it over myself. I have to go over this evening.'

She handed him a small writing pad. An inkwell and pen had appeared on the small table. 'Our own,' she pointed out, referring to the ink in the inkwell into which he put the wooden nib before writing out, in very black capitals, the bold, if inscrutable, message: 'COTTON BRING CLOTHES STADLEIGH COURT HEREFORDSHIRE URGENT. R.'

She queried what it meant.

'He'll know. Very good ink,' he remarked. 'Tell me – why did you ask about the Karenins? You know what happened to Anna Arkadyevna, don't you? Suicide. She threw herself under a train.'

Lady Helen suddenly peered at the prince, as if he was an archaeological discovery of incalculable value. 'You're certain of that, prince, are you? Did you ever meet her?'

He had to admit he did meet her. Twice, in fact. Long, long ago.

To his absolute astonishment she leaned forward and kissed him on the cheek with every sign of being delighted to do so. Before he could stop blinking or respond in any proper fashion he heard her go running down the stairs in a positive avalanche of racing footsteps. Meanwhile, he sat on the bed and contemplated the need to put on the nightshirt that had been laid neatly on the pillow.

In the quiet of the early evening after the rain he fell into a healing and dreamless sleep that lasted until quite late the following morning. Meanwhile, his hostess had gone across the river, climbed terrace after terrace of the Stadleigh Court garden and heard the organ music float out ever more loudly over shrubs and flowerbeds. The short telegram had indeed been despatched within the hour. By eight o'clock that evening railway timetables had been consulted in the house in Portland Place and a cab ordered to go to Paddington.

4

The next morning after a very late, suitably vegetarian breakfast of carrot juice, homemade bread, gooseberry jam, fresh butter and oatcakes, the prince whiled away a little time reading a two-day-old copy of *The Times* in the hope that Lady Helen would shortly come back from whatever good works she had been busy with since early morning. Approaching midday he heard a familiar voice just outside his door. It was his manservant Cotton who had just arrived with a carriage from Stadleigh Court.

He was always known as Cotton. No forename, no relatives, it seemed, no past experience except service in good households that brought with it a reputation for trustfulness, cleanliness and practicality in ways the prince could only envy. He had, for instance, a remarkable ability of quite Herculean intellectual valour for understanding railway timetables. They were second nature to him. On receipt of the telegram he had gone at once to Paddington, booked a ticket for Swindon, found a means of reaching Stadleigh Halt, been conveyed to Stadleigh Court and then been instructed to fetch the prince from Lady Helen's cottage in a carriage provided by Lord Irmingham. What is more, he came with fresh clothes.

'Cotton, my dear fellow, tell me *why*? *Why* am I being taken to see Lord Irmingham?'

Cotton could only say those were his instructions. The prince accepted the inevitable. 'To the future!' he cried as he stepped into the carriage. He was doing this, he told himself, chiefly because of the beautiful Lady Helen's unexpected kiss. So they drove away from her cottage and down the route towards the river.

'Would you care, sir,' Cotton asked politely, 'to give me an account of what happened? I have a morbid interest in the details of accidents.'

The prince was reluctant to say more than that he had been on his bicycling holiday, enjoying the English countryside and stopping at inns for the night. On the third day he had got as far as Herefordshire. 'I was travelling down a lane of some kind. It was rather steep. I had my thoughts fixed on the "sylvan Wye" of your English poet William Wordsworth. You see, I have always wondered what Mr Wordsworth's words were really worth.'

It was an open carriage with the leather roof folded down and gave a clear view of the coachman's back. The man appeared to shrug his shoulders, whether derisively or due to the reins being flicked, it was hard to say. What both his passengers could see clearly was that the back of his velvet-trimmed jacket was so shiny with wear it gave an inkling of the state of the Irmingham finances.

Cotton persisted. 'About the accident, sir. The details?'

'Yes, well...'

As many details as could be remembered were given – the black boat, the sunlit water, the man hopping about as if shot, the red rose. It was all said in a low voice because it sounded less and less significant once it was recounted. Throughout

Cotton's expression remained quite inscrutable, if attentive.

'And your bicycle, sir?'

He said he hoped it could be repaired.

'Well, sir, if I may say so, sir, I hope *you* will also be repaired soon as well.'

'Thank you, Cotton, I hope so.'

They were crossing a stone bridge at that moment. The brisk clip-clop of horses' hooves matched the sparkling sunlight on the stretch of water below the bridge as the river flowed away hurriedly into the shade of trees. The prince's attention was directed to the looping telegraph wires and the red-tiled roof of what Cotton told him was Stadleigh Halt.

'So we could catch a train, if we wished? Is the Court far from here?'

'No, sir, not far at all.'

This was true. In a reasonably short time they were passing through gates and down a long tree-lined driveway. At the end of it they confronted tall Gothic windows and tall pitched roofs of blue slate set between even taller, red-brick towers and battlements in a mixture of styles combining English baronial, Prussian military and Tudor domestic. This, then, was Stadleigh Court. Its wide front door and entrance steps faced on to a large courtyard. Their carriage swept up to these steps in proprietorial fashion with a loud grinding of shingle under hooves and wheels.

At the front door a tall, bearded man dressed like a priest in a kind of light-blue cassock was welcoming two other new arrivals. He waved to the newly arrived carriage, but continued speaking to a well-dressed lady and a young man. Liveried staff were simultaneously engaged in unloading luggage.

Immediately on arrival Cotton jumped down and announced in a loud voice, to the prince's evident annoyance: 'Your lordship, I have the honour to present His Excellency Prince Dmitry Nikolaevich Rostov, sir, of the Province of Tula, loyal subject, sir, of His Highness Emperor Nicholas II, Tsar of all the Russias. Lord Irmingham – His Excellency Prince Dmitry!'

'My dear fellow,' said Lord Irmingham, coming down the steps at once, 'how good of you to come! My daughter, Lady Helen, came over last evening and mentioned you had been in an accident. Are you, er... ?'

The prince momentarily looked daggers at Cotton. The latter raised one eyebrow and bowed a trifle unctuously without apparently noticing the disapproval, allowing the prince to respond warmly to the greeting.

'Your daughter, Lord Irmingham, your doctor and a night's rest have helped to restore me a good deal.'

'Ah, but you must be fully restored here! I insist. In any case, we are having a soiree and you will be most welcome.' Further discussion was curtailed by the introduction of the other new arrivals. They were a Mrs Emerald Stephenson and her son by her first marriage, Montgomery or Monty Coulsham. 'Just arrived from Massachusetts. Via Southampton.'

'I don't want to appear,' said Mrs Emerald Stephenson, a tall lady of middle age with a high soprano American twang, slightly altering the hang of her dress at the shoulders and in doing so making the feathers in her wide-brimmed hat perform a brief *pas de deux*, 'too provincial, but to be introduced to a lordship and a prince within two minutes of arrival sure impresses us folks used to nuthin' more socially excitin' than a common-or-garden New Haven clambake! What'll we tell our friends back home, Monty dear?'

Monty, wearing a green velvet jacket with a pink silk handkerchief hanging limply from a breast pocket, nodded and made a noise which sounded like *'privet'* to which he added the title 'prince' a second later. The prince took a moment to realise what he meant.

'Pree-VET!' he responded, not so much correcting the pronunciation by emphasising the final syllable as grateful for the attempt to greet him in his own language. *'Ochen' priatno!'*

'My son,' said Mrs Stephenson, ignoring the exchange, 'is a poet. He believes in a universal language. You may not have heard of Symbioticism but he is surely the very first Symbiotic poet in the entire world!'

This was too much for Monty. 'Mother, please desist,' he said with a sigh. 'This is neither the time nor the place.' He explained that out of respect for the ideas of Count Leo Tolstoy he had learned a couple of words of Russian.

Lord Irmingham congratulated him and admitted he had never been able to master much of the language himself, though he instantly apologised to the prince for such inadequacy. 'Well, you are all most welcome as my guests. Do please excuse me.'

With a magnanimous wave of the hand he invited them to find their rooms. The Americans' luggage led the way. It amounted to three large travelling trunks and half-a-dozen hat boxes requiring three men to carry them through the spacious hallway and up the main staircase, whereas the prince's, consisting of no more than a small suitcase and a larger case Cotton had brought from London, seemed pitifully un-princely by comparison.

He appeared, though, to be favoured as an honoured guest by being offered a room near the head of the stairs while the others were led away down a long corridor, waving their goodbyes as they went. The room had all the necessary appointments of a bedroom and the additional amenity of a bathroom. Cotton was delighted to find it contained what was known as an 'Irmingham Rapido', a design of water closet with a special siphon action. Although a German invention had recently superseded it, the fact of such a modern amenity was a clear advance on the absence of any such arrangement when they had visited the prince's Tula estate earlier that summer.

'I am afraid,' the prince felt bound to admit, 'we Russians are not in the forefront of water closet inventiveness. Tolstoyanism can clearly not compete in that area.'

'Pardon, sir. Tolst-what, sir?'

'Tolstoyanism is what it is called in England. The reason we are here, I suspect.'

A brief explanation followed, with a possibly unduly cursory acknowledgement that, apart from non-opposition to evil by violence and self-sufficiency, etc., Tolstoyanism involved vegetarianism.

'I didn't realise,' remarked a suddenly anxious Cotton, 'I would not be allowed to eat meat while here, sir.'

'I do apologise,' said the prince. 'It is all to do with the need to live in peace, you know, and avoid killing.'

'Oh, you are peace-loving, sir, I am sure of that. Well, sir, I am also peace-loving, no one can accuse me of not being peace-loving, but to be denied bacon for breakfast or beef on Sundays can be an intolerable deprivation to someone like myself. Quite intolerable, sir.'

Cotton became rather subdued by the threat of vegetarianism. In silence he set about arranging the prince's clothes and performing all the normal duties of a valet while the prince himself took a seat in a large upright armchair facing the window. The journey from Lady Helen's cottage had restarted the aching in his ribs and made his left arm feel sore again. He stared at the view, pursing his lips in frustration and annoyance. Although the view was attractive, it did not attract him to explore it immediately – a wide terrace with a balustrade, steps leading down to lower terraces and lawns fringed by yew hedges, with pine trees beyond. Presumably the gardens stretched down to the river, although there seemed to be a declivity or valley beyond offering a horizon of ruins, possibly of a castle, looking incongruously like a row of broken teeth.

Any strange place can be unsettling and the prince was unsettled. The bedroom was clean if unaired, smelled of mothballs and was furnished in a style popular, in his estimation, some thirty years before. If he were to stay here long, he would have to find some outdoor activity to distract him. But he hoped he would enjoy Lord Irmingham's hospitality no longer than was required to attend the soiree, after which he was bound to feel better and could either resume his bicycling holiday or go home to his house in Portland Place. There he would await the return of Princess Alisa from her visit to Russia. His London club, business affairs, one or two invitations to country house weekends and perhaps a little more bicycling would fill in the time.

He must have slept. He was conscious of a hissing sound. Peering round, thinking it must be Cotton, he was surprised to see Lord Irmingham's pale-blue cassock-like garment approach rapidly across the carpet towards his chair. Cotton danced attendance in an unsuccessful effort to keep the sound of footsteps and fabric to a minimum. Lord Irmingham brushed aside the attempt to calm his arrival. Instead, without warning, he confronted the prince face to face, a pair of very bright blue eyes scrutinising him with the same intensity as Lady Helen's had studied him the previous day.

'Do please excuse me. I know I am intruding. But I must ask you something, my dear prince, because I would be most grateful for your help.'

Help? The prince could never resist appeals for help. He began to rise from his chair. Lord Irmingham at once urged him not to.

'No, no, please. I would like to speak to you alone, if I may.'

Cotton gracefully took his leave and Lord Irmingham immediately lowered himself onto the cushioned window seat. Drawing up the skirt of his ankle-length garment and crossing his legs, he clasped both hands together across his chest, a gesture suggesting intensity of feeling rather than piety. Bright sunlight set up a modest corona at the fringes of his beard and accentuated the lean muscularity of his figure.

The prince could not avoid studying his face, even though it was backlit. Broad, a little pallid, with tiny veins apparent in the upper cheeks and eyebrows white like his beard, both neatly trimmed, it had the strong features of someone who obviously wished to look venerable and yet was a little unsure of himself. His eyes, for all their brilliance, were the secret. When he spoke they appeared partly hidden by a nervous semaphore of blinking. His lips were well shaped but seemed to make a movement as if tasting what he said and uttering the words in an oversweet sonorous voice.

'You must forgive me for interrupting your rest.' He asked how the prince was feeling, whether this was an appropriate time to have a private talk and assured him it would not take up much time. 'I owe you an explanation, I know. You are probably wondering why you are here.'

'I must agree with that, Lord Irmingham.'

'Well, you see, as I mentioned, you can be of very great help to me.' The blue eyes blinked more rapidly than ever. 'Prince, let us dispense with titles. May I call you Dmitry?'

'You may.'

'I am Giles. Giles Irmingham.' The sound of voices from below them, audible through the half-open window, distracted him. He looked down. 'Ah, some of my guests are enjoying the sunshine. As you probably know, since my daughter Helen must have told you, I like to entertain visitors here and encourage them to become better informed about the ideas of your famous compatriot Count Leo Tolstoy. She tells me that you know him.'

The prince acknowledged that he was kindred.

'Then it is most fortunate that you are here.' The speaker lowered his voice. 'Can I ask you if you were in Moscow or St Petersburg in the seventies?'

The question came as something of a shock. 'I was in my teens then.'

'But you *were* there?'

'Yes, I was in St Petersburg.'

'Did you ever meet or know of or have any dealings with...' the voice was lowered now to the point of being little more than a breathy whisper '...any of... anyone by the name of...' It was as if the name was too hard to pronounce and suddenly the subject was changed. 'In your teens, you say. So you were hardly likely to be in high society, in the *beau monde*, as they call it?'

'On the fringes. It was before I went off as a volunteer to fight against the Turks. In those days in particular, if you were young and a volunteer, you were quite feted in high society. In any case, my title…'

'Ah, yes, of course. So you might perhaps have known the, er, the Karenins?'

The prince let his mouth fall open. 'Your daughter, Lady Helen...'

Giles Irmingham raised his eyebrows expectantly. 'She said you knew them, isn't that right? I think she said you did?'

The prince inhaled deeply and looked down at his fingernails. 'I was introduced to *her* – Madame Karenina, Anna Arkadyevna. My grandmother knew her.'

'Your grandmother… well, well! So you actually met her – Anna, I mean?'

'I met her. Twice, as a matter of fact.'

Giles Irmingham gazed for several moments in wonderment and query at his guest. The gaze was returned with genuine puzzlement.

'She died very tragically,' the prince muttered.

'Yes, yes...' Giles Irmingham licked his lips.

'I mean, she killed herself. She threw herself under a train. It was a tragedy.'

'Oh, of course, of course. Yes, yes, I wasn't meaning...' The white beard was stroked anxiously. 'I wasn't meaning to give the impression she didn't, my dear Dmitry. No, no, of course not. We know her death was called a tragedy. It was just a question of identifying...' The eyes blinked with greater rapidity as Giles Irmingham clasped and unclasped his hands. He turned his face towards the window in an apparent effort to avoid the other's puzzled gaze. 'A question of identification, that's all. I have to make sure I have not been misled about a particular identity. It is rather important. May I talk to you again tomorrow? Then perhaps I can explain things more fully.'

The prince nodded. He was grateful for the promise of an explanation even if in the meantime his curiosity and puzzlement were not allayed one iota. He resisted the temptation to ask further questions about it. Instead he raised the question of vegetarianism. Well, no, it was not for everyone, Giles Irmingham admitted. It was practised upstairs, true, in the spirit of Count Tolstoy's teaching, but downstairs it was voluntary. That would be very gratifying to his manservant Cotton, the prince said. His host then mentioned that dinner that evening would be early since they were celebrating the birthday of their grandson, Master Charles Irmingham. He hoped the prince would join them and was delighted to learn that he would. A further snake-like hissing of his cassock then accompanied his hurried departure, though not before he implored the prince, in the politest way, not to breathe a word, not a word, about – in a whisper – *the Karenins*.

5

Dinner that evening was served in the main hall. Designed originally in the Gothic manner to house a collection of medieval armour and serve as an impressive reception room, it had recently been stripped of its exhibits and was now in semi-darkness, with its tall windows tightly curtained against the early evening light.

Descending the wide staircase, the prince was surprised to hear organ music. He soon discovered it was coming from an organ gallery in the hall. Wave after wave of frankly rather banal chords filled the air at the moment he entered, suggesting a finale. Then there was silence. He saw what looked like a narrow enclosed staircase linking the gallery to the hall and could have expected to see the organist. No one appeared. Instead Giles Irmingham came forward to greet him with a whispered explanation.

'My dear Dmitry, so glad you could come. We are all assembled ready for the evening meal.'

The prince was about to apologise for being late, though he had assumed he was on time, when his host forestalled him by changing the subject.

'It is the gentleman from the other side. His music.'

'I am so sorry, I hadn't…Other side?'

'He's from the other side of the river. He resides with my daughter. Mr Kingston is practising his composition for the soiree.'

This piece of news was almost as obscure to him as the candlelit faces of the assembled guests. The prince found himself being introduced immediately to a gaunt-faced prelate, the Reverend Ellis Chalmers of Belfast, a distinguished interpreter of Tolstoy's teaching, so he was told. His companion was Raymond Vernoncourt, described as a journalist, a much younger man with a boyish face and slicked down black hair. Also present was Julie Mayhew-Summers, a pretty young woman in her twenties with a rather sing-song voice who professed an earnest devotion to Tolstoy but was in fact more devoted to her companion, a widower and retired businessman, Rodney Palmer. He was rich, corpulent, loud-voiced, balding and wickedly 'naughty', as he liked to call himself, with the kind of intelligence and dislike of etiquette easily justified by having sufficient wealth to fend off all manner of criticism. The only other guests were Mrs Emerald Stephenson and her son Monty.

The Irmingham family, on the other hand, was represented by Giles Irmingham and his second wife, Lady Isobel. His son by his first marriage, Gerald, was seated next to his wife, Hannah, and their son, Master Charles Irmingham. The prince looked in vain for Lady Helen. She was clearly not present, but the resemblance to her in Gerald's copper hair and blue eyes was unmistakable. He was strikingly handsome and evidently charming in upper-class terms, with an ingratiating drawl and a tendency to laugh nervously at his own remarks. His wife, Hannah, a petite, good-looking blonde, clearly doted on him. She spoke little but when she did it was quite loudly and defensively. This occurred chiefly in talking to Lady Isobel Irmingham who went to considerable lengths to hide the strain of poor hearing.

The reason for the dinner being held so early, Master Charles, looked ideally pre-Raphaelite, as should any boy with Lady Helen as an aunt, the prince supposed. He was dressed for the occasion in a suitably Tolstoyan peasant smock that, for all its simplicity, served to draw attention to the way his head of curly fair hair stood up thickly like a straw crown. This gave him every right to preside over one end of the table as 'king' for his eleventh or twelfth birthday, the prince never having discovered exactly which it was.

The conversation during the wholly vegetarian meal was punctuated by bursts of excited talk, followed by periods of embarrassed silence. Carrot soup, for instance, allowed the Reverend Ellis Chalmers to express himself loudly on one or another aspect of Tolstoyanism, to the annoyance of Raymond Vernoncourt who described everything said as 'poppycock' or 'abject poppycock.' The main dish of nut cutlets and a variety of vegetables was accompanied by a more light-hearted discussion of certain Tolstoyan ideas led by Giles Irmingham, who invited contributions and opinions from the prince as 'the only one among us who is truly related to the great religious thinker.' The prince tried to respond adequately but was glad when the dessert arrived. It consisted of fruit and ice cream specially prepared for the birthday boy and was climaxed by the arrival of a birthday cake topped by an array of candles which were all ceremoniously blown out in one breath to cries of 'Happy Birthday!' and a round of applause.

Towards the end of the meal abstinence from all alcohol and any kind of liquid stimulant, including tea or coffee, led to a general conversational malaise. Julie exclaimed at the 'beautiful idea of living together completely freely and completely honestly.' The sing-song statement sounded so pert and earnest it made Rodney Palmer murmur aloud that it was all very well for people to make their own clothes but what the hell would life be like if you had to try and make your own Havana cigars ('Can you imagine *not* having tobacco leaf that had *not* been rolled on the thick brown thighs of nubile Cuban ladies?'). The remark hardly elicited a smile, let alone a titter. It left room for Mrs Emerald Stephenson to extol the attempts to create communes in the United States. Once that had been greeted with polite thanks from Lord Irmingham, she inquired whether 'that poor birthday boy' was really enjoying his birthday. She said she thought a birthday could not be a real birthday without charades.

'Isn't that right, Monty?'

'Please, mother.'

'Count Tolstoy says nothing about what you call char-*aids* and we call char-*ards*,' declared the Reverend Ellis Chalmers.

'For once in a way he's absolutely right!' said Raymond Vernoncourt. 'Charades – pronounce the word any way you like – are all so much poppycock conceived as entertainment for the upper classes. Abolish them! I say.'

'They are not poppycock at all. They are a simple human pleasure, ritualised among the poorest of our brethren into a brand of carnival and most certainly likely to receive the full endorsement of Count Tolstoy when brought to his attention. I must write to him on the subject.' The Reverend Ellis Chalmers took out a notebook.

'I find something very difficult to understand,' announced Mrs Emerald Stephenson shrilly.

'Please, mother,' Monty said.

'What is it you find difficult to understand?' asked Rodney Palmer as he cut off the end of a cigar.

'I mean the Russian soul. The Russian soul is too big a thing, isn't it? It's too grand, too great. But we have to take it very seriously, don't we? Which is why we simple folk in Massachusetts need remindin' of the simple side o' life. It ain't witches, it ain't superstition I'm referrin' to, you understand, it's just light-hearted legends, fairytales, char-*aids*, as I call 'em, which simple folk can enjoy. They believe in 'em, you know. Of course, you English don't seem to have no folklore to speak of. Why, it's all travelled abroad, I reckon. How many people here have actually seen a water nymph, I wonder? Why, where I come from, we've always had water nymphs!'

'I share that sense of loss,' said Rodney Palmer. The cigar had been lit and he blew a plume of blue cigar smoke into the candlelight, wiping the match flame out as he did so with suitably flamboyant exuberance. 'Mind you, I imagine if I went down to the river now...' he cleared his throat '... and was very quiet, and did nothing to frighten our modest English river spirits, I'd see a nymph. Long hair, of course, charmingly naked, pale of limb, curvaceous, utterly innocent, a perfect child of nature. But if you were to ask me what I would do after seeing this nymph...'

He paused.

'Well,' asked Mrs Emerald Stephenson, 'what would you do?'

'Tell her the facts of life!'

'Why, that'd sure scare her!'

'The prime reason, perhaps,' said Rodney Palmer, 'why one sees them so rarely. But what good is a nymph to us humans unless she knows the facts of life?'

'And can therefore, er, appreciate our human needs?' drawled Gerald suggestively.

'True, quite true. But it poses a moral dilemma, does it not?' Rodney Palmer blew a further plume of cigar smoke into the air. 'Innocence is not an absolute, not an unconditional state of things, but the dilemma which faces us is that a nymph who is not in a state of innocence cannot have a moral claim to be a nymph, in my opinion.'

'They have bosoms and tits!' came a boyish cry from the end of the table.

'What on earth is he saying?' cried Lady Isobel, who was too far away to hear accurately. 'What's the child saying?'

Hannah wagged her finger at him and Master Charles went extremely red.

'Yes, from the mouths of babes and sucklings,' Rodney Palmer went on quickly. He looked hard at Julie, who returned his look with a sensual, querying half-smile. 'It is a sign of a nymph's implausibility, alas, that she should flee away from human contact in this country and find a habitation and a dwelling for herself among the waterways of the eastern states of America. But, you see, their impermanence, their reticence, their shyness disarms us morally. It makes us aware how fallen and seduced we are. What is your opinion, Prince?'

'"A gap in nature" is one way of describing it. I saw such a gap on the river yesterday.'

'Pardon?' exclaimed Giles Irmingham.

'You are referring to water nymphs, I imagine?' Rodney Palmer inquired.

'No, I am referring to what I saw yesterday.'

'What was that?'

He described the black boat, the gunshot and the red rose cast on the water. 'It brought to mind, you see, Cleopatra in her barge. I am fond of English poetry, especially Shakespeare, and Shakespeare described Cleopatra in her barge as "a gap in nature".'

'I say, that's very good!'

'Poppycock!' shouted Raymond Vernoncourt.

'No, not poppycock at all!' protested Rodney Palmer. 'Not at all! There *are* gaps in nature. Consequently, in approaching the innocence of water nymphs, we confront a gap, don't we? We are inevitably placed in the wrong if we try to explain to them what is natural to us. That is "a gap in nature".'

'What is wrong,' interrupted Giles Irmingham a little crossly, 'excuse my mentioning it, is talk of a black boat and a gunshot. Surely, my dear Dmitry, you must be mistaken. I cannot imagine you saw anyone shot!'

'But I did,' said the prince quite calmly.

'Really! Oh, good heavens!' exclaimed Mrs Emerald Stephenson.

'Oh, mother, please,' said Monty and turned to the prince. 'What do you mean, sir?'

'I thought I saw someone being shot. But I was very probably wrong.'

'I am sure you must be wrong,' Giles Irmingham insisted.

'But I am sure I saw a black boat.'

The prince's repetition of his claim, stated so confidently, brought a moment of silence that led Mrs Emerald Stephenson to say equally confidently: 'If the prince saw what he saw, why I believe him. He's entitled as a Russian to see things we very likely don't see. Isn't that right, Mr Palmer? Why, if you are prepared to see an innocent little water nymph, I am quite prepared to believe the prince saw a black boat.'

Rodney Palmer bowed towards her. 'You understand me, my dear. I am gratified. Tolstoyanism should free us of the rational imperatives surrounding truth, not to mention the moral and sexual constraints to which western civilisation has so long inured us.'

'You mean genuine symbiosis?' Monty asked.

'As genuine, my boy, as flesh can allow.' And Rodney Palmer kissed the back of Julie's hand, at which she emitted a cascade of giggles.

That night the prince found it hard to sleep, not only because he had obviously upset his host but also because he was very puzzled. The colour combination of the light counterpane on his bed reminded him of Lady Helen's remarkably deep blue eyes and the way they were offset so brilliantly by her abundant, copper-red hair. He could not imagine why she had not been at the dinner, especially as it had been to celebrate her young nephew's birthday. He could only hope what kept her away was not his presence. He had asked after her, but she had been described as 'busy'. He did not press to know what that meant. So he contented himself with superimposing the image of her deep blue eyes and copper-red hair on the remembered, long-cherished image of his dear wife, Princess Alisa, the one merging into the other into a pure velvet blue in the darkness beyond the flickering radiance of the bedside candle. He knew emotional betrayal lurked there, unreal and unlikely though it might be; so he blew the candle out and the images slowly decayed into a ghostly whiteness as the oblong of the window, still open, concentrated all the light in the room.

The night was warm and close. An owl hooted. It was a reminder how unused he was to the noises of the countryside, despite the days he had spent on his bicycle tour. He had been too tired at the end of each day to notice. Now the outside noises served to reinforce the secretive and mysterious air of Stadleigh Court and his reasons for being there. The name *Karenin* crept into his thoughts. Why had Giles Irmingham asked him about it and been so adamant that it shouldn't be mentioned? And why had he been offered what was obviously a very good guest room, with a beautiful view over the gardens and all the most desirable facilities, including an Irmingham Rapido?

Consumed though he was by such doubts and queries, he apparently could not help himself from falling headlong into a hectic dream. He was running, running very hard, along a rocky hillside, and the running became a kind of gliding. Bullets whistled above his head and the shell-shattered earth fountained up directly in front of the Grivitza Redoubt. A huge pain like a spreading inkblot drenched his whole body. He tried to raise his right hand to fend off the explosion, but the echo of it resounded sharper than any owl's cry and brought him upright. He awoke to find himself sitting up in bed fully conscious.

Greyish darkness surrounded him. His forehead was covered in beads of sweat.

There came a quite audible clicking noise. The door handle to his room was being moved.

A fearful creeping sensation, like a rat's claws, ran along the crown of his head.

Who?

The tongue of the door lock had been moved back. He knew Cotton hadn't locked it. It was being held back by someone outside, at the head of the stairs. The next moment the door slowly opened. An enlarging beam of light fell across the carpet. The door shut quietly and a figure approached.

'Mr Rostov? Sorry, sir. I mean prince, Prince Rostov... Ah, ya'r wekkit, sir!'

It took two or three seconds to put two and two together. In the gleam of the oil lamp held up to aid identification the prince recognised the youthful but drawn face, the bulges of little sacs below the eyes and a distinct sallowness in the lightly freckled cheeks.

'Dr Parkinson, what on earth...'

'Did I wek ya, sir? My sincere apologies.'

'No need for all that!'

'No, sir. Sorry, sir. It's second nature to me now, the accent. How are you? How is your arm? And the rib?' He placed the oil lamp next to the extinguished candle.

The prince protested quite justifiably that it was hardly the right time for a consultation. James Parkinson gave a low chuckle. He announced he had heard his patient was coming to the Court from Lady Helen the previous evening. Now was the opportunity to undo the tight bandage and take a look at the wounded left arm, only to find the bandage already undone.

'You're better, aren't you?'

The prince explained that he had taken a bath.

'I see. May I just…' James Parkinson frisked professionally. 'Bruising, I think. Take it easy, that's all. No bicycling down steep lanes, understand?'

His patient acquiesced.

'Well, Prince Rostov, sir, I don't know really how to put it to you, but you are Russian, aren't you?'

The prince could hardly deny it.

'Then it's about your compatriots, sir.'

'My compatriots!'

'Yes, sir, Russians, sir. One of them's very seriously ill. I cannot make him or the others understand he must go into hospital. Otherwise there'll be no chance. Can you help me, sir? It's very, very urgent!'

'How can I help?'

The doctor explained he was at the end of his tether and his voice contained such a genuine note of fatigue there could be no doubting him. 'They won't let him, you see.'

'Who won't let him?'

'The servants. They seem to be in charge. Lord Irmingham said it was up to them.'

This was extremely puzzling and intriguing. 'These are Russian servants?'

'Oh, yes, sir. *Most* Russian!'

'And you want me to talk to them? Where are they?'

'Upstairs. Yes, I want you to persuade them he must go into hospital.'

'Upstairs? Here, in the house?'

'I will be eternally grateful Mr – sorry, Prince – Rostov, sir.'

There was enough here in what he had heard to intrigue the prince sufficiently to point to the dressing gown at the end of the bed. It was of blue silk with red piping to the wide lapels and a crest on the breast pocket picked out in gold thread. 'One of my little luxuries,' he murmured as he was helped to put it on after pulling on his slippers.

The glow of the doctor's oil lamp showed the way. It was hard to believe there were any compatriots of his at Stadleigh Court, but he followed the young man's stooped back out of sheer curiosity. Practically soundlessly they went along the corridor at the head of the stairs and round a corner. The door facing them had to be unlocked. It swung open softly and was re-locked just as softly and he found himself being led up a flight of curved stairs. The oil lamp showed a dado to shoulder level and above it rows of framed paintings whose glass fronts flickered and glimmered in the passing light. They climbed two flights and two small landings. The air smelled stuffy and unused. At the top was a larger landing containing such oddments as a pile of books, an old pair of boots, an umbrella and a portrait on the wall before which a light burned very dimly in the manner of an icon flame. He had no time to see who it was. The doctor turned to him with a finger to his lips and whispered that he hoped *he* was now asleep.

The hope was extinguished almost immediately. Muffled yet distinct, at that very instant came a yell of agony that made the doctor rush to a door and swing it open without knocking. The prince followed him.

The first thing he knew was a darkness filled with the stench of the sickroom. It was so repulsive that he staggered backwards and masked his mouth and nostrils with the lapel of his dressing gown. The smell, though, was less dreadful than the sight. Within the ring of light cast by the lamp a couple of candle flames could be seen set either side of a bed on which a naked man was lying. He had a strong, muscular body, the lines of his torso clearly silhouetted by the fact that he was enduring some kind of spasm. His back was arched steeply in a wrestler's bridge that made his body unnaturally and hideously rigid. His skin glistened with sweat and fluid exuded from his anus, his eyes and his nose. The door was hurriedly shut to prevent another yell being heard, only for the spasm to pass practically at once and the muscles to relax. The pale body flopped back exhausted.

An elderly woman dressed in black, with a black shawl over her head, leaned forward at once and began wiping the man's eyes and mouth. He lay there apparently oblivious to her repeated appeals for divine intervention and divine mercy. Even the way she stroked his cheeks was accepted as an endearment merely incidental to the pain that tautened his neck muscles and forced his sweat-soaked hair back into an already soaked pillow. Seeing the prince and reacting to his instant query about her patient, she quickly covered the man's nakedness as best she could with a small blanket.

So this must be one of the Russian servants, was the prince's first thought. About to ask more questions, he suddenly caught sight of an old man standing near the foot of the bed. He was dressed in an antiquated, elegant waistcoat with embroidery round the buttonholes and a long, shabby frockcoat so aged and stiffened by use it looked like a toga carved from stone. He did not turn to look at the new arrival but remained fixed in predatory watchfulness. The prince could not help following the direction of his gaze.

He was gazing at the sick man's face. What he saw, as the prince now saw, was the sardonic smile, the lips curled back as far as the gums, the features contorted in pain and the sweaty pallor. They were all characteristic symptoms. There had been faces showing the same symptoms during the war against the Turks. What he was seeing, the prince realised, was the *spasmus cynicus* of tetanus poisoning. It was unforgettably a sign of what Hippocrates called the disease of wounding.

'Lockjaw,' he muttered, peering down with the lapel still held firmly over his nose and mouth.

'What?' asked James Parkinson.

'Lockjaw. Isn't that what you call it? Look at the jaw.'

'Oh, my God!'

'You didn't know?'

'To be honest, I didn't know what it was. I tried various antidotes.'

'I've seen it before. *Curare.*'

'*Curare*?'

'You have to use *curare.*'

'Oh, my God, of course! Why the hell didn't I think of that!' A series of rapid, remorseful gestures culminated in the young doctor striking his forehead with the palm of his hand. 'I think I might have some, you know. I studied the use of *curare...*' He explained that he been interested in tropical medicine during his medical training. He picked up his medical case and said he would go back to his consulting-room at once. 'Thank you, prince. I'm very, very grateful to you.'

The prince assumed he meant he would be returning to Lady Helen's. He seized his arm for an instant. 'He's been shot, hasn't he?'

'No.'

'Surely he's been shot?'

'No.'

'I heard a shot. He must have been shot! Surely it was because of him you were brought here? I mean, at tea-time at Lady Helen's?' He was certain the lockjaw victim was the man he had seen hopping about in the water. 'Remember? When it suddenly started to rain...'

'No. Sergius here...'

'That's his name?'

'Sergius or Sergei, yes. It was his mother I came to see first of all. He only complained of feeling ill a bit later. You're right, he thought he might have been shot. I checked him thoroughly, I can assure you. But there was no sign of a pellet wound or anything like that.'

'No injury of any kind?'

'Perhaps a small cut on the sole of his foot, but otherwise only a few ordinary scratches. Ah, lockjaw, of course... Boris,' the doctor said, turning to the elderly retainer, 'Boris, this is Mr – sorry, no – Prince Rostov. Please, tell him in Russian,' he implored, 'that I must go and get some medicine at once.'

The prince obliged and added a question of his own. 'Had he,' indicating the sick man, 'been down at the river the previous day?'

The old man leaned forward like an unwieldy bird and, as if pecking his way into the lamplight, opened and closed his mouth several times. Judging by the way he peered at the prince, he obviously noted the crest embroidered on the dressing-gown pocket. His expression slowly transformed itself into one of servile and awesome wonderment.

'Your excellency,' came the breathy, quavering voice, 'your excellency,' and bending low, to the prince's dismay, he seized his right hand and kissed it. Yes, he had been down by the river, the young master had been, the old man conceded. So he *had* heard Russian spoken on the banks of the "sylvan Wye"!

'Thank you. That explains...'

But all explanations came to nothing when the old man, still holding his hand, persisted in addressing him as if he were heaven-sent: 'God be with you, sir, God bless you, sir, God keep you! You are an angel come to save us! The soul... the soul of our poor young master, sir, is about to fly into the highest heavens, and I see you are an angel, sir, come to our aid, our saviour... Our dear mistress will bless you, sir, our mistress, sir, will bless you everlastingly... everlastingly... for coming to our aid!'

If this were not embarrassing enough, the old woman fell on her knees at that moment and joined in the supplications. James Parkinson shrugged his shoulders, raised the oil lamp and raced from the room. Practically at once the sick man was convulsed by a further spasm, but was soon calm again when the old woman resumed her gentle wiping of his features.

'Who?' the prince asked in the silence. 'Who is your mistress? Is it Lady Irmingham?' There was a muttered response that the prince could not hear.

'Who?'

Boris hung his head. 'She has ordered the windows

closed, your excellency. I cannot say. Forgive me. I will light your way downstairs.'

6

The prince had to assume it was his hostess, Lady Isobel, who was being referred to as the 'mistress' and the victim of lockjaw was therefore her 'son'. Boris refused to answer any other questions. He led the prince determinedly out of the sickroom and went slowly ahead of him, step by step, down the curved stairs, holding a candle shakily aloft and sprinkling 'excellencies' over him like so much holy water.

Puzzled as he was by the strangeness of it all, the prince quickly fell into an unbroken asleep when he returned to his bedroom until woken by Cotton's arrival with his breakfast the next morning. Had he heard anything about other Russians at Stadleigh Court? No, Cotton hadn't. Did he know if Dr James Parkinson was at Stadleigh Court? No, Cotton didn't; he had no idea there *was* a doctor at Stadleigh Court. As for the tower and its inhabitants, he knew nothing about it or them. But he did know one thing for certain.

'And that is?'

The prince looked steadily at his manservant as Cotton straightened himself a little stiffly after having failed to answer the previous questions.

'Lord Irmingham,' he announced, 'has informed me that he would be most grateful if you could call on him at ten o'clock. In his study, sir. Can I run some hot water for you, sir?'

'Thank you, Cotton, I'll...'

So it very likely meant, the prince supposed, that Lady Isobel – and no doubt Giles as well – wanted to keep the sickroom secret, because the victim of lockjaw was very likely a cause of shame to the family, although why this 'son' should have been Russian and allowed to fester in such an unhygienic state, with windows closed and two such elderly, incompetent servants in charge, was outrageous. He felt in duty bound to protest at such a state of things and, once bathed and dressed, he went down the main staircase fully prepared to express his outrage to his host.

Maybe it was the stained glass in the window at the head of the stairs, or maybe the elaborately carved griffins and dragons on the newel posts that suddenly reminded him of Lady Helen and made him wonder what she had made of these things as a child. She must have come down these stairs. Had she played on them as the prince had enjoyed playing on the stairs of his grandmother's house in St Petersburg? Had she played at sleigh-riding down these stairs on tin trays? Had this been a treat of her childhood as the St Petersburg stairs had been a treat of his? He fantasised happily over these questions as he went slowly down step by step. Suddenly the fantasies stopped just as he found himself facing the doorway to the Gothic hall.

'Ah, prince!'

It was a woman's voice. He saw his hostess approaching down the hallway at that moment carrying a wicker basket. The fact that it was Lady Isobel gave him what he hoped was the chance to ask about the victim of lockjaw, but she anticipated him by inquiring about his health: 'You're probably still recovering, aren't you? I noticed you were probably not at your best last evening at dinner. I think you probably shouldn't have accepted Giles's invitation. We'd have understood perfectly well, you know.'

'My ribs, Lady Isobel, are feeling much better, and so is my arm.'

'Good. That is such good news.'

Her manner was sympathetically well bred, authoritative and trim, very like her slightly severe English good looks. The prince dismissed any idea she could be Russian. In any case, she was far too young to have an adult son, which made him anxious not to cause offence by asking about the sick man's health. So he excused his failure to be at his best during last night's dinner by saying he had been tired.

'You slept well, I hope?'

This gave him an opportunity to mention the sickroom. She stared back in utter bewilderment.

'Who?'

'Your son, Lady Isobel. He's sick, isn't he?'

'My son!' She gave him the sort of fixed, strained look that a near-sighted person gives when spectacles have been mislaid. 'Sick! Good heavens, no! I have no children, prince!'

He apologised. Naturally he was shocked by her fierce denial. He explained that the doctor had mentioned a mother.

'Oh, that is too much!' Then she checked herself. 'I think I know now why Giles invited you here. Really there are times when...' She seemed to lose her train of thought for a moment and then quickly offered apologies of her own. 'I'm afraid my husband and I do not see eye to eye over certain matters.' She smiled weakly at sharing such a disreputable confidence.

He again apologised for jumping to the wrong conclusion. It was hardly surprising that a raw nerve might have been touched with the mention of the sickroom, something that might best be left unmentioned, and was grateful to her for changing the subject.

'As you may have gathered from last night's dinner,' she went on, gesturing rather casually with her free hand. 'Our guests, you see... Giles is not as selective as he should be. I hope you were not offended.' A guardedly feminine look followed this. 'Oh, about Dr Parkinson's patient – yes, well, they are your compatriots, prince, and he, Dr Parkinson, I mean – such a nice young man, isn't he? – He would naturally come to you. I think he's found a cure.'

He said he was delighted.

'That was the news this morning, prince'.

'The news... You mean the doctor said there had been an improvement? Then it may have been my suggestion.'

'Yours, prince?'

'I said I thought the patient had lockjaw.'

'Really! Is that infectious? I wish some of our guests had locked their jaws last night!'

The prince smiled, but his reply was serious. 'No. It can be alleviated and cured. It is known as the disease of wounding and has very unpleasant symptoms.'

'How do you know this?'

He explained briefly about his experience during the Turkish campaign and reiterated that he thought he had seen the man with lockjaw shot two days previously.

'I thought you said you might have been mistaken about that. We are very pacifist now, you know. No guns or anything military in the Gothic hall.'

'Lady Isobel, I admit I may have been wrong about a gunshot. But Dr Parkinson's patient displays all the symptoms of the disease of wounding at an advanced stage.'

'Good heavens! Surely it can't be wounding!' She frowned, touching a finger to her lips. 'I wonder whether...'

'Who is he?' the prince asked curtly, annoyed by her apparent ignorance. 'And who are those two elderly servants? It may seem rude of me to ask, Lady Isobel, but I find myself involved. Who is his mother? The man is dying...'

She conceded that much but cut short all further discussion for a moment or so. They had passed through the hallway and were already in warm sunshine at the head of the steps by the front door. She again raised her free hand, this time to shade her eyes.

'My husband,' she said quietly, speaking as much to herself as to her guest, 'has many Russian associates, you know. Some have stayed here for long periods. They often only speak Russian or French and I have no head for languages. By the way, prince, you yourself are obviously an exception.' She had turned and looked at him rather artfully. 'You speak the most perfect English.'

'Not altogether perfect,' he had to admit.

'Yes, well...' Aware she might be embarrassing him, she gave a second smile. She seemed to smile by numbers rather than spontaneously. 'There are exceptions to any rule and you are one. Tell me a little about yourself, if you would. Are you beset by guests when at home, for example?'

It was an odd sort of question. The prince had to admit that the Tula estate had had its share of hangers-on, but it was his brother's problem, not his. He had business interests. Timber, for example.

'Do you go back often?'

'Oh, at least once a year. In the summer. I regard England as my home, though.'

'That is very nice to hear. How often nowadays one hears English people decry their own heritage! I think a heritage is essential. We Irminghams have the heritage of this place and it is our solemn duty, I feel, to preserve it and hand it on intact to the next generation.'

He found the claim a little trying. 'It must cost a lot – keeping up appearances, I mean.'

'Prince, you are right! Poor Giles is at his wits' end trying to find ways and means. Of course, we do not see eye to eye exactly over certain things. My husband is an idealist, you know. He would prefer to live very simply if he could in the manner of your great writer...' she flicked her fingers in a way that was hardly lady-like, '...dear me, who am I thinking of? I am getting so forgetful.'

'Tolstoy,' he reminded her.

'Ah, yes. Thank you. My memory for names gets worse and worse.' She announced she was taking the basket to help with gathering roses. 'Oh,' she added, startling him by suddenly exclaiming: 'I thought it was! There's Gerald!'

She lowered her voice and confided that the prince had met him at dinner. There he was, Gerald Kempson, striding towards them across the wide shingle forecourt. He had an energetic, brisk step that made him seem to dance in his riding boots and jodhpurs. In the bright morning sunlight he displayed his sister's looks more clearly than at dinner the previous evening. It was the shape of his face that struck the likeness. The well-defined pink lips and curved eyebrows were part of it, but its square-ish structure and the brilliance of the eyes were the real identifying features, although the removal of the peaked cap he was wearing on seeing his stepmother and the prince showed the reddish stubble on his jaw-line along with his copper-red hair, banishing all suggestion of femininity from his general appearance and manner.

'Gerald dear, have you been riding?' Lady Isobel asked. The question was rather unnecessary in view of his jodhpurs and she at once made a grand introductory gesture towards the prince. 'You remember our Russian guest, Prince Rostov, don't you?'

Gerald shook his hand politely. The sensual Monna Vanna gaze of the eyes sent instantaneous, covert messages so immodest they seemed to implicate the prince in knowing more about the sexual gossip at Stadleigh Court than anyone. He flinched slightly and responded to a polite query about horse riding by mentioning that his bicycle was being repaired. 'The prince had an accident while bicycling. That's why he's here,' Lady Isobel pointed out.

'Ah, yes, of course. Do please excuse me.' Gerald kissed his stepmother lightly on the cheek. 'I've just come over to have a word with Hannah.' Why this explanation sounded false the prince could not say. The speaker dry-washed his hands a little awkwardly and concluded with: 'So nice to meet you. I mustn't keep you waiting.'

He nodded and left. The prince had the distinct impression he was a little wary of both of them. Lady Isobel herself, perhaps detecting her companion's puzzlement, rather self-consciously seized the prince by the arm and made sure he accompanied her to gather roses.

They crossed the forecourt towards the rose garden and in a very short while, in an impulsive rush of confidentiality, she divulged that she came from a county family. He had no precise idea what this meant, but it was clear she simply adored being Lady Isobel Irmingham of Stadleigh Court.

'Ah, I see my helper's already at work.'

Entering through wrought-iron gates, she indicated someone stooping among the rose bushes, but the first person they came across was the previous night's birthday boy, Master Charles Kempson. Dressed in corduroy trousers obviously too short for him, he was crouching down and studying something very closely. When Lady Isobel cried out cheerily 'Hello, Charles dear, more creepy-crawlies?' he answered by holding up a glass jar.

'He was given a fishing rod for his birthday. Collecting worms, I imagine,' she said. 'The dear boy is terribly curious about nature. Ah, Julie dear, how kind of you!'

Julie Mayhew-Summers, in a large straw hat and white dress, was busy cutting roses and laying them carefully on the brick path. As soon as Lady Isobel arrived, she took the basket from her and began heaping roses into it.

'I started before you came,' she explained from her kneeling position and not looking up. 'Sorry I've got dirty hands. Can't do the polite thing, I'm afraid. Can't shake hands.'

'Julie,' said Lady Isobel with a light laugh, 'is known as the Unruly. She is devoted to my husband's ideas.'

'Communes,' said Julie the Unruly, snipping. 'Love the idea of communes. Absolutely love them. Living communally and working communally – what a difference it would make, wouldn't it? And true cooperation. That's the secret. Anarchism. One has to go the whole hog, in my opinion. Do you know Prince Kropotkin?' Glancing sideways at the prince, she snipped off a long stem.

'No, I'm afraid I don't.'

'A little gnome of a man. Such a charmer. Your roses are lovely this year, Lady Isobel. I just love work. No one should be idle, should they? It's what your Tolstoy teaches. He is so right. I adore him.'

'My love is like a red, red rose,' came a fluting American voice. Montgomery Coulsham in a large floppy hat and a reefer jacket was walking towards them, accompanied by his mother. She wore a long green silk dress cut to flare out below the knee and matched her son with a wide-brimmed hat trimmed with feathers. A few paces away he stopped and pointed statuesquely towards a remoter part of the rose garden.

'How does it go now? "For the foam-flowers endure"' he intoned, '"when the rose-blossoms wither And men that love lightly may die – but we?" Swinburne.'

'Monty!' exclaimed Mrs Emerald Stephenson.

'Please, mother.'

'I sure do wish,' she said, 'you'd give us some warning when you're going to recite! This is the prince. How are you, prince? Better?'

'Swinburne,' Monty repeated, unabashed. 'Delighted.' He gave a nod towards the prince but did not offer his hand. 'Thoughts from a forsaken garden, you know, and hardly appropriate to where we are now. Miss Julie, will you, er, permit me join you in picking these rose-blossoms even though I am, er, doomed always to be one of those men that love lightly?'

Julie sniffed and began talking energetically to Mrs Emereald Stephenson.

Lady Isobel quickly guided the prince away. It was rude to her guests, that was obvious, and he was so struck by her brusqueness he could not bring himself to speak until they had gone some distance along the sweep of gravel walk beside the house and were out of earshot.

'Your guests, Lady Isobel...'

She glanced back imperiously. '*That* is what I really can't stand!'

He asked what she meant.

'I mean the guests Giles insists on inviting. Are you a Tolstoyan, prince? Somehow or other I don't think you are. I can't see you making your own clothes or not eating meat. I would be the first to admit that is not at the core of your great writer's teaching. But I am sure that American lady wouldn't dream of making her own clothes. She dresses far too fashionably for that. As for that silly son of hers... Really, I can't think what made Giles invite them! There'll not be much financial reward from having them here, I'm sure of that. Mr Palmer does contribute something, so Giles tells me. I will be blunt, prince. Are *you* going to contribute?'

He could have been equally blunt with her. 'I am not a

Tolstoyan,' he admitted, 'but I admire his moral stance. As for contributing...'

She at once confessed it had been impolite to ask. 'No, no, it was simply that you asked about the cost. I will be quite candid. I dislike foreigners. Giles has always had to accommodate himself to their needs and spend endless sums supporting them. The long and the short of it is I find myself more and more out of sympathy with our guests and the need to influence people. We would be much better off if we weren't involved.'

It was a candour that surprised but it showed she had sufficient confidence to be open with him. They had reached the tower at that point in their walk and were already in its shadow. He judged it was four floors high, a large tubular structure set at the south-eastern corner of Stadleigh Court. In keeping with redbrick appearance of the rest of the house, it had a faintly Tudor look, but unlike the adjoining elevations it seemed strangely shut up. All the casement windows were closed as if it were midwinter and not a warm summer morning. It prompted him to point out what must be the sickroom.

Lady Isobel heaved a deep sigh, swallowed and looked away. 'I leave all that to Giles. I have grown very cynical.'

'Cynical?'

'Yes. I have no idea who lives there.' She made another of her casual gestures. 'They are your compatriots, they are Russians. Giles won't tell me who they are.' She turned and looked at him. He saw her eyes were brimming with tears. 'It is too much, you know, too much for a wife to bear! To think that I have to learn about them from a stranger! Or from what

Giles grudgingly tells me! In my own home! It is so unfair, dreadfully unfair!' A lace handkerchief was drawn quickly from her sleeve and pressed to her eyes.

The potentially difficult moment was defused by the sound of a door opening and rapid steps on the shingle. Lord Irmingham hurried towards them, his light-blue cassock flapping at his ankles.

'My dear, I saw you with Prince Dmitry! I thought...'

The sight of her husband had a startling effect. She gave a loud sob, waved the handkerchief protestingly in his direction and without a word fled past him towards the open door at the base of the tower.

'Isobel dear!'

He peered round at the prince afterwards, eyelids flickering busily in slightly accusing confusion, and asked what the matter was.

The prince cleared his throat. 'Your wife did not know what was going on in her own home. I was in the tower last night and I told her. One of my compatriots, a Russian, is dying. I was going to ask you, Lord Irmingham...'

'Giles, please.'

'Giles, I was going to ask you who they were.'

His host gave him the benefit of a long stare and stroked his beard. He raised his eyebrows, looked down at his feet and nodded. 'Yes, yes, yes, I owe you an explanation. Last evening you mentioned something about a black boat and a gunshot. Yes, yes, it's all quite possible, I'm afraid. I shouldn't have tried to deny it. It's very worrying, of course it is, and my wife, poor thing, is quite overwrought by it.'

Small glassy drops of perspiration stood out on his forehead as he spoke.

7

Consumed by a mixture of courtesy and curiosity, the prince followed Giles into Stadleigh Court through the door at the base of the tower. It was carefully locked behind them, a procedure familiar from the previous night. A flight of curved carpeted stairs, with a dado at shoulder height surmounted by glass-fronted pictures, led up to a musty-smelling first-floor landing. It seemed vaguely recognisable to the prince and confirmation came when he realised they had reached a point close to the door used last night for going up to the sickroom. Giles meanwhile showed him out through the door into the corridor no distance from his bedroom and, after carefully locking it, hurried him in another direction. He soon beckoned him into what turned out to be a study.

'Caught sight of you from here,' he announced as he directed the prince towards a leather armchair. 'Do have a seat.'

The manner was as brusque as Isobel Irmingham's, but more from nervousness than a wish to command. As he sat down, the prince noted that the window from which he had presumably been seen had leaded panes and fancy pre-Raphaelite coloured glass round the edges. It was now brilliantly sunlit and its colours shed a frosty imitation of their pigments on the book-lined wall opposite. A loudly ticking clock on a carved wooden mantelpiece also drew attention to itself, although its glass face glittered so strongly in the sunlight that it was hard to see what time it told. The prince consulted his watch to find it was scarcely more than nine-thirty.

'I am not, I hope, keeping you from something else?'

The question made him replace the watch instantly and explain that he had been told the meeting was not due until ten o'clock.

'I'm so sorry. I should explain about my wife, you see. There are reasons why she, and of course you, my dear Dmitry, may seem to be kept in the dark... They are delicate, very delicate.'

Judging by his red-rimmed eyes and pale complexion, Giles Irmingham's night had been even more interrupted than the prince's. He seated himself in an armchair opposite, inquired whether his guest had breakfasted well, appeared reassured by the answer, ran his fingers along the arm of his chair and began speaking in a quiet, confidential voice.

'You know, don't you?'

'I am not sure what you mean.'

'It's about last night.'

'What about last night?'

'You said you had been talking to my wife Isobel about what you saw in the tower last night. Well, I know all about it.'

The prince was uncertain: 'You mean the doctor told you?'

'Yes.' Giles leaned forward attentively and made little quivering movements of his outstretched fingers. If they were intended to urge the prince to speak, they succeeded. He described roughly what he had told Lady Isobel. The other's pink, unhealthily veined cheeks above the white rim of beard began to break into a smile.

'So it was you who mentioned *curare*! Why on earth didn't young Jamie think of that before! Lockjaw! Well I never!

'Jamie – you call him Jamie, do you? He has a quaint habit of pretending he is Scottish.'

'Yes, he does. I have no idea why. He's only been with us three weeks or so. And of course he's not very experienced. We had an old country doctor here until a couple of months ago. He had heart trouble and retired to the south coast. We're lucky to have young Jamie. His experience is limited, true, but he makes up for it in conscientiousness.'

'He said he had some *curare*,' the prince said, 'but who is the victim? Who is Sergius? Your wife appeared to know nothing about him.'

The clock on the mantelpiece embarked on a loud Westminster chiming of the three-quarter-hour. It was almost as if a signal had been given for confessions to begin. Giles coloured a little with embarrassment and looked at the prince with piercing honesty as he framed the following remarks.

Certain things had to be kept from his wife. That was what it was all about. The reason – well, they had only been married eighteen months. No excuse, of course, but maybe there would be a better understanding of things when the prince heard what he had to say. So far, though, *every single thing* (both hands were raised in a pleading gesture to lend further emphasis) *every single thing* depended on secrecy. So Lady Isobel simply could not be told everything because it would be hard to believe everything and there were also issues of, er, security and identity. As if to offer an incontrovertible justification, Giles stretched across to his desk, shuffled among papers, raised puffs of dust and ended by finding two volumes that he seemed to have laid ready. The prince took them. They were two volumes of Tolstoy's *Anna Karenina* in Russian.

The prince said it was Tolstoy's final masterpiece before his 'conversion'.

'Exactly.' Giles was evidently pleased. He then asked: 'But would you say it was true?'

The question seemed quite innocent and easy to answer, save for the likelihood of a trap and the prince hesitated. 'Of course it's not really...'

'You're doubtful whether it's really true, aren't you?' The sentence was finished for him. 'Yes, that's the trouble. It's a bit like what you called "a gap in nature". Very good, that. Yes, it *is* like "a gap in nature"! Who is to say where fiction ends and fact begins? Or vice-versa? Now I won't beat about the bush. You told me, didn't you, that before you went off to fight against the Turks you were living in St Petersburg? Don't I remember you saying you were living with your grandmother?'

'In St Petersburg I always used to stay with my grandmother.'

'And your grandmother had certain connections, I think?'

'She had connections in high society, yes.'

'Exactly. That's what I thought. You see, my dear Dmitry, you're the very person I need.' He reached out for a paper knife and waved it idly. His hand was noticeably shaking. He raised the tip of the knife very carefully to his lips and then lowered it before saying, though not directly to the prince: 'You are quite free of any financial embarrassments, I imagine. It is rather important that you should be."

'Well, I...' This was carrying bluntness a shade too far for the prince's liking. He pointed out that his affairs were his private concern unless, of course, he was being asked whether he might make a contribution to the Tolstoyan commune.

'No, no, it's not about that. I know it's bad form to discuss such matters. Following Tolstoyan example, since you mention it, I felt I had to be sure. Because a lot of money, yes, a lot of money is involved. You see... Oh, how can I put this?'

At this point Giles threw down the paper knife, heaved himself out of his chair, put his hands behind his back and did what the prince recalled certain Oxford dons doing. The burdensome weight of scholarship would be demonstrated by a hunching of the shoulders and a lowering of the head, followed by two heavy steps taken across the carpet, the head then raised slightly, followed by a moment or so of hesitation as a good deal of care was taken to think carefully what to say, followed then by a further two steps, at which point there would be a slow, neatly executed about-face, the back straightened, the procedure restarted and the words uttered.

'My father built this place.' Giles spoke straight ahead of him at either bookshelves or the window. 'He caught the capitalist bug. He made his money out of the very extensive business he did with your country in the days when big profits were to be made. He married into the Stadleigh family, which is why this is called Stadleigh Court, and the Stadleigh wealth helped him move up in the world. Being an inveterate, red-blooded captain of industry, he simply couldn't be content until he had made himself into an aristocrat and received a peerage. Call us nouveaux riches if you like. We Irminghams don't really mind. My father married money and made the most of it. That's all that matters.'

He paused to study a particularly tight-packed section of books on the shelves.

'I did the exact opposite. I did not marry money. My first wife had a hereditary title and not much else. So my daughter Helen has a title in her own right and not a penny to her name. My son will succeed to my title and my second wife, bless her, is county but not an heiress. I know I let the side down a bit. Still, that's not the point.'

He laughed and in a more jovial tone began talking about his mother. It appeared to be a rambling tale at first, but gradually it achieved coherence and relevance. His mother had been very fond of riding and whenever she accompanied his father on trips to Russia she had included among her entourage a favourite groom of hers. He was called Wilson, an expert equestrian. In addition to having a good eye for horseflesh he had a fondness for drink. Giles's mother was persuaded to let this man Wilson stay in Russia, in good employment, but the result could probably have been foreseen. His fondness for the hard stuff and Russian conviviality turned him quickly enough into a drunkard. His wife died and he very soon sank to the bottom, leaving behind him an orphan girl called Hannah.

'I can't pretend it's an edifying story.' He stopped right in front of the prince. 'It had a happy ending, at least in one sense. The girl Hannah was befriended by someone you know. Or knew. Many, many years ago.' He folded his arms across his chest and breathed in very heavily. 'You have the answer literally in your hands.'

Holding the two volumes of *Anna Karenina*, the prince began unwillingly to realise that he was being asked to accept something quite literally beyond belief. There were degrees of plausibility he could not begin to imagine. Yet memory reinforced the plausibility rather than denied it and concerned literally what he held in his hands. Where exactly, then, does biography merge with the creative imagination to achieve a blend so real it might seem to transcend fact and make fiction a reality? How could he deny to himself the reality of what he remembered and yet simultaneously face up to the knowledge that memory itself might be a fiction?

***

The sound of harness bells and carriage wheels hissing through slushy, thawing snow along the boulevards and the ice already flowing on the wide reaches of the Neva and spiders' webs of cracks forming in the canals. I was seventeen, an officer cadet, accompanying my grandmother on a very secret journey into a part of St Petersburg I couldn't remember save for the fact of the sun shining on my face with that incredible, heatless brilliance of early springtime. We alighted and I trailed up steps in the wake of grandmother's thick, ankle-length fur coat and then up another of those St Petersburg staircases, not as wide, true, or as grand as grandmother's, until the reception rooms were reached where I remembered having to wait perhaps as much as half-an-hour while grandmother was received alone. Afterwards, suddenly, double doors opened and this astonishing woman came out. She came up to me, held me for a moment at arms length, then drew me slowly towards her, to my faintly resisting embarrassment, and pressed me to her, saying quietly: *'Seriozha! Seriozha!'* and her perfume, her femininity, her sensuality engulfed me with a quickening, enchanting sweetness.

***

'Yes,' he said, shaking himself out of the momentary daydream, 'I remember, of course I remember.' In fact, he remembered his second visit to Anna Karenina more vividly even than the first, but Giles was already saying: 'Well, she befriended Hannah Wilson. Now my mother had also taken considerable trouble to keep in touch and knew about this. I don't say she exactly approved. The lady's reputation was, well, shall we say hardly *de rigueur*? The scandal surrounding her relationship with that guards officer, Count...'

'You mean Count Vronskii?'

'I do mean him.' Giles ran his hand a trifle nervously over his mouth and beard and slowly retook his seat opposite. 'That scandal had all sorts of repercussions, as you know. It even affected my father's business interests. Her husband, Karenin, was a very influential man. My father and Karenin were friendly. I can even go so far as to say that, without my father's initial help, it is doubtful whether Karenin would have become as rich as he has. And he has become very, very rich.'

'I didn't know that.'

'Oh, yes.' He gave an airy wave of the hand. 'He gave up his official work, you know, and devoted himself to mining and the manufacture of steel. That's where my father was able to help him.'

'Did he marry again?'

'No, no, he didn't remarry. He threw himself into his work. He became an industrialist and a millionaire. And that's what I want to talk about now. Because, you see, two weeks ago he died, a very old man. It was thought he died intestate, but it seems not. He died leaving all his wealth to his wife.'

The statement was plain, matter-of-fact, unembellished and for that reason it had such a ring of reasonableness the prince did not immediately apprehend its latent meaning. A husband would naturally leave his wealth to his wife. He sat upright.

'But Anna Karenina, Anna Arkadyevna is dead! She threw herself under a train!'

Giles stared back at him for as long as half a minute, during which he began to shake his head slightly as if he had heard something palpably true but almost beyond the bounds of probability.

'No, she isn't. She's not dead. She has been living here for a dozen and more years. Here at Stadleigh Court. Or – how can I put it? – *someone* who claims to be her has been living here all that time. That's what I want to find out, you see. Is she really who she says she is?'

It was not a direct question, it seemed, more a vague speculation. He at once appeared to concede as much by rising to his feet and looking blankly out of the window. The prince waited. It crossed his mind for one appalling instant that his host was mad. Then he corrected himself by recognising that he himself might be thought mad if he claimed he had met Anna Karenina on two occasions. All he could rely on was the reasonable certainty that his memory was trustworthy.

Silence gathered round them, consumed by the loud ticking of the clock. The prince was at a loss to know what to say. Giles broke the spell.

'Oh, of course, you know and I know, we all know the legend. It is arguably a legend, a myth. I mean, of course, the incomparable myth of her death, the way she took that journey to the station, the sense of the worthlessness of her life, her ignoble wish to avenge herself on the man for whose sake she had sacrificed so much, and then the inevitability of her tragedy, symbolised by the inexorable steel rails on which she threw herself and the famous final image of the candle, *"...the candle by which she had been reading the book so full of life's alarms, deceits, wretchedness and evil flared up more brightly than ever, illumined all that had previously been obscure, flickered, started to gutter and was extinguished forever."*'

'Images of light and dark were what gave a pattern to her life – that and, of course, her vitality, the way she moved through her society world as if she were waltzing away her life to suit its rhythms whereas in reality she was always trying to dance herself out of the ballroom and into a freedom of her own choosing. She never succeeded. She was locked into that futile waltzing by bonds as rigid as the steel rails governing her life from start to finish. That was her tragedy.

And her only escape was suicide. We all supposed it, of course. Even I supposed for a time that Anna killed herself like that. What other evidence did we have?'

The prince opened his mouth to speak and Giles anticipated him: 'Yes, her lover, that guards officer – Count Vronskii – I knew you'd want to mention him...'

Again the prince was about to interrupt and Giles was too quick. He made his points with judicial forcefulness, using his right index finger to slice the air each time: 'That's the only real evidence, isn't it? Didn't he claim to have identified her? A body covered in blood – that's all he identified. And he, after all, had driven her to it, hadn't he? When you think about it, it was only his testimony that pronounced her dead and he, a man with a bad conscience, toothache and God knows what else, probably glad to be rid of her, he couldn't be sure, could he? – in his state of mind, I mean? – whether it really was *her* blood-stained corpse laid out there among other corpses at the railway-station? And her legal husband, Karenin, did he see her? No, apparently not. On the authority of one man – one man, mark you! – she was accepted as being dead. That's the sole evidence. But she wasn't dead! No, she wasn't dead at all!'

The prince tried hard to disregard these final emphatic claims, but was provoked by them into an ironic, imitative response: 'Oh, no, she's not dead! *Slava bogu, ona vsyo yescho v zhivykh!* She's alive! *Ona zhivyot, konechno zhivyot zdes!* She is living here at Stadleigh Court! Of course, of course! Really, Giles, you mustn't overstrain either my credulity or my goodwill!'

'You may mock, Dmitry, my dear chap. I don't blame

you. I've had mockery from several quarters, some very close to me, indeed my nearest and dearest. But I ask you to be serious. Please be serious.'

'I will be serious about one thing,' the prince said curtly. 'I know Vronskii is dead. He was killed in the Turkish campaign. As for the claims you're making about Anna Arkadyevna, I can't take them seriously at all. Vronskii was absolutely crushed by what happened to her. I don't believe for a moment he gave false testimony, as you're suggesting. In any case, how did she get here?'

'I was coming to that.' With a flourish Giles seized the two volumes of *Anna Karenina* and replaced them on the desk. 'She came here largely because of my daughter-in-law, Hannah. She was Hannah Wilson then. As soon as the girl heard about it, she was in touch with my mother and the upshot was that Anna was secreted away on one of my father's ships.'

'How serious were her injuries?'

'Pretty bad. Both legs were broken, I believe, and she had a terrible blow to her forehead. Severe concussion, you know. For months it was touch and go. Even when she finally got here, she was an invalid for a couple of years. My father had her very carefully looked after. There was always a nurse in attendance.'

'But didn't anybody guess who she was?'

'Here? In the depths of Herefordshire? Of course not! Why should they?'

'Well, didn't she want to go back to Russia?'

'My father assumed she would once she'd fully recovered. But no, she had lost her nerve. "The zest is gone," she would say – she spoke good English before she came here – and her zest for Russia had quite gone. She virtually became a recluse. Her great pleasure was horse riding. It was the one thing that got her outside and she would ride in all weathers. Until her beloved horse stumbled one day down by the ford and threw her. She injured her face and her hip. That upset her so much she's hardly been out since.'

'You mean she's just lived here by herself?'

'No, no. She had two personal servants, old Boris and his wife. They came… Oh, I can't say exactly when. That was until very recently, you see. Then, just over a month ago, her son turned up. Sergius.'

'Oh, her son! Sergey Alekseevich! That's who he is!'

'Sergius is her son, yes.'

'Her son by Karenin, of course.'

'Of course.'

'The lockjaw victim?'

'That's right.'

'Well, well, what a happy outcome!'

'Happy?'

'I mean happy for her,' the prince said. 'Her greatest regret was that she had had to give up her son. Don't you remember how she tried to see him on his birthday?'

'Oh, that, yes.' Giles sounded slightly at a loss and gave another airy wave of the hand.

'What about his father? Did he let him come? I would imagine he'd never have allowed it.'

'Oh, yes, towards the end Karenin relented. He even wanted to make it up with his wife. His son came as a kind of peacemaker, well, something like that... But Anna wouldn't go back. She said she couldn't let herself be seen. It all stemmed from her riding accident, I think. Since then her behaviour's tended to be a bit abnormal, even a bit irrational. You know, things like insisting she wouldn't speak English any more, an obsession with taking baths – we had to have a bathroom specially made for her next to her bedroom – and fear of certain noises, fear even of going out, fear of visitors... Oh, we've had quite a lot of trouble, I can tell you!'

'I see.'

In fact, what the prince really saw was the likelihood that this strange guest at Stadleigh Court had outstayed her welcome. By several years, it seemed, judging from the irritable tone of the last remark.

'The young man, who grandly calls himself Sergius for some reason, had been on bad terms with his father before he arrived and has been thoroughly uncooperative ever since. His mother dotes on him and won't hear a word against him. The trouble is they're both convinced they've got enemies on all sides. But they don't take proper precautions. The news of Karenin's death has made them more suspicious than ever and yet earlier this week she insisted on an idiotic escapade.'

'What?'

'Oh, she insisted on conducting some sort of obsequies down by the river. They were for her late husband, I think.'

'In a black boat? In a boat with a canopy draped in black?' the prince asked excitedly. '"A gap in nature" as Shakespeare described it! You remember, I told you...'

'Yes, yes, yes.' Giles frowned slightly. 'Of course, of course, you had that accident with your bicycle. Well, that afternoon she was apparently carried back by Sergius. She calls him Seriozha. She'd apparently hurt herself while getting out of that boat. Oh, what a fuss!'

'But surely *he* was hurt, wasn't he?'

'It was utterly silly of both of them! That's the real truth!' Giles disregarded the other's query and restarted his impatient pacing. He went on in a loud voice, his face now pink with irritation: 'They behave as if they owed me nothing! Nothing! But my father spent God knows how much on ensuring her contentment here, and I've spent thousands every year and it's about time I got something back! She did try to be less demanding since her accident, I admit – we didn't have to keep a horse specially for her, special horse shoes, that sort of thing – but since the arrival of her son, she's been hopelessly unreasonable and irresponsible! They both have!'

Realising he had said a bit too much, he stopped and stared down at the carpet.

'Look,' he began again, with every appearance of having regained his self-control, 'I must have trustworthy testimony. Do you understand what I mean? I must have someone who can say authoritatively, confidently, clearly that this is Anna Karenina. Now tell me, please, how well did you know her?'

'I met her twice. The first time very briefly. The second time we had a long talk.'

'Can you remember what it was about?'

'It's a good many years ago, you know, but I think I can.'

'Good. Then I suggest you try talking about exactly the same things. That'll give you some standard of comparison. You see I want you to help me prove she is Anna Karenina beyond any reasonable doubt. And then, if you would be good enough to make a sworn statement witnessed by my lawyer, she can be treated as a beneficiary, a genuine claimant.'

'Claimant?'

'For the Will, Karenin's Will.'

'Ah, that had slipped my mind!'

'My dear Dmitry, that is what this entire matter is all about! I need the money. She is quite willing to let me have the money if it is legally hers, but it has to be proved that she is who she claims she is. You see my dilemma.'

'I do, I do.'

'And you will help, will you?'

'Of course. What do you want me to do?'

'Dmitry, my dear chap, I counted on this!' He leaned down and clasped the other's right hand between his own two hands. He then released it and stood back and once more stared out of the window. 'I think we ought to strike while the iron is hot, as it were. I mean we ought to go and see her immediately, if you are willing. She won't have time to think of excuses and your own impressions will be as fresh as they can be in the circumstances. I'll introduce you, if I may, as someone she knew in the past.' He lowered his voice. 'She has a weakness for younger men. She and my son Gerald – oh, never mind! We are men of the world, aren't we? I hardly need to spell everything out in detail. Let's go.'

The prince took several seconds to absorb this revelation. The casual candour of it could seem shocking, yet it tended to validate the claim that *she* was living here. A vision of the woman he had once known as so attractive and vital, holding court like Catherine the Great in this out-of-the-way place and characteristically taking a lover – well, on reflection it was hardly all that unexpected! He felt a genuine tremor of excitement at the sudden prospect of seeing her again, this time not as the daunted, impressionable adolescent he had been all those years ago, but as a man with a great admiration for women and a taste for their company.

'Right,' he said.

***

They went by the route the doctor had taken the previous night, through the locked door, that is, and up the stairway to the landing on what he assumed was the second floor, where the air evidently had little chance of escaping but contained distinct whiffs of cooking smells. He did not remember this from the night-time visit, though it struck him as quite natural that meals should be prepared in this tower occupied exclusively, it seemed, by his compatriots and unvisited even by Lady Isobel. Yet, as he climbed higher, following the cloth of the light-blue cassock tautening along Giles Irmingham's back, he could not overcome increasing doubts. The fact of Anna Karenina's presence here seemed beyond belief. This would have remained his firm conviction if he had not suddenly came face to face with the portrait on the top landing, before which there still burned a single feeble candle flame as if before an icon.

In a flash it all came back. He remembered it from St Petersburg. It had hung in the small reception room where she had received him on his second visit. At first sight it reminded him only too keenly of the Repin portrait of his dear Princess Alisa that hung in the drawing room of their house in Portland Place. That portrait never failed to keep her image vividly alive during all her absences.

Seeing the Anna Karenina portrait now, in daylight or as

much morning light as filtered from a skylight, it was much more than so much oil pigment artfully brushed on canvas to simulate life. It was Anna Arkadyevna in person, a vital, charming woman with curly black hair, bared shoulders and arms. A thoughtful half-smile parted soft lips covered with a slight down and she gazed at him triumphantly and sensitively out of embarrassingly candid eyes. She wore a dark-blue dress and looked just as if she were about to extend her beautiful bare arms towards him and hold him to her and whisper the seductive name 'Seriozha' in mistake for her son, yet ready to embrace him as her lover.

'*Akh, kakaia krasavitsa!* My God, Giles, I remember this!'

The prince's exclamation was not matched by anything equivalent from Giles. He was preoccupied. He was standing by the open door to the bedroom and waving to someone inside.

'Hannah, my dear, you remember the prince, Dmitry...'

Hannah Kempson came out of the sickroom carrying a tray. She looked happy, calling over her shoulder in Russian: 'All right, Boria, I know, I know. The doctor'll be back after lunch. Ah, Giles!'

'My daughter-in-law, Hannah.'

The introduction was polite but hardly necessary. She explained she had been busy assisting with a bed-bath. The prince naturally asked after the patient.

'So much better, it's scarcely credible. He has accepted a little food and we have managed to get him into a nightshirt at last. But he is still very, very weak. I think we owe you a lot, sir. You suggested the cure, didn't you?'

She had spoken the last sentence in Russian and the prince replied in the affirmative. The brief exchange clearly pained Giles who was somewhat impatiently about to guide the prince towards another door when a further loud burst of Russian speech filled the space of the landing. Boris, the elderly retainer, approached in a majestic waddle.

'Your excellency, you are our saviour! Your excellency, how can we possibly repay such loving kindness! Your excellency, the young master is better! He is better! It is a miracle!'

The prince's hand was seized and received a drenching from the old man's wet kisses.

'Your excellency, our lady has expressed the wish... to receive you, sir... to thank you, sir, in person, sir, for saving our dear young master's life, sir.' The kissing became frenzied. 'Oh, your excellency, it is a great privilege and we would be deeply, deeply...' He drew in a long, quivering breath and then blurted out a stream of words, still firmly gripping the prince's hand '...if you would be gracious enough to accept, your highness, sir, gracious enough, sir, to accept the invitation of our dear mistress, of our lady, of Anna Arkadyevna herself...'

'Enough!'

The prince drew his hand back. Boris opened his lips several times tasting air, like a baby suddenly deprived of a nipple.

'Your excellency, sir,' he murmured reproachfully.

'Boris, my friend, you are kissing me to death!'

'Oh, your excellency, sir, pardon me, sir, no, sir.' He swayed forwards and backwards and his face literally burst into an explosion of wrinkles. 'Sir, you are permitting yourself a ribaldry, I perceive. Gracious sir, how gratifying! This way, this way, be so good...'

A waddle, a shuffle of extremely ancient buckled shoes and the smell of long unwashed underwear, not to mention the frockcoat so stiff with age it fitted the elderly, stooped figure as much like a turtle's shell as a stone toga, gave notice that there was no option but to accept the inevitable. Boris and his accompanying odour were to be followed, as the prince now followed behind him through another door.

8

He entered a room with curved walls matching the shape of
the tower. The first thing he noticed was a heavy, foursquare
table covered in a tasselled green cloth, upon which stood a
bubbling samovar and glasses. A number of other large pieces
of furniture, along with some rickety upright chairs, were
scattered randomly on a worn Persian carpet. Everything was
characteristically Russian, he felt, including the room's dusty
stuffiness.

'Dear mistress, dear mistress,' came Boris's wailing
quaver of a voice, 'our saviour, his excellency, Prince Rostov,
is here.'

Sunlight caught dust motes and made them sparkle so
brightly it was hard to see who was there. Then, just as it
had been difficult to discern the figure in the boat, the prince
took a while to realise that someone was reclining on a high-
backed dark leather sofa, dressed in black, with a black veil.

The black shape remained motionless despite Boris's
announcement and his insistence that the prince should
approach. He felt overwhelmed by a sense that he was
about to confront a corpse. Then a thin white hand suddenly
emerged from the black garments and languidly offered itself
to be kissed.

The prince did what was expected of him. He bent
and kissed it. The fingers were small, beautifully shaped

and smelled of rose water. Perhaps he found himself at that instant peering a little too keenly at the veil without being able to discern any features. The hand was then withdrawn and used to beckon the elderly manservant.

'Help me up a little, Boris, if you would.'

It was a voice of quiet, feminine authority that matched the elegance of the movement as she sat upright with Boris's help and then skilfully, delicately adjusted the skirt of her long garment to suit herself. This was the vitality, the poise, of Anna Arkadyevna as the prince had known her in St Petersburg. He could not doubt that for a moment. She herself forestalled any further doubts by waving towards a chair and saying confidently and strongly, as if they were the closest of friends: 'I learned, my dear prince, only this morning how helpful you have been.'

'Madame,' he said a little nervously and equally nervously sat down in a rickety gilded upright armchair.

'You may have found a cure for my darling Sergei, my dear Seriozha. I cannot say how grateful I am. He is very precious to me, you know, and anything that can alleviate the pain must have some quality of the divine about it. In that sense you have indeed been a saviour to us.' She adjusted the sleeves of her black garment. 'You are content that I speak our language? Russian is not strange to you?'

'Oh, no, madame!' He was disconcerted to hear the voice coming from behind the veil as if from behind a heavy curtain that scarcely moved at all when she spoke. 'I imagine you have not had much opportunity to speak our language...'

'Prince, you are right! For many, many years I tried to speak only English, but it strikes me one cannot change oneself. I now prefer my native language. I believe – yes, I think I can tell from your face...' she leaned forward to look closely at him, still without revealing any of her own features '...I believe I knew you a long time ago, Prince Rostov. You were very young and your looks, well, like mine... have changed. Do you remember me?'

'Of course, madame. It was just before I went off to the Turkish campaign.'

'Oh, please, do not mention that! I hate to remember that war! Do you smoke? Boris, where are the cigars?'

He said he did not smoke.

'My friend Gerald does,' she said. 'So many men do nowadays, I understand.'

Both of her white hands now fluttered commandingly and a little irritably as if trying to disperse cigar smoke. It was a signal for Boris to begin doing what was expected of him. The ritual included a slow pouring of sepia-coloured tea into glasses set in fretted silver holders, a topping up with hot water from the tap of the bubbling samovar and the placing of the silver holders on little saucers beside sugar lumps. All this was watched with a kind of momentary absorption as if the ritual would be bound to end in the old man's shaky movements causing a spill. Attention was suddenly diverted by her voice coming from behind the veil: 'So, prince, we are in your debt, I understand. My poor, poor boy, he was so terribly ill. I trembled for him, as you can imagine. He had only been with me here such a short time and we had been out just once... He thought he had been shot, you know. It is quite possible, because we have enemies.'

'Surely, madame, not here.'

'Oh, my dear prince, you cannot imagine!' Her voice fell to a whisper. 'We have enemies all round us! This house is full of our enemies! Please draw your chair closer so we can talk quietly. I find loud sounds so distracting these days.'

'Not Giles, not Lord Irmingham surely?' the prince asked, the chair creaking beneath him as he moved forward.

'No, no, Giles has always been my friend. But there are others. People wish to know who I am, you see. Threats have even come to me...' She pressed her veiled face close to his ear and whispered something about a bath.

'Excuse me, I didn't...'

'...*in my bath*! Think of that!'

She was crazy! Probably like Giles!

'*In my bath*, my dear prince! And I am not imagining it! I know dear Giles thinks I do, but I do not! I do not! For a recluse like me it may seem easy to imagine things, but I am not imagining anything!'

'Madame, surely...'

Boris was hovering close by, having poured the tea and awaiting further orders. His eyes met the prince's with the distressed look of a child who did not know what to do. An instant later they were fastened on his mistress, leaving the prince with an increasing sense that both of them were equally deranged.

'Thank you, Boris, that will be all,' she announced.

'Mistress.'

Boris then bowed, shuffled backwards, bowed again and no doubt through long habit managed to avoid crashing into any of the furniture. Before leaving he crossed himself with broad sweeps of his arm in front of an icon and rather theatrically turned, bowed again and beat a retreat through the door.

'Oh, he is so devoted. I need devoted friends,' she said. 'I think, prince, I can count on your devotion.'

He assured her she could.

'Oh, I am so grateful! I am sure you can understand.' She reached out and patted his hand. For him there was no escaping a sense that she had moved far beyond politeness in her gratitude and was even assuming the right of a seraglio queen to make a covert overture to love. 'I feel I can be perfectly intimate with you, my dear prince. I can tell you now quite sincerely that *there are enemies here*. I have enemies. I know I have. That is why I hardly dare go out. Why I want the windows closed. And you will soon find you have enemies, too, now that you have come to see me.'

'Oh, but why?'

'You will find out.'

She lifted her veil and took a sip of the tea. It was done so skilfully he did not catch sight of her face. He recognised that the sipping of the tea was a move designed to quell further discussion. The veil was impenetrable, that was that. He knew he had no right to ask why she wore it. Instead he sipped his own tea and asked after her health.

'I am all right. Nerves, as always.'

They both drank in a momentary silence.

'I remember your portrait outside, madame,' he remarked in an effort not to talk about her nerves. 'But may I,' he added, 'presume upon your good nature and address you in a less formal way? May I call you Anna Arkadyevna?'

'Oh, of course, my dear prince! Please do address me

as Anna Arkadyevna. I am so unused to being called that. Like the portrait, you understand, the name belongs to my past, not my present self.' It pleased him to hear her give a little laugh. 'Don't you remember, prince, all those years ago, how we talked about such important things? We talked about painting, I think. The realism of French painting, for example.'

'Oh, I do remember. I was a great enthusiast for the return to realism in those days and the French struck me as exhibiting such a sense of poetry in their respect for the truth of reality.'

Again she gave a light laugh. 'I am laughing,' she said, 'in the way one does when one sees a portrait that has captured a very good likeness. What you've just said captured exactly French art as it was then, their painting and their literature – Zola, I mean, and Daudet. Perhaps it's always the case that one's concepts originally have their source in invented, conventional figures and later combinations occur, as it were, so that invented figures become boring and the time comes to think up more natural ones, figures that do more justice to reality.'

'That is absolutely right!' The prince could not have agreed more.

'You have met my little pupil, have you?' The glass appeared from underneath the veil and was placed on an occasional table. The sudden change of subject took him off guard.

'Who?'

'Hannah. Hannah Kempson, as she now is. She has been taking such care of my poor Seriozha. I think she may have fallen a little bit in love with him.'

'I was told she brought you here.'

'She did, yes. She was my only real success, you know. I have had a life full of failures, my dear prince, and she is my only success.'

'What do you mean?'

'I failed to make a success of my marriage. I failed over my son. I failed over Count Vronskii. But over dear Hannah – no. I expended so much love and care on her and she repaid me by literally saving my life. I call that a success.'

'Oh, that is most certainly true.' She was living in the past, he thought, but that in itself tended to prove it was the real Anna Arkadyevna speaking. He took a chance and made a remark very similar to one he remembered making at their first meeting.

'Anna Arkadyevna, forgive me if I speak familiarly...'

'Please.'

'Anna Arkadyevna, if you had devoted a hundredth part of the energy you devoted to Hannah to the more general purpose of educating Russian children you would have done a useful and important job.'

She gave no sign of taking offence. The elegant hands drew apart in unaffected candour: 'That may be so, but I couldn't. I was encouraged to take an interest in the school on the Vronskii estate. I went there several times. The peasant children were very nice, but I wasn't drawn to it. You mentioned my energy. Energy is based on love. But you can't force love, you know. I loved Hannah, I don't know why.'

'I understand perfectly,' he said. 'One cannot put one's heart into schools and institutions like that and I think that's precisely why such philanthropic institutions always produce so few results.'

'Yes,' she agreed, 'I never could. *Je n'ai pas le coeur assez large* to love a whole home of beastly little girls. *Cela ne m'ai jamais reussi.* So many women have gained a position in society in that way. But you see I never wanted a position in society. And now, of course...'

A dismissive flutter of the hands elegantly put the subject to rest.

One thing was now clear: the natural, easy way of talking was exactly what the prince remembered from their meeting in St Petersburg. Like that earlier time, Anna Karenina moved the conversation along with confidence and fluency. She described without embarrassment and with hardly any hesitation how she had entrusted herself completely to Hannah, how Hannah had tended her on the voyage to England and how she had eventually arrived at Stadleigh Court and very slowly recovered from her injuries. He was naturally dying to ask exactly what had caused them. Almost casually she gave him the answer: 'I was pushed, you know.'

'Pushed! But who...'

'I simply cannot say, but I know someone pushed me.'

'Someone pushed you!'

'Yes, yes, someone pushed me. I think that's what happened.'

Oh, it couldn't be otherwise! The vivacity was still there, after all these years, and though she might be prey to all sorts of fears, not least that of showing the terrible injuries done to her face, she gave no impression of being frightened of life.

'I cannot tell you how pleased I am to hear that,' he said. 'I know it is the generally accepted version...'

'The *published* version,' she pointed out.

'Oh, yes, of course!'

'And what people read they tend to believe.'

'Yes, but you are clearly *alive*! And if I may say so, it is because you are alive that I was asked to come here by Giles, by Lord Irmingham. You are an heiress, you know.'

'Oh, *that*!'

'It is most important apparently. He needs the money so badly.'

'Of course he does, poor dear! I love his idealism.'

'But you have always preferred realism, Anna Arkadyevna.'

'Always,'

'Yet I would never have thought you sentimental.'

'Sentimental? What do you mean?'

'I was riding my bicycle and had an accident. It was just down by what I think is called the old ford. As I lay there I could hardly fail to see a strange sight – a boat decked out in black, with a black canopy. It sailed out into the sunlight and I think you cast a red rose on the water. It was you, wasn't it, Anna Arkadyevna? Giles said you did it in honour of your late husband.'

He knew he was taking a risk in mentioning the episode, but the silence that greeted it made him regret it at once. There was no way of telling what the effect was. Neither the veil nor the elegant hands gave any sign of reaction, so it took a little time to realise what was happening.

Her whole body quivered under the black garment. He assumed at first it was due to anger. Then he realised she was not so much quivering as shaking and he felt alarmed. By quick stages the rapid movement transformed itself into the beginnings of a shoulder-heaving mirth, accompanied by a ripple of unaffected, girlish giggles from behind the veil, which in turn gathered momentum and ended in a long peal of laughter. She threw her head back. Then, as the laughter subsided, a hand stretched out to the occasional table beside her, found a handkerchief and again disappeared beneath the veil, soon to be followed by a lengthy nose-blowing.

'Oh, my dear prince! No! In honour of my late husband indeed!'

Again a little trill of laughter followed by more sniffing and nose-blowing. He apologised for supposing she had been annoyed and, as he spoke, noticed on the occasional table where the handkerchief had been lying a small silver-framed photograph of someone who looked very like Gerald Kempson.

'No need to be sorry.' She again patted his hand reassuringly. 'You weren't to know. No, it was a little outing for me, a little ceremony. Oh, it's too silly to talk about. You are quite right, I am sentimental.'

'May I ask what kind of ceremony?'

'Oh, it's too silly to talk about! It was for my poor Frou-Frou!' She seemed ready to abandon the subject and then added: 'Of course, my poor boy thought he had been shot. Could he have been?'

'The doctor could find no sign of any injury. Yet I could see he was suffering from what has been called the disease of wounding. I thought he had been shot, you see, because as I was lying on the riverbank after my accident I distinctly heard a shot fired.'

'You did!'

She had sat up. Though the black material of the veil was thick, he felt sure he could distinguish a pair of glistening eyes looking at him intently.

'I wasn't sure. Now I think I was mistaken. Did you say it was a ceremony for your horse?'

'Oh, yes, it was in memory of my lovely Frou-Frou who was shot. I have tried to hold a little ceremony each year, but not with a boat as this time. I can't think now how long ago it was. I fell off, you see, and hurt myself quite badly. This time I stupidly tripped as I got out of the boat.' She seemed to suppress an embarrassed laugh before suddenly saying: 'Oh, prince, you know I have enemies! They are all round me. But you will help me, I am sure. Please give me your hand. I must go and see how my son is, how my dear Seriozha is.'

By that time enough had been said for the prince to be sure beyond any reasonable doubt. The lady in black to whom he now offered his hand *was* Anna Arkadyevna Karenina. She *was* the Anna Karenina to whom he had talked in St Petersburg all those years ago. The awkward way she rose from the sofa even with his help and took one or two steps leaning on his arm demonstrated her age and her frailty and if this was not as he had remembered her, her commanding manner was the same. She had seemed then so elegant and commanding but never unnatural. Now the pressure of her weight on his arm was more authoritative than actual. She asserted this slightly fussy authority in directing him hurriedly across the room and out on to the landing, whispering that she was anxious to find out how the cure was working.

Ever attentive, Boris, hearing her voice, rose from the chair set outside the sickroom and announced in a pronounced whisper that the young master was sleeping. This naturally put her in two minds.

'Oh, what a good thing that is! When will the doctor be coming?'

'I cannot say for sure, dear mistress. He said he would make a visit some time after midday.'

She remarked something to the effect that no one in England ever seemed to do things at sensible times. The prince remarked that he had long grown used to the English custom of lunch at one o'clock and not dinner in the Russian manner at three o'clock in the afternoon. She then sighed.

'Well, prince, I can see there is no alternative.'

'No alternative?'

'I will show you my secret place.'

He looked round at once expecting to see the naughty look of a society lady who had just permitted herself a daringly rude *double entendre*, but her disguise was impenetrable. Unsure whether she was serious, he felt a light tug on his arm, playful as well as authoritative, urging him across the landing. With one hand still resting on his arm, she began a slow step-by-step descent of the curved stairs. She pressed down on him at each footfall. He had to brace himself each time to receive the pressure even though it was not great, because he was reminded of his bruised ribs.

'When I say a secret place, of course it is not really secret at all. You see, there was a time when I enjoyed bathing in the river on hot summer days like this. Then I had my accident. So my good friend, my protector, dear Giles, he built me this secret place. Oh, they have been good to me here! I know I have not shown my gratitude as I should. *Mais je ne suis pas ingrate*. It is so hard, don't you find? To be grateful, I mean. It was a defect in my education, I suppose.'

They arrived by gradual stages at the lower landing. Here were the cooking smells again and the sound of pans being moved about beyond a half-open door. She guided him down a further flight towards a length of landing and a door that turned out to be her bedroom. His gentlemanly reluctance to enter it provoked a characteristic laugh and a reassertion of her authority in urging him onwards into its unaired atmosphere. Scents of perfume and powder fought a losing battle against the room's general stuffiness, just as the pretty pink ruffled cover on the large bed and the similarly pink drapes over the windows formed a theatrical, light-operatic backdrop against which he glimpsed, in a succession of mirrors on wardrobe doors, their own two figures moving obtrusively and darkly like villains. Slowly they made their way through this boudoir.

'Voila, mon ami!'

She threw open a further door. He had supposed her 'secret place' would be an elegantly furnished little study or private sitting room. Instead he was being shown a bathroom. True, the walls were wood panelled, but the pipe-work and enamelled furnishings, including a cast-iron bath on lion-claw legs, were ordinary, if fairly new and unstained. He felt quite let down by this unremarkable example of English plumbing. Her veiled head, though, was turned towards him in obvious expectation of shared enthusiasm.

'Oh, very nice, very nice indeed,' the prince murmured, aware that in a practical sense this bathroom was not architecturally part of the tower. His practical attitude did not stop her from saying in a prattling way: 'Oh, I do love it. And I don't show it to anyone. It's my secret. I do so enjoy my baths, you see. It's been such a pleasure having a bathroom all to myself.'

In further demonstration of the bathroom's delights, she leaned forward and opened a casement window slightly. It immediately admitted a fresh flow of air and the warmth of morning sunshine. Along with it, a little to their surprise, came a sound of voices. He glanced out and saw several of Giles Irmingham's guests gathered along the balustrade almost immediately below. The difference between the tower's seclusion and the guests' free-and-easy life was most striking.

'Anna Arkadyevna, don't you ever feel cut off? I mean when all the windows are closed...'

'No!' The hooded head gave an emphatic shake. 'This window into my lovely bathroom is the only one I open. Oh, I have friends here, too, you know. And now that my dear Seriozha has come, why should I leave?'

'I can understand that, of course. As for myself, well, I don't know that I would choose to spend much time here.'

'You speak as if you won't be staying long, prince. Am I right?'

It was an awkward moment. He had never anticipated he would have found himself in any way emotionally drawn to this black-clad, nun-like Anna Karenina. Yet her clear preference for the dolls-house world of Stadleigh Court seemed suddenly very touching. He could see she needed the protection offered by the place. She had about her the vulnerability of a very gifted, easily hurt child. Perhaps this was what had made Giles Irmingham's father and then Giles himself go to such lengths to ensure her security and anonymity for so long.

That and something else. In a totally unexpected way, while he looked at her, there came a sound from far away on the other side of the river. He did not recognise the sound clearly at first. Like a fingernail drawn scratchily across glass, it identified itself after a while as the shrill, clear note of a locomotive whistle. In a further instant came its fainter echo and the distant rumble of wheels.

As if it had been a gunshot, she pressed herself against him and held him so tight he could hardly breathe.

'Protect me! Protect me! Protect me!' she whispered.

'From whom?'

'From my enemies! They are all around me! They think I should not exist!'

9

'She is imagining things.'

It was the prince's verdict once he had returned to the study, but he knew he was not imagining his own feelings. The force of his emotional attachment to the Anna Karenina who had hugged him at their first meeting now overwhelmed him. He was in love as deeply as a boy first consumed by love. Older, of course, vulnerable, willful in a childlike, self-absorbed way and yet charming despite the rather pitiable charade of her veil, she still had the power to set his heart racing. It was a guilty love, naturally, that challenged fidelity to Princess Alisa, not to mention the way Lady Helen's beauty had suborned him, but in Anna's case he knew how Gerald Kempson would feel as her lover. He felt a similar need to offer a loving protection, to enfold her, keep her safe and ward off all her fears.

'Oh, I know, I know. Enemies! She is imagining she has enemies!'

This was Giles's emphatic response to the prince's verdict. It suddenly awakened a momentary suspicion. Perhaps the prince's imagination had played tricks on him. Just as her insistence on having been pushed to her death seemed unlikely, he wondered whether he had been wrong to suppose that, only a moment previously, once he had left the tower and the door had again been locked behind him, he had seen someone watching him from the end of the corridor. Had there been someone there? Had it been one of her enemies? Maybe he blinked. He looked again. No one was there. So he had made his way quickly along the corridor to the study.

'That's been the trouble recently,' Giles went on a little irritably. 'They're imaginary, these enemies, I feel sure. And why she imagines she hears threats in her bathroom beats me. We only had it put it in about a year ago and she never complained about anything then. As I've assured her, just as Hannah has and, er, my son Gerald...' Giles caught his breath at this point '...there's really no reason for her to be frightened.' In his solemnly sonorous way he then announced that they were all trying to observe the precepts of Count Leo Tolstoy, so it was very unlikely anyone would use violence against Anna Karenina. 'But you are sure about her identity? You would swear to it in a court of law?'

'I would.'

The prince surprised himself by his very certainty. Apart from his own feelings, so many things had been convincing. Her voice, for one thing, the elegance of her gestures for another, but it was the subject of her conversation, so spontaneous and so intelligent, that left no doubt.

'She spoke exactly as I remember from our meeting, oh, what, two decades ago? I remember it like yesterday!'

Giles said he perfectly understood. He shook the prince's hand and broke into effusive thanks. Then he suddenly snapped his fingers.

'Your bicycle, my dear chap! It slipped my mind. I heard from the other side, from Irmingham, that it's been repaired.'

'From where?'

'Ah, yes, Irmingham! That's what the place is called on the other side of the river. If you're going there, do give my daughter my love. Naturally I hope to see her tomorrow at the soiree. And, my dear Dmitry, what you've said about the lady in the tower will be of the utmost importance. But do keep it secret, I beg of you. My lawyers will be here tomorrow and I would ask you to be prepared to sign written testimony, if you have no objection.'

He said he had none.

'Then can I arrange a carriage for you if you're going across to Irmingham?'

The prince said he would prefer to go on foot because he felt in need of exercise. Giles responded with a series of sonorously issued instructions as to how to get there and a renewal of his heartfelt thanks. With these ringing in his ears and relief at freeing himself from the reclusive, hot, airless atmosphere of the tower as well as his host's irritability, the prince returned to his bedroom.

Stimulated by the meeting with Anna Karenina, he found himself on reflection just as much puzzled and dismayed by it. He felt sure he could not be wrong about her identity. Her fear that had led to the concealment offered by the heavy black veil could not of course hide her natural vitality even if it might hide her injuries. It certainly did not conceal her obsessive, possibly unreal, concern for "enemies". Could it perhaps conceal her true identity? Was he wrong in being so certain that she *was* Anna Arkadyevna Karenina? He swept the doubt from his mind. No, he would refresh himself by walking to 'the other side', as Giles enigmatically referred to the village named after him on the other side of the river.

He had hoped on returning to his bedroom to find Cotton. There was no sign of him. Instead he found the newly cleaned and mended white linen cycling clothes neatly laid ready. Whether or not it was fitting dress for a stroll in the country before lunch, he could not say, but he fancied he would look rather up-to-date in a sporty English way. A glance in the mirror confirmed the impression. Canvas-topped shoes and a Panama hat completed the outfit.

Having been told to go through the rose garden, he did so. On the way he chose a tight-budded red rose for his buttonhole in celebration of the pleasure of the fresh air after the stuffiness of the tower. Although he felt a liberation of sorts, he could not throw off a feeling of anxiety and sadness. Just as the bruised ribs and wounded arm were reminders of the cycling accident, retrieval of his Rudge Explorer promised further freedom, he thought, yet doubts as to his own motives grew more marked and oddly more palpable as he made his way slowly down the sunlit stone steps and the terraces, waving the Panama hat languidly from side to side in front of his face to fend off flies.

He met no one. The English were clearly not going out in the midday sun. The neatly manicured garden, the terraces of lawn, the lines of yew hedges, the curving paths and stone steps – all seemed so normal in the heat. So why on earth did he have a feeling of being covertly watched? Why did he sense hostility in such normal surroundings?

Giles had told him to take the steep path down to the riverbank through the trees. The glistening surface of Wordsworth's "sylvan Wye" soon became visible through the darkly shuttering shapes of the tree trunks, although when he reached the bottom of the slope he faced not water but the planking of a footbridge and his weight caused a distinct sharp creaking that skittered across the quiet surroundings like a stone across water.

The river had its customary majestic calm flow. He paused at the centre of the bridge and looked downstream. Two figures could be seen some hundred metres away. To his amazement, one of them appeared to be wearing a bowler hat. It could only be Cotton standing there! And with water up to his knees!

What on earth was Cotton doing down by the river? The prince crossed the rest of the footbridge and walked down the overgrown path along the river's edge, remembering vaguely that this was the way he must have come in Oswald Holmcroft's trap. Willows and alders and reeds, though, provided an effective shield from the two figures he had glimpsed, but after a short walk Cotton's voice became distinctly audible and speaking with a great deal more enthusiasm than usual.

'A very nice one, young Charles, sir! That's right! Well done!'

A large willow hid him until, as if a door had opened, there he was. His black trousers folded halfway up his white thighs, he was standing some distance out from the bank and making gestures that looked as if they might be appropriate for cricket, but since the prince knew it was not a game usually played in mid-river he soon realised Cotton was giving directions about how to use a fishing rod. In his black bowler hat, looking a bit like a policeman, though still wearing a tie, coat and waistcoat, he was showing the long-legged Charles Kempson how to cast.

'Now again, young sir! Farther out, this time! Swing it right up!'

The boy, naked save for corduroy shorts and a floppy-brimmed straw hat, was standing a short way downstream with the fishing rod raised in the air.

'Caught anything yet?' the prince asked.

'Sir!' Cotton swung round in astonishment and almost toppled into the water.

The boy turned and pointed negligently to a wicker basket on the bank containing a large fish. The brightness of the sunlight on the water's surface and the faint pallor of shadow from the straw hat lit up his young face in a most striking way. He had the same Monna Vanna beauty of his aunt and his father but much fresher in the sun's brightness than it had been the previous evening at dinner or in the rose garden earlier. He looked at the newcomer, absorbed the prince's image, as it were, gave a faint smile of recognition and turned back again to the business of casting.

'I hope you have no objection, sir,' said Cotton. 'Young Master Charles wanted someone to come fishing with him. I had some time to spare and I took the liberty...'

'I never knew you were a fisherman, Cotton.'

'Oh, yes, sir. My father taught me.'

'That was very sensible of him. I thought I saw you down here and wanted to make sure. Can we expect fish for lunch?'

Cotton said he did not know. He was preparing to make his way back to the bank, but the prince urged him to stay where he was and explained that he was off to Irmingham to retrieve his bicycle. As he waved his hat at a fly buzzing close to his face he saw something else.

A small grey cloud, like a faint fog bank, had appeared farther downstream. On the calm, glittering, sunny reaches of water it looked more like a swarm of insects than drifting smoke. He asked Cotton what it was and received no more than a shrug in reply. The boy heard and pipingly his young voice rang back: 'Stubble-burning. In the Irmingham fields. If you're going to see Auntie Helen, don't go through the smoke, go up the other way by the old ford.'

The other way by the old ford the prince repeated to himself, both in order to conceal his ignorance of what 'stubble-burning' was and out of gratitude for being warned about the smoke, which had suddenly grown much thicker. He merely said, 'I see,' gave a grateful wave, wished them both luck and turned back the way he had come.

'Stubble', of course, referred to a man's beard. But 'stubble' as an agricultural term meant nothing. Certainly something was burning. Whiffs of a smell like bonfire smoke momentarily filled the air round him. They lessened and then vanished once he re-entered the shade of the trees.

He walked quickly upstream, noticing as he went how the river widened and presumably grew shallower. Everything began to marshal itself into the correct relationship of shape and colour he remembered from the site of his accident. Even the cows still stood dutifully in shallow water in the shade of trees near the far bank and were no doubt ready to disperse should the black boat appear. In no time the willow against which he had propped himself came into view. There also was the narrow lane down which he had cycled. Its high banks topped by hedges on either side made a sunlit oasis for butterflies filling the air like thrown confetti. He stopped and looked around him and understood at once why it was known as the old ford.

In that instant the quiet of the scene was faintly interrupted by the odd creaking sound of someone crossing the footbridge downstream. Why it should have sent a sharp twinge of panic up his spine he did not know. He quickened his pace, knowing how conspicuous he might look in his white linen bicycling clothes, and began climbing the lane, telling himself that *if* this was the way to Irmingham, as Master Charles had seemed to indicate, then he was doing the right thing.

Butterflies fluttered in delicately tinted kaleidoscopic patterns against the dark green of the steep sides and the hedgerows, obliging him to keep his eyes down. It was this that drew his attention to something in the thick grass. At first glance it looked like a lump of stone. On closer inspection it turned out to be a heap of stone fragments. The growth of grass over several seasons had virtually hidden them, so that what he saw was little more than a grass-covered mound.

'Ia natknulsia na… Vot!'

It seemed he had stumbled on the cause of his accident. Coming fast down the slope towards the river his front wheel must have struck the fragments, concealed as they were in the grass, and he had been thrown forward. His ribs ached now in recollection.

Simultaneously he was reminded that something had caught his eye and it prompted him to look round. As he did so a butterfly alighted on what looked like a short length of bare wood set high up in the hedge. He peered up at it only to see what looked at first like bare bone, curved, whitish, but obviously part of a small tombstone. Faintly visible were the words *In memoriam* already green with lichen and below them, again discoloured, the barely discernible shape of a horse's head, or so he supposed, because the stone in which the words and the horse's head were carved had been cracked diagonally right across. The only certainty was that this fragment glittered whitely in sunshine against the dark jade of the hedge. This was what he must have glimpsed as he sped downwards.

The rest of the inscription presumably lay in the mound at his feet. Why, though, had this memorial or whatever it was been placed here, atop the steep side of this lane and in the shade of the hedge?

'*Kto zhe postavil byi... esli ne ona?*'

Who would have put a memorial to a horse, *if* that's what it was, *there*, precisely *there*? Who? He felt sure it was connected with Anna Karenina, connected with the ceremony he had witnessed, connected with 'A little outing for me...' Hadn't she said something like that? 'Every year I have a little ceremony,' she had said. He fingered the tight red rosebud in his buttonhole as he remembered the red rose floating on the water.

What if this broken headstone commemorated the place and the date of the death of her favourite horse? What if this was the site of *her* accident? What if she hadn't been performing some strange obsequies in memory of her late husband, as Giles imagined, but simply been remembering her dead horse and her own injury? Of course she was a sentimentalist after her fashion! The idea of decking out the boat in black would have a macabre appeal for her, much in the way that her own black garments and black veil, no matter what they might hide, confirmed the macabre notion that she was already dead.

So why had it been smashed to pieces? Was this the work of her enemies? And was it all related to some special date?

He would go to Irmingham at once. Lady Helen would be able to shed some light on it, he felt sure. It took him therefore very little time to climb the lane, which he soon found rutted with parallel cart tracks that had very likely been created by the traffic of heavy horse-drawn vehicles long ago. It rose less sharply towards the top and the steep sides gave way to overgrown hedges that framed the beautiful vista of river and trees he saw as he glanced behind him.

Looking to his right, he was quite taken by surprise at the glimpse of another vista. Visible through the thickness of the hedgerow was the silvery glimmer of steel rails. They were some distance away and vanished in a curve from his line of sight. So he must be standing above a short tunnel! The locomotive would whistle no doubt as it emerged from the tunnel and the tunnel exit would act as a megaphone for the rumble of wheels.

Well, well, another little mystery solved! By now, though, he had reached the crest of the ascent and there, to his relief, he found a signpost shaped like a thick-fingered hand that announced the way to *'Irm ..gham'* in faint, weather-beaten letters. Somewhat strangely it directed him to nothing more obvious than a stile in an overgrown hedge.

Twinges from his ribs made him pause. He sat on the stile to have a rest, facing the way he had come and the phrase "a gap in nature" suddenly came to mind. Why had he felt there was "a gap in nature"? Why, though, should he have experienced "a gap in nature" on that particular date? He had explained to himself the boat and what it signified, or so he thought, and yet the threat of the unknown or even the supernatural implied by the phrase seemed as real as ever. The very idea that Anna Karenina should be alive was in itself unnatural. He found it equally unnatural that here, in the apparent tranquility of rural England, he should feel such a sense of menace. The feeling of being observed, of eyes covertly watching, of being pursued, became exceptionally strong, due no doubt to his unfamiliarity with the very rural quiet of the place, and he had literally to shake himself out of such a silly mood before continuing on his way.

The small field on the other side of the stile sloped towards a dense hedgerow interspersed with trees that stood silhouetted against a blue sky. Recently it had been cut and piles of hay lay about. Otherwise there was no real sign of a path as such. He hesitated. He had a fear of trespassing. In Russia he had been used to wandering freely. In England he knew it was sheer foolhardiness to tempt a farmer's lethal anger by trespassing on his land. Looking keenly round to see if there were someone he might ask, or indeed if the sense of being covertly observed actually amounted to anything, he could see no one. The sun came beating down on the piles of hay that emitted an attractively warm smell. The only sound apart from birdsong was a distant crackling not unlike the chatter of foliage in a light breeze.

He would go where the signpost pointed. He would make his way through the dry, ploughed field in the hope it was the shortest way to Irmingham. The slope of the field, if nothing else, seemed to suggest a path and until he was about half way across everything was normal. Then suddenly the air was filled with clouds of smoke. It took him completely by surprise. Billowing from behind him with a strong bonfire smell, it forced him to press a handkerchief close to his nose and start running quickly towards what looked like a gate into an adjacent field. He had no sooner reached it and pushed it open than more smoke funneled through the gap. Momentary panic made him rush onwards until, to his horror, he came face to face with an inferno. Flames and smoke leapt into the air and filled it with particles of burning straw.

All of a sudden he seemed to have no choice. The smoke rose so thickly that it made his eyes smart and virtually blinded him. He could not see where he was, let along turn back. A moment later came the sound of a shot. Disbelief was instantly followed by a panic sense that he was a target. Guns were obviously being fired close by. He dived for the ground and lay flat. All pain from his ribs vanished momentarily. Something whistled very close to him. Then there were more shots. Just as frightening was the crackle of burning straw. His lungs ached from the inescapable, ground-hugging smoke. In its swirling motion it seemed to creep and weave like an animal among the charred stalks.

He simply could not imagine what had happened.

Stubble-burning, yes, but gunshots?

Was he somehow again at war with the Turks?

A handful of soil fell on his hair. He was sure now he was a target. If it weren't for the smoke the shooter's aim would be a lot more accurate, because there was no doubt that one set of gunshots came from somewhere very close indeed. Then it shocked him to find a rabbit crouching beside his face.

He exchanged one brief glance with it before it dashed away. Despite smoke, bruised ribs and loss of dignity, the shock made him follow the scared rabbit's example. He instantly scrambled back towards the hedge. Luckily he found a ditch and tumbled gratefully into it.

Silhouetted against the white smoke and the sky was the figure of a man. Foreshortened as he appeared when viewed from ground level, he could have been any height. He was certainly wearing a peaked cap and had a scarf over the lower part of his face. He was carrying what looked like a twin-barreled shotgun.

The prince held his breath. The man had only to look slightly to his left to see him. Their two pairs of eyes would meet. The gun would be leveled. Icy shivers ran along his scalp. Or perhaps the man was simply shooting rabbits. Nothing worse. The thought was consoling but hardly reassuring.

With a crackling much like Chinese firecrackers, the line of dry stalks just above the ditch caught alight and burned furiously. In an instant the smoke hid the man. A breeze played with the flames for a while, made them flare and dance and the stalks crackled until, just as suddenly, the smoke cleared and direct sunlight beat down. The prince tried hard not to attract attention by coughing. He pressed the handkerchief to his lips. Nothing happened. The acrid smoke burned in his lungs and his eyes were streaming.

Panic was quickly replaced by resentment at his own apparent cowardice and anger at the whole ridiculous situation. To be intimidated by anything was irksome. To have been disabled by the pain from his ribcage after his accident was one thing; being panicked by gunshots and rabbits was almost more hurtful. Not only had the prince's dignity suffered, his common sense had been affronted and, worse still, his white linen suit had been smudged and stained.

Peering above the level of the ditch, he saw that the stubble farther down the field was still burning vigorously. It caused clouds of dense smoke, although closer to him the light breeze did no more than ignite little points of fire that flared into brief life and ended in quickly dispersed wisps. There was no sign of the man with the gun. Although he could not deny he was shaken, he knew a Russian prince could not do otherwise than put a brave face on things. He picked up his Panama hat and placed it on his head in defiance of caution and good judgment. If he were going to be shot at, he wanted to be a presentable target. Having brushed his clothes free of straw, twigs and soil, he looked round with wary dignity and saw little more than a sloping field darkened by burnt patches. Apart from the continuing crackle of stubble as it caught alight nothing was audible; nor was anything visible save for smoke and hedges. Not a soul about. It was cause for mild relief.

Unsure whether to return the way he had come, or indeed where to go, he was alarmed by a noise of rapid hoof beats and crunching wheels. A head and cap similar to Oswald Holmcroft's could be seen bobbing along above the hedge on the far side of the field. The cap had no peak or was worn reversed and was therefore unlikely to belong to the man with the gun. In a moment it had vanished.

Had Oswald Holmcroft been shooting at *him*? The idea seemed absurd, but a doubt lingered. If he had been, why?

Why should Oswald Holmcroft want *him* dead or injured? The whole idea was as absurd as his present situation. All he did know now beyond a shadow of doubt was that on the other side of the hedge there must be a lane. He stumbled quickly off in that direction.

The hedge was at right angles to the ditch and he followed it until it curved sharply and revealed another gate. Three men were leaning on it. They were so absorbed in talking that his approach caused them to stare as if he were an apparition out of hell. The prince knew his appearance could be theatrically devilish, the soil matting his hair, his face streaked with sweat and his white clothing smudged by a combination of soil, grass stains and burnt stalks.

'I am looking for Irmingham,' he said in his most Russian-accented tones and confessed he had lost his way.

'Where you bin, sir?' said one of them, removing a pipe from his mouth. 'You bin burned? You looks like you bin in the burnin'! You shouldna bin in the burnin', sir!'

'I agree with that. But I've also been shot at, you know...'

'You shouldna bin in the burnin', sir! No, sir, not in the burnin'!'

'I am fully aware...'

'Did un say shotart?'

'Excuse me?'

'Did un say shotart, sir? You bin shotart, you said.'

'Oh, shot, yes...'

'Varmint's wot's shotart! Rarbits! Varmint's wot's 'em are! Good for eatin', mind. The gentry, sir, wot's shotart the rarbits.'

'Would Mr Holmcroft have been shooting?' the prince asked as politely as possible.

"'Olmcroft. 'Olmcroft. Oo-arrgh, oo-arrgh, 'ee were un!'

'Thank you. Which way is it to Irmingham?'

'Yarnder, sir.'

'Oh, thank you.'

They drew open the gate for him and gave directions. He was told he would be able to see the church tower after a short walk. So he followed their directions and went down a well-used lane that sloped towards the river in a meandering, gentle way and was replete with the usual fairly tall hedges, overhanging trees, butterflies, birds and countryside detritus, such as an old leather boot without a sole and a scrap of cloth attaching to a twig in a hedgerow. It was all manifestly English, manifestly rural, manifestly peaceful. The very idea of being shot at was so incongruous it was hard to believe he could have been caught in crossfire only a short while before.

Approaching the church and the line of houses which he took to be the main street of Irmingham, he began to be seriously worried about his dishevelled appearance. To appear before the beautiful Lady Helen Swanning looking so grubby would be a repeat performance and perhaps give her the impression he was incorrigibly accident-prone. He thought of turning back. Too late. There she was, walking towards him carrying a sickle.

'Good heavens, what *have* you been doing with yourself, prince? Anyhow, it is very nice to see you again.' She asked after his health, listened politely to his brief account and then said: 'I have been very busy, you see. I have just been bonking.'

'Excuse me?' Rural Herefordshire seemed to offer a treasure trove of fanciful agricultural expressions.

'Bonking,' she said, wielding the sickle lightheartedly. 'Thistle bonking. In the churchyard.'

'You mean the churchyard is...' The churchyards of his native Orel region did more for local procreation than countless stove-tops or bath-houses.

'Full of thistles. And rabbits. Much worse than last year. Father disapproves of killing them, so there's been a plague. They've got to be controlled somehow.'

'I see. By the way, your father asked me to give you his love. He hopes to see you at tomorrow's soiree.'

'Oh, how nice of him! Yes, I'll be there. But you... you say you've been shot at?'

'As I said, I have been through "the burnin", as it's called.'

'I heard them shooting rabbits not long ago, but surely, prince, they weren't shooting at you?'

'I wish I were sure.'

'What you need is a good clean-up. Come on. I'll see what I can do.'

He loved her practicality. It was so different from the kind of instant soulfulness, not to say soulful coyness, a Russian girl might have brandished at him as a mark of her concern. In her cotton blouse, through which he had no difficulty seeing well-formed breasts and solid pink nipples, and in her long worsted skirt, to which burrs and thistle-heads still remained attached, Lady Helen had such a practical, outdoor, efficient look she seemed wantonly to downplay her attractiveness. It was hard to disregard this because her workaday clothes simply enhanced her natural beauty and yet left her apparently quite unaware of its allure. He was suddenly stabbed by the naughty idea that she was at heart quite cool, even scheming. She studied him, he saw, from the shade of her wide-brimmed hat.

'I think your ribs may still be hurting.'

He explained that the need to escape smoke and gunfire at first quelled all the pain, only for it to reawaken once he was on his feet again.

'Are you sure they were really firing at *you*?'

'Quite sure.'

'The local people don't mind if the rabbits get shot. They stick lighted straw down the burrows. The idea is to smoke them out. Of course, it tends to mean all the stubble catches alight. After a couple of hot days round here everything's tinder-dry. What exactly were you doing in "the burnin'"?'

'Your nephew, Master Charles, told me to come this way.'

'You were coming to see me, then?'

'Of course. Is there any other reason why I should come here? Except, of course, to retrieve my bicycle.'

She laughed and pushed open the gate to her front garden. 'Come in, prince. We've only met twice and on both occasions you've been in need of assistance. You must try and break the habit. As a matter of fact, I asked about your bicycle yesterday and they said it would be ready today. I sent word this morning.'

By the time he had been led into the hallway, past the temporary consulting-room, he was so exhilarated at seeing her again in her familiar surroundings he was scarcely listening any more. The sweetly perfumed atmosphere of the low-ceilinged sitting room where he was offered a chair remained exactly the same. This time, however, there was no likelihood of sudden rainfall. She flung herself down in an armchair with a flower-printed cover, giving the first signs of exhaustion, and let her hat and the sickle drop to the floor.

She sat there and they looked at each other. The prince flattered himself with the sense of being welcomed by her and the possibility that she was glad to see him and had perhaps even thought about him as he had thought about her. For some moments of silence it felt very pleasant just to sit and rest.

He had not realised how tiring the morning's events had been. The surrounding quiet, interrupted only by the buzzing of an insect, was a delightful substitute for conversation. After a minute or so he tried hard to think how he could broach the question of the smashed headstone without mentioning Anna Karenina. She, perhaps amused at his embarrassment, allowed herself a private smile while he could not help thinking how readily he and his dear Alisa usually talked about all manner of things, as is customary among Russians and makes them so different from the usually withdrawn English. The number of times he had sat in English train compartments with not a word spoken for hours at a time was amazing. This time he plucked up courage and asked what made her smile.

'It was odd about Oswald,' she said. 'I showed you his history of Cromwell, didn't I?'

He asked what she meant.

'I don't mean about the history, but odd he should have found you there, prince. I was thinking, you see, that hardly anyone uses the old ford nowadays. I can't imagine what he was doing there.'

'Shooting rabbits. He said he had been shooting rabbits, or "rarbits" as the local people apparently call them.'

'Ah, local talk! Yes, well...'

'I found some broken stones in the lane, you know,' he said. 'I think they must have caused my accident.'

'Stones?' There was hardly anything remarkable about finding stones in a lane and he scarcely expected her to respond, but she suddenly exclaimed: 'Oh, yes!'

'There was some kind of memorial stone...'

'A horse was killed,' she said quickly. 'I think it tripped or something crossing the ford. It was all quite some time ago.'

'*Her* horse?' he asked pointedly.

She ran her tongue round her lips. 'I think my grandfather had a little tablet erected. The horse was a beautiful animal. As I say, it was all quite some time ago.'

'And was *she* hurt?'

'I don't know who you mean.'

She spoke the words quite coldly, deliberately turning away as she said them. The subject was apparently not to be discussed. He was diplomatic enough not to pursue it. A warm invitation to stay for lunch was gratefully accepted, which allowed her to re-assume her practical manner and suggest they should both tidy themselves in preparation for it. Jane was ordered to provide a jug of water in the consulting-room so he could wash and she would change her clothes upstairs. An atmosphere of amiable compliance neatly hid the certainty that the invitation to lunch was a distraction quickly devised by Lady Helen to avoid any mention of the lady in the tower.

The prince recognised this and was quite ready to acquiesce. He was not going to betray his promise to Giles. No, he would simply enjoy Lady Helen's company over lunch, provided of course he made himself presentable for it. The mirror above the basin in the consulting-room mirror showed him all he needed to know about his messy appearance, so the soap and the jug of water were most welcome. He washed as vigorously as young Dr Parkinson had washed, but had to wait a short while for Jane to return with his jacket which she had taken to brush and then sponge to remove the worst stains.

It was not exactly the prince at his smartest who stood in Lady Helen's sitting room that lunchtime, although he felt his appearance was a great deal better than in 'the burnin'. Grateful for the renewal of the wash and brush-up, he stared through the open French window at the sunlit garden. Lawn, roses, far trees and bright star-like flashes from the glass panes of a greenhouse where light filtered through the flickering movement of high foliage – that was what he saw, but it was the sound that caught his attention, the faint sound of a train whistle. His thoughts turned back to Lady Helen. He ran through the likely reasons for her talking about Oswald Holmcroft.

Intuitively he felt she did not talk about Oswald Holmcroft as someone with whom she seemed to be emotionally involved, although he knew he could be wrong. There were other reasons, the prince told himself. They seemed related chiefly to her father and his belief in the simple vegetarian and pacifist ideals of Tolstoyanism; whereas Oswald Holmcroft seemed far less seriously committed to them. He had another agenda. It could well be, of course, that the memorial to a dead horse had been smashed for some good reason. The suspicion suddenly spurred him to wonder whether Oswald Holmcroft's connection might become clear from his work as a historian.

The prince looked round the sitting room and saw what he wanted. In its smart binding with gold embossing the history of Oliver Cromwell enjoyed pride of place on one of the bookshelves. He opened it and, a little to his surprise, the thick pages fell open at page 117 and his eye was immediately caught by a footnote. He drew in a long breath. It was part of the answer, if not the complete answer, to the riddle of the headstone and perhaps the reason why it had been smashed.

He snapped the book shut and replaced it.

10

Lady Helen re-entered the sitting room in her usual pink dress accompanied by someone the prince had never seen before. Quite unaccountably he felt a twinge of jealousy on seeing this stranger. She made the introduction.

'This is Carew, prince. Carew, may I introduce Prince Dmitry Rostov, your compatriot. Carew is our translator, you know, and the one who knows more about the teachings of Count Tolstoy than anyone. Anyone here, I mean.'

Carew? The prince conjured with the name a moment, running it round his Russian tongue. 'Oh, yes.' He remembered Oswald Holmcroft had mentioned the name. He said he was very glad to meet a compatriot.

A small man of about fifty limped towards him with the aid of a walking stick. He had a furrowed, angular face, a gunmetal beard whitening at the tips and moist, round eyes of soft blue almost hidden by spectacles. His unnecessarily firm handshake was accompanied by a rather chirpy reference to his red shirt: 'My *rubashka.* Appropriate, eh, my dear Prince Dmitry?'

'Oh, indeed!' A true Tolstoyan! thought the prince. 'Most appropriate,' he added, trying not to sound even faintly sarcastic since the red shirt, the *rubashka,* belted at the waist, tended to emphasise the wearer's thickening waistline.

Carew Kingston leant on his stick and subjected him to

a penetrating scrutiny for several moments before admitting rather too magnanimously that it was a great honour to have a Russian prince in modest little Irmingham.

'I gather you've been in what they call "the burnin"'?'

The prince apologised for the signs of dirt on his clothes, but Lady Helen said there was no need for apologies. She mentioned she had herself only just changed out of her working clothes.

'Work, ah, yes,' Carew Kingston muttered, 'the simple agricultural life, pacifism... Most important in Tolstoy's teaching.'

'Not when you are mistaken for a rabbit,' said the prince.

'Mistaken for a rabbit?'

'If you're being shot at, I mean.'

'Who would want to shoot at a Russian prince, I wonder?'

'Oh, Russian princes have always been targets.'

'Well, you are not a target now,' said Lady Helen. 'I am sure you two will have a lot to say to each other. Do speak Russian if you wish. We will be having lunch soon.'

'No, no, that would be most impolite.' Like the way he had gingerly gripped the prince's hand and crinkled his eyes in an ingratiating smile, the way Carew Kingston spoke English signaled an unusual eagerness to be accepted as friendly and affable. He pointed out that they had not embraced in true Russian style. 'It is not, as they say, a *done thing*. Am I right?'

The prince agreed it was not the English way.

'Poor Carew has trouble with his legs,' said Lady Helen. She invited both of them to sit.

'It is when I play.' He demonstrated keyboard movements

with his fingers. 'The organ at Stadleigh Court has heavy pedals, you know. I find my legs are very tired.'

'Carew has taken to composing.'

'Oh, really. May I ask what?'

'Small things, small things.' The reluctance to discuss his work seemed genuine. 'You are long a resident in England, prince?' The questioner seated himself slowly without waiting for an answer. 'For me it is always a question of a mother tongue – or should I say a mother's tongue? My mother was Russian, my father English. But my father had no money and left me nothing except my name and my command of English. Whereas my mother left me a native command of Russian, a little money and a sense of exile.'

The prince sat down. 'You are a translator, I think?'

'Oh, yes, I am that kind of hybrid creature. Exile is for translators.'

'I do try to help,' Lady Helen pointed out.

'Oh, I am forever ably assisted in my everlasting search for perfection by Lady Helen. For whom, of course, perfection is, as it were, a native clime – may I say that?'

'You may!' she laughed. 'Though it makes me sound absurdly Shakespearean!'

'Ah, Shakespearean,' sighed Carew Kingston, 'what a thing that is!'

The talk turned to next day's soiree at Stadleigh Court. Such soirees, it seemed, had been held regularly throughout the summer months and had attracted actors and actresses, public figures and celebrities from the literary and academic world as well as some press attention; but this one was to be the last for the season. Carew Kingston's organ recital was an innovation, but Lord Irmingham always said a few words on the aims of Tolstoyanism at the end of each soiree and this one would be no exception.

'And we allow no stimulants,' said Lady Helen. 'None of the refreshments contain any meat. It is all strictly vegetarian.'

'It all happens naturally,' said Carew Kingston. 'For instance, I hope to start playing...'

'Each one is different. There is no planning,' said Lady Helen.

'Someone will sing. Someone will give a talk.'

'This time there is the reverend, the Irishman, I can't remember his name...'

'And there is Julie to help me,' said Carew Kingston.

'And that poet,' said Lady Helen. 'I can't remember his name. My father mentioned him.'

They spoke as if there were no end to the possible delights of the soiree. The prince raised his eyebrows and smilingly asked if there would be many converts. It was not intended as an ironic question. If anything, he sought information. Carew Kingston took him at his word: 'You yourself, sir, are of the Tolstoyan persuasion?'

The prince said he wasn't.

'Then may I ask why you are here?'

His accident was quoted as the answer. He had been invited, he said, by Lord Irmingham and was on the point of mentioning Lady Helen's part in it when he intercepted an anxious blue-eyed glance from her and remembered Giles's stern admonition not to say a word about the *Karenins*. It gave Carew Kingston a chance to say: 'Of course, *we* are all converts. There must be two or three in this area. Perhaps more. Educated people. All converts. Of course, it will be many, many years yet before we can expect Count Tolstoy's teaching to become influential throughout the world. But in our small way we continue our work.'

He exchanged glances with his hostess. It was hard to tell whether something more than mutual interest lay behind that exchange of looks. Against his better nature the prince felt a renewed spurt of envy, which he knew to be completely unjustified, but it drove him to remark in a spirit of playfulness as much as defiance: 'I am a Tolstoyan in another sense.'

'What is that?' Carew Kingston looked at him over his spectacles.

'My grandmother was a Bolkonskii and I am a descendant of the Moscow Rostovs.'

'I am sure we are not all so privileged.' Carew Kingston pushed his spectacles back onto the bridge of his nose.

'I am sure of one thing,' said the prince.

'What is that?'

'Tolstoy's reputation will survive as a creator of great novels, not as a religious thinker.'

'You mean,' said Carew Kingston, 'that our greatest author does not live in the real world?'

'Oh, no. I mean the world of his fiction is so real. That is what matters.'

'No, pardon me, that is *not* what matters. What matters is the real world, the world we live in. We do not live in a fiction. It does not exist. In any case, Tolstoy has himself repudiated all his literary work before his conversion.'

A sparkle of triumph shone in the bespectacled eyes. It did not annoy the prince. What puzzled him were the assumptions. He had to assume his compatriot was so dedicated to Tolstoy's teachings that the truth of his fiction meant nothing.

'I might not exist if that were true,' he remarked. 'Certainly my grandmother would not have existed.'

'Well, of course.' Again the spectacles were adjusted.

'And Anna Karenina might not be dead.'

This of course was risky. To the prince's relief, no flicker of query, let alone alarm, crossed Lady Helen's face. Carew Kingston gave a pitying smile. 'My dear Prince Dmitry, Anna Karenina is dead, we all know that!'

'Of course.'

The prince tried to look innocent. Carew Kingston leaned forward and started saying in an earnest, whispered Russian, hissing the words a little as if he were frightened of being overheard: *'She committed suicide by throwing herself under a train and Tolstoy, her creator, has himself repudiated her. Her spirit is laid to rest, surely. And not before time. Because the worst thing she did was to destroy a noble, decent man. And that was unforgivable.'*

The ferocity of this last remark was startling. *'You mean her husband?'*

'I mean...' Carew Kingston blinked and his face twitched. *'Yes.'* He avoided the other's eyes, *'I naturally mean her husband. She ruined his life.'*

'You adopt a perfectly correct Tolstoyan view,' the prince remarked cordially, only too aware how keenly Lady Helen was watching. At the same time there was a distinct softening of Carew Kingston's expression as he glanced at her.

'I feel I have a fatherly role,' he explained. *'I teach, you*

know, the correct Tolstoyan view. I love my pupil, she is like a daughter to me...' he smiled as he spoke *'...and I hope my pupil feels some respect, some love, in return.'*

'I am sure she does,' the prince politely agreed, more than ever aware how embarrassing this might be to Lady Helen if she could understand the Russian.

'She is so beautiful, is she not, that men are likely to fall in love with her at first sight? I think you, prince, are not immune. Are you?'

The question was allowed to hang in the air. There was a moment of silence in which the fact of the quiet room itself, the low beams, the twinkling brasses and the summery outside heat reasserted itself. The eyes behind the spectacles sparkled brighter than ever. Then Carew Kingston broke into English.

'I am so sorry, my dear Lady Helen. You understood perhaps what we were talking about?'

'Oh...' she twiddled her fingers. 'No, not everything, I'm afraid. I am so unused to hearing the language spoken, you know. I do wish I knew it better. It sounds so musical and strong.'

'It is a very good language for love and for argument,' said Carew Kingston, rising slowly. 'Forgive me, Lady Helen. Forgive me, sir. I must go across to the Court. A final practice before tomorrow's soiree.'

There was general agreement that they would be at Stadleigh Court to hear his composition during the soiree. The small man smiled and bowed. He then leaned on his stick and walked slowly out of the room.

'You haven't really, have you?'

The question was asked in a low whisper as soon as they

were alone. The prince could not be sure what Lady Helen meant, so he denied he had said a word about the lady in the tower.

'Is it a secret? Should I have said something?'

Why on earth was he confessing that much, even if only in a whisper? Her eyes, which smiled approvingly, suggested clearly enough that she probably knew what her father wanted.

'Well, no.' Her quiet voice and the way she raised her hand close to her lips indicated a need for care. She threw back her head to loosen a strand of red hair from her cheek. 'I mean so few people round here know about her. What I do know is that father has pinned his hopes on her. I know he is relying on you to testify that she is who she is.'

He said he was quite ready to testify. Then he changed the subject. 'My compatriot is in love with you, you know.'

'Oh, I'm sure you're exaggerating.' He watched her closely and saw her blink uneasily and look away. As if to make amends, she simply added: 'He is very serious-minded, very dedicated. I have only known him for a year or so, since coming to live here. I used to live over at the Court, you see, before father remarried. Isobel and I didn't get on. Two rather bossy women. That's one thing. The other is something even more embarrassing.'

Naturally this was intriguing. The prince tried to look suitably attentive.

'Oh, I owe you an explanation, I know that, my dear Prince Dmitry. Isobel and I are both bossy. Isobel wants to rule the roost over there at the Court. I couldn't stand it, so I came here. In due course, when there's enough money, father wants to come over here and join me. In our commune, you see. Meantime, I'm the one to inherit the Court. That's the arrangement at present. And the other thing is that the lady in the tower has taken my dear silly brother as a lover. With my sister-in-law's consent and connivance. Which disgusts me so much I can't bring myself to talk to her. And that's the reason I wasn't there last night for Charles's birthday dinner. You may have noticed.'

He had to admit he had. Although she had flung out her last sentence like a challenge, he did not rise to it. It was startling enough to be confronted by the animosity so latent in her attitude and therefore at the root of relationships in the Irmingham family. It was not the time, he felt, to become involved in the very slightest. Seeing how she flushed, he asked with an airily whispered nonchalance: 'Tell me, how long have you known of her existence – the lady in the tower, I mean?'

'Oh, a few years. But I've never been sure...'

'Sure, you mean, about her identity?'

'Yes. Of course, I've always trusted father. He's always believed in her.'

That was it! *Believed in her!* 'So who else knows?' he asked.

'I don't think anybody knows except father. Oh, and Gerald, of course, and Hannah, my sister-in-law. But not anyone else outside the Court, I mean.'

'So Oswald Holmcroft wouldn't know?'

'Oswald?' This was possibly one question too many. She brushed a strand of hair away from her eyes. 'No!' She was so emphatic the shock of the negative came like a gust of cold air. 'He's insisted on denying it! He's even got up a sort of statement! Like Carew, like my stepmother, he insists she doesn't exist!'

The prince was stunned. 'You've seen this, er, this statement?'

She nodded. 'I made two copies of it.'

'Why?'

'For father and for Oswald.'

'I see. So these people – Oswald, your stepmother, Mr Kingston – they would be her enemies, would they?'

She looked offended. 'Oh, no, not really enemies, just people who don't believe. I don't think she's really got enemies.'

'She thinks so.'

'Well, I know father thinks she's a bit, you know, frightened, but it's not serious. He says she says she hears things in her bath – I mean what nonsense! He's done so much for her, you can't imagine. Shall we have lunch? I see Jane's waiting for us.'

Food suddenly seemed very attractive and put the whole problem of Anna Karenina to rest. He gave no further thought to it as he accompanied his hostess into a small adjacent dining room where a cold lunch was laid ready. A window was open to the garden. Hot summer midday air swept in and around them as they sat and talked over the meal. Flies and wasps came in with the warmth, but were hardly noticed. He was entirely consumed by Lady Helen's beauty, the glitter of her eyes and the way her features lit up as she smiled. She poured out ice-cold lemonade and he knew he had never tasted more delicious lemonade in his entire life than the lemonade Lady Helen Swanning poured out for him that lunchtime, the delicate golden hairs of her bare sunburned arm catching the sunlight as she leaned across the table to lift the jug.

Conversation continued quietly and intimately, all queries about Oswald Holmcroft being avoided in the near-certainty that there was no likelihood of an emotional connection. The prince was now quite certain that the historian of Cromwell was scarcely more than a platonic friend who would call in on Lady Helen for tea or receive insight into Tolstoy's thinking from Carew Kingston. True, his behaviour could be considered eccentric in some respects and a footnote in his book certainly needed questioning. As for the organist and composer, the conscientious, dedicated, rather humourless lifeline between Tolstoyanism and the erstwhile Tolstoyans of the neighbourhood, the prince was quite simply puzzled. She anticipated him by asking: 'He speaks good Russian, does he?'

'Your organist? Oh, yes. His composing, what exactly is it? In what sort of style?'

'Oh, it's a new departure for him! His mother taught him to play the piano – she's buried here, you know, in the churchyard – but he's only taken to playing the organ and composing in the last few months.'

'Is that so?' Swallowing the last of the delicious lemonade, he contented himself with the thought that the forthcoming soiree would soon provide an answer. She rose from the table and asked what his plans were for the afternoon.

'I, er...'

He would have liked to continue their conversation but as he followed her into the hallway he could not help noticing something hanging on one of the clothes hooks. His conscience was pricked.

'You must forgive me,' he said in offering warm thanks for the lunch and the lemonade. 'I realise I have a call to make.'

Did a shadow of disappointment show in her eyes? She raised her chin a little imperiously and he at once bent forward, boldly seized her hand and kissed it, saying: 'It has been a great pleasure, Lady Helen.'

She was clearly taken aback, but her lips then formed an unforced, rather surprised smile.

'For me, too,' she admitted.

He reached up and took Oswald Holmcroft's cape off its hook.

***

To have the warm air of the hot afternoon flowing against his face and the wheels of the Rudge Explorer turning smoothly under him was a delight. More than this, it was the exhilarating sense of freedom, of momentary release from life's slow pace into the speed of racing air that lifted his spirits and made him want to sing aloud. After only two meetings with Lady Helen he was in the gloriously elated condition of feeling totally at peace with the world.

Of course, it was nonsense. He was elated simply by the natural joy of being alive. Whether it was no more than a romantic illusion of the moment he had no way of knowing, but at that instant his happiness seemed an endless beam of sunlight down which he glided on spinning wheels. It was enough to evoke the beautiful Monna Vanna features and the lustrous red hair for all surrounding nature to be transfused by a Wordsworthian contentment, to induce a mood of oneness with the hedgerows and trees and majestically flowing river, a readiness to accept that this tranquil rural corner of England could be heaven on earth.

11

A house, or one with some of the features he had been told would identify it, came into view at the end of a straight, tree-lined drive. He supposed it could be called vaguely 'Mediterranean' in style, or that was as Lady Helen had described it, since it sported at ground level a covered verandah with elegant wooden supports elaborately encased in a lacework of wisteria, above which were the square white frames of bedroom windows peering out of ivy-clad brickwork. Above that was a low-pitched roof looking a bit like an outsize coolie hat that had been pulled down over the stubby ears of chimneys at either end.

That was as far as the 'Mediterranean' style went. A bust of Cromwell on a plinth beside the front door proclaimed it was the house of an admirer, as did a seventeenth-century cannon perched next to a little pyramid of newly painted cannonballs. Such military objects instantly struck the prince as so out of keeping with the other features of the house that they distracted him and made him brake far too loudly after swooping – as he hoped, gracefully – into the gravel forecourt.

From the outside the house appeared deserted. Although the bust of Cromwell and the cannonballs seemed to identify the owner, closer inspection made the prince hesitate, since there was no name-plate or sign of an address. The lion's-head knocker on the stout oak front door seemed to suggest an unexpected defiance, not to say hostility. He felt like leaving the cape in the doorway and cycling away at once, except that questions needed asking even in face of the challenge posed by the cannon pointing directly up the driveway and the lion's head staring at him defiantly. He had not associated belligerence with Oswald Holmcroft. He could of course excuse all his questions as mere guesswork by airily assuming how silly he was in supposing that there was any truth in Anna Karenina's fear of "enemies", not to mention the reason why the memorial to her horse Frou-Frou had been smashed. Then the decision was made for him.

There were loud shouts. A male voice, undoubtedly that of the historian of Cromwell, was issuing instructions.

'Stand clear, please! Please stand clear!'

The shouts came from the other side of a wall running between the house and what appeared to be stables and a barn. The loud instructions were repeated and drew attention to an archway. The prince quickly steered his bicycle towards it and alighted. As he walked through the arch he was quite expecting to be confronted by a conventional English scene of lawn and flowerbeds and perhaps others like himself who formed the audience for the shouted instructions, only to find himself staring at tawdry wooden structures that might have been in a fairground or offered for sale in an auction of unwanted theatrical props. They so obscured his view that he had to peer round them to see the source of the shouts.

It was of course Oswald Holmcroft. On a large patch of un-mown grass some twenty or more paces away he was bracing himself against the crozier-shaped object the prince had noticed in his trap. Resting on it was a weapon resembling

a thin trumpet with its round mouth pointing in his direction.
No one else was visible so far as the prince could see and
he naturally wondered what had caused the instructions to be
issued so loudly. Another loud shouted instruction followed
instantly.

'I say,' the prince called out, 'Mr Holmcroft! Oswald!'

Too late. An ear-splitting blast occurred, something
whizzed past his left ear and a lump of wood fell off the
wooden structure with a loud rending sound. It knocked both
him and the Rudge Explorer to the ground.

It was not so much the prince's past life that sped past
him as he lay in a momentary daze. His imagination provoked
an array of vaguely suggestive reasons why the historian of
Cromwell might have wanted to kill him. A loud flapping
sound, though, quickly dispersed such concerns. Homemade,
slipper-like shoes raced towards him across the grass. A
moment later a pair of large red knees came into view. Oswald
Holmcroft leaned down, his head and shoulders blocking out
the sun.

'My dear fellow, I'm so terribly, terribly sorry! What on
earth have I done? Are you hurt?'

More apologies followed coupled with anxious enquiries
about injuries, but it quickly turned out that only the prince's
dignity had been hurt and no damage had been done to the
Rudge Explorer.

'My dear chap, I'm so glad! Here, let me help you up!'

This was far too much like a repeat performance. At their
first encounter Oswald Holmcroft had looked down at him in
roughly the same way and said roughly the same thing, so the
prince preferred to get up on his own. Once on his feet and

his clothes straightened, he looked suspiciously and a trifle angrily at the other's anxious, solicitous, sweaty face, noticed that the schoolboyish cap was worn back to front and added tacit insult to injury by stooping down and untying the cape from the bicycle rack. This was all too much.

'What on earth must you think of me!' came the chastened exclamation. 'My dear prince, I never for a moment intended to injure you! And thank you, thank you! Very thoughtful of you to bring my cape back. Your bicycle, I see, is repaired. How is your rib?' Reassured to hear it was better, he went on to utter more grateful thanks for the return of the cape before concluding in faint justification: 'But I did shout several warnings, you know. And I didn't expect you.'

The prince agreed.

'I always shout warnings, you see. Loud warnings. Even if there's nobody about. On account of my mother chiefly. Her hearing is, well, not so good. But you are a victim, you see, of an experiment of mine.'

'An experiment?' The prince asked the question a little shakily. Having been shot at once that day, he felt he had to be doubly cautious. 'What sort of experiment?'

It was very hot in the windless shelter of the stretch of grass. He stooped down to retrieve his fallen Panama hat and put it on.

'Yes, yes, an experiment! In the name of historical accuracy! I wasn't aiming at anyone, you see. Good heavens, I'm a pacifist! After all, your Count Tolstoy teaches not to confront evil with violence. No, no, I was conducting an experiment, an experiment on historically scientific lines, that's to say. That's the reason I found you down by the old ford in the first place.'

'What exactly do you mean?' All manner of suspicions sprang to mind but all the prince could say on the spur of the moment was: 'So you *did* shoot him?' without mentioning Sergius by name.

'Who?'

'The man down by the ford.'

The remark was greeted quite blankly and followed by a frown. 'Oh, yes, you said something at Lady Helen's about that.' Oswald Holmcroft wiped his face with the cape. 'No, no, I didn't shoot anyone! Of course not! I was referring to shooting rabbits. I used this, er, support or stand... Here, let me show you.'

He hurried across the grass towards where he had been standing earlier and urged the prince to join him. It was a preliminary to a little lecture. He began dilating on the need for the right conditions in which to conduct his experiments and the sort of support needed to achieve reasonable accuracy. This involved showing off the crozier-shaped rest. Described as his own invention, it offered reasonably firm purchase for the heavy, ancient weapon perched on it. He showed how he could swivel it with ease in any direction, collapse it to walking-stick size or, as he laughingly admitted, follow the shooting star of a rabbit's tail dashing over a field.

'I go with my old trap,' he explained, 'get this thing out, stick it in the ground and take aim. Sometimes it works well, sometimes it doesn't. Of course I don't usually use this matchlock for anything but experiments. I use my sporting rifle for shooting rabbits.' He adjusted his cap, bringing the peak round to face forwards, pointing out it was easier for him to take aim when worn with the peak backwards. 'But for my experiments and for shooting generally this is a perfect scientific instrument. It saves my shoulder, you see. Recoil. Know what I mean? I have just been practising with targets.'

He made the prince look behind him. Standing close by the archway were the dilapidated wooden structures that he had seen when he arrived. One depicted a helmeted foot soldier in the act of advancing. His belted topcoat was so shot through with holes that the aggressive pose seemed manifestly foolhardy. It was hard to see how he remained upright. The other target was larger and more elaborate and the evident reason why the prince had been knocked to the ground. It was a wooden figure of a plumed cavalryman on a charging horse brandishing a sword. The tip of the sword had been shot away, something very unpleasant had happened to one of the horse's legs and there was clearly a recently made half-moon hole in the side of the plume where the wood had splintered.

'There!' Oswald Holmcroft announced. 'You see you personally experienced the force of the weapon! Mind you, I don't imagine that last shot would have been, er, fatal. I wasn't aiming at the plume. That came off, I'm afraid, by mistake. Sorry about that.' He turned apologetically to the prince with his hazel eyes literally glistening. He was emerging now in his true role as a historian of the latest kind – accurate, scrupulous, honest – whose technical accuracy over weaponry and battlefield tactics during Cromwell's campaigns had to be beyond reproach. 'The role of the matchlock musketeer at the time of Cromwell, prince! Just imagine it! There you are, your weapon primed, taking aim! What you've really got is a kind of small cannon, lethal only up to about thirty yards!

A matchlock required clement conditions, preferably dry and windless. So you've got to be very, very careful to ensure each shot pays off! Now for a number of years I've been...'

He checked himself, looked down, stirred the grass at his feet with the puckered, clumsily stitched tip of his shoe and apologised.

'Sorry. I can become an infernal bore...'

'Please go on.'

'In that case, well...' Changing his tone, he folded his arms and spoke more formally. 'For a number of years now, you see, I have been endeavoring to acquire the skill needed to prepare a matchlock and fire it. I think I can say I have mastered the technique. Not without personal injury and many failures, mind you. As a weapon it had poor mobility on the field of battle, which is odd when you think that Cromwell's great success as a general was due largely to the mobility of his tactics. The great thing was, I believe, that the musket helped to immobilise cavalry. Provided it enjoyed some cover and protection. A horse was a much bigger target than a man, as you can appreciate, and could be scared out of its wits by a musket discharging in its face. I mean, who wouldn't be? I mean, pardon me for mentioning it, but just now, you know, you came within an ace... I hardly need add anything more, need I?'

He looked contrite. Again the prince agreed but there was no stopping the explanations, which became even more copious and candid. It transpired that the experiments had been conducted under various conditions and in various situations, all of which were expounded in a little too much detail for the prince's comfort, especially when it came to a description of the sort of injury that could be inflicted on a horse.

'You say you experimented... on a live horse?' he asked, frankly shocked. It struck him as very un-English and most certainly not gentlemanly by English standards. In any case, it was in very poor taste.

'Well, yes, I suppose I might be said to have done that.' An uneasy laugh. 'No, not really, I really don't mean that.' He changed the subject. 'This morning I had no luck at all. I tried to bag some rabbits on the other side of Irmingham, where they're burning the stubble, but the smoke got in my eyes and I gave up. Which is why I felt I needed a bit of practice...'

'I see. In that case, can I ask you...'

The question was interrupted, not at all rudely, but rather surprisingly, by a shrill overloud female voice. So engrossing had been the technical explanation of the matchlock musket and its uses that neither of them had noticed the approach of a small, round-faced woman. In a whisper the prince learned she was Oswald Holmcroft's mother and that he, as an only son, shared the house with her.

'Oswald dear!'

'Yes, mother.'

'Oswald dear!' She was advancing on them across the grass carrying a basket. 'Oswald dear!'

'Yes, mother.'

'Have you stopped firing?'

'Yes, mother.'

'Oswald dear, do answer me!'

'I have, mother.'

'Oswald dear, who are you with?'

'Mother, this is Prince Rostov, a Russian.'

'Who, dear?'

'Mother, please do take out your earplugs. I want to introduce... Oh, let me help.'

Mrs Holmcroft submitted with an uneasy smile to her son's not very deft efforts to remove the large cotton-wool plugs from her ears and gave a little cry when they finally both popped out.

'Oh, thank heavens for that! I am so glad you've stopped your banging.' She announced she had just been to the kitchen garden and showed her basket full of vegetables to prove it. 'Will you be staying to lunch?' she asked the prince. 'We are so late today.'

He explained as courteously as he could that he had already had lunch and wanted to be back at Stadleigh Court shortly.

'Oh, what a pity! Some other time then. Oswald dear, lunch will be ready in twenty minutes.'

She went off quickly towards the house. Her son took the opportunity to explain that his mother was staunchly opposed to his 'experiments' and insisted on protecting her ears. He also explained that she liked to cook lunch for them, with the help of kitchen staff, but was getting slower and more forgetful. 'You were about to ask me something, prince, weren't you?'

'I was going to ask you, why were you down by the old ford on the day you rescued me? Was it connected with an experiment?'

On hearing the question, Oswald Holmcroft stood stock

still and put a finger to his lips. The slow sideways swivel of his hazel eyes hinted at a sudden realisation that the question might not be entirely innocent. He looked up at the sky and then down at his fee before removing the matchlock musket from its crozier-like stand.

'What exactly do you mean?'

'I mean a coincidence.' The prince did not blink. 'Though I suppose it could also be called an anniversary. The date... am I wrong? I think you know what I mean.'

The historian of Cromwell shouldered the musket. He had indicated that they should go in the direction of the house across what was not so much lawn as grassland. It was suddenly clear to the prince as they made their way to the house that his question had rattled his host and he pressed home his advantage.

'The anniversary of the accident to the horse Frou-Frou. Remember the horse Frou-Frou?'

The other did not answer and quickened his pace.

'I know I am guessing, but I'd like you to listen to what I have to say. You probably know there is a Russian lady, a compatriot, who has resided at Stadleigh Court for many years. Did you know that? You must do. Didn't Lady Helen say something about the Karenins when we were having tea?'

Oswald Holmcroft gave a slight nod, but avoided the prince's querying gaze and appeared to be sweating more copiously. He wiped his face with the hem of the cape.

'Some years ago,' the prince went on, 'it's my guess she had an accident on her horse Frou-Frou. It suffered some injury down by the old ford and had to be destroyed. I am guessing, of course.' The prince looked for some kind of reaction, but his listener just went on wiping his face as he walked. 'She herself was so shocked – I am guessing, I know that – so shocked she virtually became a recluse and ever since has worn black, on the example, of course, of your own dear Queen Victoria. But she has made a habit of acknowledging the anniversary of the horse's death. Each year on that date she has conducted a little ceremony and marked the site of her accident with a red rose.'

This was apparently too much for Oswald Holmcroft. His historian's professional pride would doubtless be at stake if he did not know about such a special local event.

'Of course, I have heard about something of the sort, prince. You yourself mentioned it at Lady Helen's.'

'And you denied it, in so many words,' he was reminded. 'Which was probably unwise, because I believe you know quite a lot about it.'

'I do?'

'A small commemorative headstone was made. I will of course ask her or Giles Irmingham when I next see them...' As he spoke he noticed a sharp change in Oswald Holmcroft's expression. 'It was set high up in the bank of the lane running down to the ford. I wasn't tall enough to see all the lettering but I saw enough, I think, when I was there this morning. Unfortunately it had been smashed. Pieces had fallen down and become buried in the grass. I am guessing, I know, but I think that must have been why I had my accident. Bang! I hit it with my front wheel... I think you know the rest.'

'So you think that caused your accident?'

'I'm certain.'

'Well, I'm so pleased your bicycle's been mended. I feel I ought to pay for it. How much...'

'Just tell me,' the prince insisted, 'why were you there?'

Silence. Then truculently: 'You know so much, you tell me.'

It was defensive and somewhat ingenuous. There seemed no reason to stop questioning him. 'You don't normally go there, do you? You were there, I suspect, because you knew my compatriot – let us call her the lady in the tower – would be there to conduct her annual ceremony at precisely that time on that particular day. You would know it because you were responsible for it.'

'Pardon me.' The tone was aggrieved and slightly challenging.

'On that particular day, at that particular time, some years ago you were concealed in the shade of the overhanging willow ready to test your musket. You knew when the train would be passing, when the whistle would sound, and at that very instant you would fire. You did fire – and you either killed or seriously injured a most beautiful horse, Frou-Frou. Do you know why I am saying this?'

Oswald Holmcroft darted a pale, anxious look at the prince and said nothing. They had reached the verandah steps.

'Because,' he said, 'as I checked in your biography of Cromwell, you state in a footnote on page 117 that you yourself had satisfactorily demonstrated that you could disable a horse at thirty paces. Being a scrupulous historian, you gave the date on which you conducted the experiment and I guess – purely an informed guess, mind you – I guess it probably happened on the date the horse Frou-Frou was maimed or killed. Can you deny that?'

Oswald Holmcroft shook his head.

'You tried to destroy the evidence of any connection by smashing the headstone, didn't you?'

Again silence.

'But a couple of days ago I think you were at it again. As I lay there in the shade of the very same overhanging willow I distinctly heard a gunshot at approximately the same moment as the train whistle sounded. I'm not guessing now. You were shooting, weren't you?'

'What do you mean?'

'I think you may have shot the wounded man over at the Court. Don't you remember, I mentioned it at Lady Helen's while we were having tea?'

'Shot?' Cromwell's biographer went several shades paler. 'I denied it then and I deny it now. You can't mean it!'

'I do mean it, Mr Holmcroft.'

'No, prince, please, I must insist... I must insist I was not aiming at anyone. And I did not shoot anyone, that's the truth.' Oswald Holmcroft spoke so earnestly his voice literally shook. 'I was shooting at rabbits!'

The prince looked straight into his hazel eyes. Shaded by the peak of his cap, they blinked back at him moist with apprehension. They were all the evidence he needed that his guesswork had done its work.

'Who could have shot him if you didn't?'

'I did not,' the other muttered. 'Come with me.'

Of course, there was no evidence. The prince knew that Sergius, or Sergei, or Seriozha, as his mother called him, had not received a bullet wound. If the young doctor was right, then something else must have caused his injury. So all he said was: 'But you admit, don't you, that you did kill Frou-Frou?'

He grunted. 'Please, not so loud. Come into my study. I will explain. There are areas of any historian's work where rumour and conjecture impinge upon historical fact and have to be clearly identified...'

His voice, if thinned by the spaciousness of the garden, acquired a booming forthrightness the instant they entered the house. A short passageway smelling of polish led to a book-lined study considerably larger than Giles Irmingham's. It was cluttered, as any good working study should be, with books and journals piled high on the floor and tables and windowsills and demonstrably betraying the absence, at least recently, of any tidying female hand and even of much effective dusting. But sunlight and warm air pouring in through a half-open window facing onto the area at the back of the house banished concern for dust and untidiness. The room suited Oswald Holmcroft's own character, appearing sunny on the outside, judging by his bright hazel eyes and suntanned complexion, yet basically business-like, serious, inventive, brisk and, above all, celibate in its schoolboyish unconcern for the frivolous and any concession to such irrelevant matters as art or good taste.

'Yes, yes, yes,' he said, standing the musket in one corner, as if he wanted to dispose of anything to his discredit with a conjuror's alacrity. 'I admit that, prince. You are a highly intelligent man, sir, the first person to realise what happened, I grant you that. My only defence is that it happened before I was attracted to Tolstoyanism. Since then I have become a changed man. Cromwell and your great writer have much in common. His view of society and Cromwell's have a remarkable similarity, you must know that... Except for one utterly essential difference, so utterly essential, you see, that I know I am fully within my rights to doubt all your insinuations about injuries to horses or shootings and so on and so forth. Accuse me as much as you like, prince, but I have one completely cast-iron defence. You look puzzled? Please do have a seat.'

A somewhat worn armchair with wooden arms seemed the obvious place to sit. As the prince sat down, he had the sudden and almost intuitive sense that he might have overplayed his hand by accusing his host of such callous – not to say murderous – behaviour. He readied himself for what he supposed would be a deserved rebuke. Oswald Holmcroft, by contrast, appeared suddenly affable and gentlemanly. 'Some cordial, prince?'

'Thank you, that would be very pleasant.'

'Another of my little Tolstoyan fads.' He handed across a glass of pink liquid. 'My mother helped make it. Local fruits. On a hot day it is a most refreshing drink. Tell me why you're puzzled, prince.'

The drink was sipped and tasted mostly of raspberries. The prince crossed his legs quite contentedly. 'What puzzles me is why? Why you aimed your musket in the first place, why you shot?' There was no immediate reply, so he added: 'Why do you hate Stadleigh Court? I think that's the question. And I think you may have already given me the answer.'

'Ah, yes, I think that *is* the question.' Oswald Holcroft took a seat in a similar armchair beside him, his suntanned face turned towards the prince with a faint smile of gentlemanly triumph. 'You're right on both counts, I think – question and answer. You have been good at guessing, prince. Very good.'

He took a sip of his own drink. 'Yes, that is the real question. In my case, because the Irminghams are usurpers. Under the Protectorate we, the Holmcrofts, were the true masters here.'

'I guessed that was it.'

'But the main reason, prince - my personal reason, a reason of my very own as a historian...' his face leaned very close as he spoke '...is because Lord Irmingham's a charlatan, an out-and-out charlatan! He's an idea-monger! He's a poseur! He pretends to be a follower of your great writer, but he is really doing a terrible disservice by giving sanctuary and succour to the lady you referred to as the lady in the tower who is at best an imposter and at worst an out-and-out fiction!'

'Ah,' the prince sighed, 'I see!' He countered the other's fiercely contentious statement with a world-weary heave of the shoulders and a dismissive, 'I heard the same thing this morning.'

A suspicious look was darted at him. 'You did! Who from?'

'He is called Carew Kingston.'

'Well, he is a compatriot of yours, he should know!' The claim was made almost joyously. 'And of course he's right! There has to be respect for the truth! That is paramount!'

'So what is the truth?'

Responding with a little chuckle, Oswald Holmcroft rose, opened a desk drawer and handed across a sheet of paper, urging him to take a careful look.

'There are only two copies,' he pointed out. 'Irmingham's got the other. But it states our case. And we've all put our initials and signed it because Irmingham himself won't countenance the truth.'

What the prince held in his hand was a brief, handwritten statement, headed <u>TO WHOM IT MAY CONCERN</u> in bold capitals, which announced *'categorically and without fear of contradiction'* that Anna Karenina committed suicide in 1877 by throwing herself under a train.

'Any attempt,' the statement concluded, *'to claim that the said person survived that event and is alive and resident at Stadleigh Court in the county of Herefordshire must be regarded as totally false and insupportable in the light of all the known evidence.'*

Four initials and four names were appended at the bottom of the statement – B.P. (Bernard Pares), O.H. (Oswald Holmcroft), C.K. (Carew Kingston), I.I. (Isobel Irmingham).

'Well, well.'

The presence of Oswald Holmcroft's name and Carew Kingston's was no surprise. Lady Isobel's caused a shock at first glance, but a moment's reflection made it seem less remarkable.

'Bernard Pares? Who is he?'

'A young English historian of great probity and promise,' came the answer, followed by a somewhat regretful acknowledgement that hardly anyone in England had a proper knowledge of Russian literature and culture, let alone the kind of scholarly ability required to sift fact from fiction in dealing with Russian history. 'Yet young Bernard Pares has. I was glad he was so forthright. Whoever claims to be the lady concerned is an imposter. As a fiction, of course, she cannot exist, in any case. All the documentation has been passed to Lord Irmingham.' Oswald Holmcroft retook his seat at this point, his tone one of disdain mingled with a certain scorn. 'How could I or anyone else shoot at a fiction? The idea is absurd! And so how could I possibly wound her horse?' He complacently licked his lips. 'Nothing in the world will persuade me that that person, whoever she is, is Anna Karenina! If she exists, she's an imposter! And as for that headstone, it was a nonsense, erected for the same silly reason that his father built that pretentious place, Stadleigh Court! Just for show! To show off! That's why I smashed it.'

'How did you do that?'

'By standing up in my trap. It was the only way I could reach it.'

'I thought as much.'

He gave the prince another look, this time of mild approval for good guesswork. 'Yes, I struck the thing with the butt of my rifle.' The admission was conjured out of sight with great swiftness. 'But I make no apologies about the horse. If it really was real, of course.'

'You mean, it would be hard to prove it was real?'

'Precisely.'

'I see. Once your experiment was over, the horse didn't matter, was that it?'

They exchanged quite candid looks. The prince had to acknowledge that the historian of Cromwell had made a reasonable case.

'I only regret...' The round hazel eyes glittered with what might have seemed sympathy and a readiness to make amends, except for a schoolboyish suggestion of malicious glee in their sideways glance '...you had that accident. I'm sorry about that.'

'So you were to blame! You were the indirect cause of

my accident and the Good Samaritan who came to my rescue! I am very grateful to you. More important, I am in your debt in another sense.'

The irony was inescapable. 'You are?'

'Yes, I would never have met Anna Karenina otherwise.'

Oswald Holcroft now raised his chin slightly and licked his lips, evidently wondering whether to believe the last remark or not. Finally he permitted himself a smile. 'A joke, prince, is that it?'

The prince did not answer directly. Instead he swallowed what remained of the cordial in his glass and asked politely: 'Would you permit me to have that document?'

'Why, of course, prince. It is cast-iron, you must agree. The Anna Karenina you mentioned is a fiction – and dead, of course. She is not the lady in the tower.'

***

Cheerily he swung a leg over the saddle of the Rudge Explorer, waved his hand and pedaled away up the long straight drive. Again, no one was about and everything seemed silent and deserted.

No "gap in nature", then, he had to conclude. On the face of it, nothing more remarkable than a sentimental woman's desire to celebrate the death of a favourite horse, a dangerous, schoolboyish experiment by someone who should have known better and a malicious, if understandable, act of vandalism in smashing a headstone in a disused lane. But beneath it all was something much less innocent, much more complex – deep-seated resentment, for example, of the Irminghams by the

Holmcrofts, a modern historian's obsession with experiment in the name of truth, and, worst of all, a conspiracy, so far as could be judged, by Anna Karenina's enemies to deny her existence or, quite probably, render her non-existent if they could.

The wind blew in the prince's face once more as he cycled down a pleasant gradient, making the rim of his Panama hat flap slightly without blowing it off, just as it did not blow away his thoughts. It concentrated them.

What had happened to Sergius? Why was he sick with lockjaw? How could he suffer from the disease of wounding if there had been no wound? If he had not been shot, how could he have been wounded?

Oswald Holmcroft was denying what the prince knew to be true. He was denying that Sergius existed, let alone that he was a victim of lockjaw. He was denying Anna Karenina was alive and well and living in Stadleigh Court. All his denials simply meant that, for him, everything was permitted, not to say justified, even the shooting of Anna Karenina's son or her horse. According to his document, then, he had a cast-iron defence, which would very likely stand up to scrutiny in a court of law. The prince knew he had to challenge that. Was it any wonder, in that case, that Anna Karenina was so obsessed with "enemies"?

In some twenty minutes of rapid pedaling he found himself once again free-wheeling down the steep lane towards the river. It rose up towards him in its placid, blue-green brilliance, enticing with its coolness and offer of something pristine and magical. Naturally he took care to brake before reaching the smashed headstone and the sharp squeaking caused a shrill, frightened flapping of wings as a disturbed moorhen rose off the water and flashed across to the far bank. He drew to a stop, climbed off the bike conscious of the slight nagging from his ribcage and took a long look at the water. The level had dropped noticeably since he had last been there. More reeds were exposed on the bank and even a modest area of pebbly beach had appeared at the water's edge. It was possible to see fairly clearly where the old ford had been, since shallows had formed above a kind of raised causeway near the riverbank.

He took a while to decide. Then he removed his shoes and stockings, rolled up his trousers and waded in. It had struck him that if a lead bullet could be found of the kind fired by a musket, that at least would be some sort of proof. There was of course very little likelihood of this. What he was about to do could be dismissed as eccentric, not to say plain silly, yet as soon as he felt the cool, caressive flow of the water round his ankles and calves he was delighted by the pleasure of it on such a hot day. The water, moreover, was clear. He could see exactly where he was going and waded on. In a short while he found himself nearly halfway across.

It seemed likely that the crossing might be made on foot, which was very surprising, and he was on the point of turning back to fetch his Rudge Explorer when suddenly he slipped. The water at once came up to his neck and he thrashed about wildly. The shock literally took his breath away. He could swim, of course, but the sensation of succumbing to the immersion, glimpsing the sun above him like a white porcelain plate fragmenting before his very eyes, caused him to thrash more frantically than ever. He could find no foothold.

A strong current dragged at his feet and sucked him down. Instinct and good fortune, he thought afterwards, saved him. For several moments he struck out blindly in a desperate dog-paddle, going under more than once but managing to raise his head back above water sufficiently to gasp in some air. As soon as that much buoyancy had been achieved, he began a breaststroke and saved himself. He was at the mercy of the river's flow for a short while and then managed to swim into calmer water until his hands touched stones. By that time he realised he was back again on the causeway of the ford.

The once smart bicycling suit clung to him with a sodden, dragging tenacity as he managed to stand upright, shivering, his teeth chattering. The water reached only to his knees but the very pressure of the wet clothing seemed to prolong the sensation of drowning. He spent a while inhaling deep breaths. It was ignominious, of course, standing there drenched. No Russian prince should allow himself to be seen in such a state.

Bozhe moi, kak eto unizitel'no!

Luckily he saw no one around him. Nothing but tree-shade and a few cows. He crossed himself and thanked God.

Cautiously, one short step at a time, he made his way towards the bank on the Stadleigh Court side.

Suddenly something glinted.

He stopped, one foot poised.

He drew his foot back.

He balanced.

He bent forward to look more closely.

It was there!

It shone among the stones!

He stooped down, picked it out of the water and studied it.

It was the proof! All the proof he needed!

12

'You are, sir,' said Cotton, 'in need of some addition to your wardrobe, if I may say so.'

The prince had to admit that, having been through fire and water, he was temporarily reduced to the silk, monogrammed dressing-gown that Cotton now held up for him. Studying himself in the mirror once he had put his arms through the sleeves, he came to the conclusion that a cycling accident, a bruised ribcage, "the burnin'", indiscriminate gunshots, a blow from a heavy wooden plume and immersion in Wordsworth's "sylvan Wye" had left him dressed more suitably for the *Promenade des Anglais* than for Stadleigh Court.

'As a boy or scarcely a man, Cotton, I endured enemy fire,' he said philosophically.

'Yes, sir.'

'And the Bashi-Bazouks. And being wounded. But today, Cotton, I have been under fire here in rural Herefordshire and I am not at all sure I like it. To be shot at like a rabbit for no good reason is undignified. What is more I have left my bicycle on the other side of the river.'

Cotton said he would fetch it.

The prince thanked him. 'My one consolation,' he added, 'is our great poet Alexander Pushkin.'

'Your great poet, sir?'

'I will try to offer you his words in English, Cotton.

"Vsyo, vsyo, chto gibel'iu grozeet..." Something like: "All that threatens peril…" *"Dlya serdtsa smertnego"* "For the heart of mortal man…Yes, all that threatens peril for the heart of mortal man, er, *"tayeet"* – "conceals, yes, conceals…" *"Neiz'iasnimy naslazhden'ia – Bessmert'ia, mozhet byt', zalog!"* "conceals inexplicable joys, the guarantee perhaps of immortality!" These lines, Cotton, now make me feel a lot better qualified for everlasting life.'

'Very gratifying, sir. I will endeavor to have your linen bicycling suit cleaned and pressed by tomorrow. The only other apparel is…'

'Please, Cotton, not now. There are perils that threaten. I feel them.'

'Yes, sir. Forgive me, it was insensitive of me. To be shot at as if you were a rabbit reminds me. I was informed by Master Charles that Lord Irmingham is very much against it, sir. The taking of life is very much against his principles. I think he also disapproves of fishing, even though he is not actually against it. So Master Charles tells me.'

'You have an interesting source of information there, Cotton. Tell me more.'

'Sir, I have been told things in confidence which I feel I cannot divulge. But he is an inquisitive young gentleman. He has, er...' Cotton cleared his throat '...er, a natural curiosity about the opposite sex, you understand.'

'Oh, yes.'

'A peep-hole interest, I think.'

'Not uncommon at the beginning of puberty.'

'True, sir. Except his powers of description are remarkable for one so young.'

'What does he describe?'

'The shape, sir...' Cotton again cleared his throat '... pardon me, sir... the shape of a lady's bosom. He has even shown me little drawings. He says that the Venus on the stairs is not a good example. There is a much better example in the Rubens Room.'

'The Rubens Room? What's that?'

'I understand it is a paneled room specially imported from Holland, sir. The first Lord Irmingham had it brought over in pieces and installed here. It contains a painting by the famous painter, Mr Rubens.'

'Very interesting, Cotton. I must find this room. For the time being, though...'

For the time being he had other things on his mind. He was particularly anxious to see Dr James Parkinson. For his recent overnight stays at Stadleigh Court the doctor had been allotted a small bedroom next door. He had not been there since the prince's sodden return from the river and was presumably attending his sick patient in the tower. It was precisely about the sick patient that the prince wanted to see him. He was pretty sure he had found something that could very likely explain what had happened.

It might also prove that both the sick patient and his mother were not fictions. The possibility of such proof was now uppermost in the prince's mind. To confirm her identity, to claim she was real, made him doubly sure she deserved to be protected from "enemies". At the same time he was fairly sure his visit to her this morning had provoked or was connected with some kind of peril. However irrational it might be, he felt the gunshots in "the burnin'" posed a threat of the very peril that can conceal inexplicable joys. Whether or not they guaranteed immortality was another matter. But he felt they guaranteed his right to be the only person in England who could verify for sure that Anna Karenina was alive and well and living in Stadleigh Court, Herefordshire.

'For the time being I am content,' he said, drawing his dressing-gown tightly round him.

'I am glad to hear it, sir.'

'Please let the doctor know I am anxious to see him.'

'Certainly, sir. And I will see to your evening dress, sir, as soon as possible.' Cotton bowed and left the room.

The prince let his gaze wander reflectively towards the scene of the garden. The sun was low and shadows were lengthening. Pink-tinged clouds looking like so many meringues on a plate of porcelain blue sky made a tasteful contribution to the tranquil early-evening scene. Possibly offering incalculable joys for the heart of mortal man, they were as transient in their beauty as the momentary quiet that seemed to possess Stadleigh Court. There was no organ music to be heard. Only a distant lowing of cattle accompanied by the faint tolling of a church bell for evensong came through the open window.

What caught his eye was Oswald Holmcroft's document. It lay on the windowsill in a triangle of sunlight. He had tried to peel back the folded sheet but the paper, sodden after being in the river, simply tore wetly apart and he had put it on the windowsill to dry.

> *(B.P.)Bernard Pares,*
> *(O.H.)Oswald Holmcroft,*
> *(C.K.)Carew Kingston,*

(I.I.)Isobel Irmingham.

He recited the names to himself. The order seemed arbitrary. Why did these four people want to deny her existence? What did they have against Anna Karenina?

It was easy enough to understand why in the case of Bernard Pares. He was a young historian trained to tell the difference between fact and fiction. Anna Karenina was a fictional heroine who had committed suicide. By no stretch of the imagination could she be said to exist. Oswald Holmcroft's hostility could be ascribed to the same respect for truth, though coloured by a longstanding personal dislike of the Irminghams. Carew Kingston was hostile because, as a dedicated Tolstoyan, he acceded to Tolstoy's wishes and repudiated all Tolstoy's writings before his conversion. As for Lady Isobel, she was no doubt hostile to all her husband's Russian connections. Whether correctly or not, she held them responsible for the drain on the Irmingham finances and the possibility that she would lose her heart's desire, which was to remain mistress of Stadleigh Court.

None of these could be considered serious reasons. Certainly not serious enough to justify Anna Karenina's own fears. They might be her "enemies" but they hardly seemed to pose a threat to her life. Something in the document might offer a clue, the prince felt intuitively, and it was annoying to have to wait for the paper to dry before examining it again.

'The doctor, sir,' said Cotton.

Carrying his leather medical bag, Dr James Parkinson stood in the open doorway. Tall and looming, his very presence was signaled by an accompanying medical odour. He had looked tired before, but now he had the pale, drawn look of someone without sleep for several days.

'You wanted to see me, prince?'

The prince asked after the victim of lockjaw.

'Worse.' The brogue was there, but very faint. 'I think I'll have to spend the night here just in case I'm needed.'

'You mean, the *curare*'s not working.'

'It's in short supply. More's being ordered, but it won't be here until the day after tomorrow. He's exhausted by the return of the spasms. Which is why, as I say, I think I'll have to stay here. And you, prince?' He had noticed the dressing-gown. 'You're not unwell, are you?'

'No, no.' He explained what had happened and why he had been reduced to wearing a dressing-gown as the only dry garment left to him apart from evening dress. It allowed him to go in a princely manner to a chest-of-drawers beside his bed and carefully unwrap something from a still-wet handkerchief. 'I wanted to show you this.'

The object had to be handled rather gingerly less due to its weight than to the sharpness of the protruding short, spiky, rusted nails. He asked the doctor what he made of it. The latter obediently studied what the unfolded handkerchief now revealed.

'An old horseshoe?'

'Found in the river down by the old ford. Where I saw your patient hopping about in the water. He wasn't shot, you know. He had probably stepped on this.'

'On this? Oh, but surely...'

'I almost trod on it myself this very afternoon.'

'Yes, but...'

'You know as well as I do that it only takes a pinprick. Tetanus has extraordinary power as a toxin.'

James Parkinson conceded that much. Then he paused, peered at the horseshoe inquisitively without letting it come too close to his face, pursed his lips and muttered something about cow manure.

'That could do it, of course,' he said. 'I'll have to take a closer look at the soles of his feet. It's a fancy piece of metal.'

It was a horseshoe made from high-quality steel that had retained something of its gleaming newness although the nails had rusted to the sharpness of pins.

'It was made for a fancy horse,' the prince pointed out. 'Frou-Frou.'

'Frou-Frou?'

The answer to the query was curtailed by a rapid knocking on the already open bedroom door and the sudden noisy entrance of Giles Irmingham, saying: 'Dmitry, my dear chap, do you mind? May I come in? I'd heard you'd almost drowned.'

He closed the door behind him. 'How are you? I mean, I can't have you falling ill just when you're about to swear an affidavit before my lawyers. They're due here from London tomorrow... Oh, I say, what have you got there?'

He was shown the horseshoe. A cursory inspection at first suggested he considered it not only obscene but wholly irrelevant to his immediate concerns.

'A horseshoe with rusty nails... So?'

'It belonged to the horse Frou-Frou.'

'I've no idea what horse it belonged to...'

'It belonged to the horse Frou-Frou and may well have been the cause of the injury to the sick man in the tower.'

'Let me have a look.' A closer inspection revealed the

Sheffield stamp. *'Frou-Frou Stadleigh'* could be discerned in the metal. He admitted that special care had been taken to ensure a regular supply of such shoes. 'Where did you find this?'

The prince explained and the doctor chipped in with his own bit about tetanus.

'Tetanus?'

'As the prince knows, it is very poisonous.' Dr James Parkinson spoke slowly and rather officiously as if he were giving evidence at an inquest. 'If my patient stepped on this accidentally and then had to carry his mother from a boat up the bank of a river covered in cow manure, it is very likely he could have been infected. That is my explanation, Lord Irmingham. He may have stepped on it before that, too, when practising with the boat, getting it ready, launching it...'

'I see.' Giles did the natural thing. He handed the horseshoe very quickly back. 'Not nice.'

'Deadly,' said the prince. 'Possibly deadly. But also possible proof.'

'Proof? Of what?'

'Proof she is alive and well and living here at Stadleigh Court.'

'Ah! I see!' The long beard was stroked.

'If the horse existed, surely the rider also existed.'

'Oh, Dmitry, my dear fellow, I see exactly what you mean!' Giles Irmingham exclaimed. 'Well I never! That's very, very good. Very, very good.'

***

Despite lack of clothes and the possible lack of dignity, the prince felt his Russian soul glow with pride in the sure knowledge that his honour was intact. He had discovered proof of a kind that could provide moral reassurance when required to swear an affidavit the following day. He could still, of course, be making an over-hasty commitment to a 'truth' that had all sorts of ramifying implications. The names of Bernard Pares, Oswald Holmcroft, Carew Kingston and Isobel Irmingham again beat a little tattoo in his brain. He insisted Giles should listen to him. In private. The doctor withdrew at once.

Giles sat down in the window seat where he had sat previously. He raised an expectant eyebrow. 'Dmitry, what is it?'

The prince maintained a candid scrutiny of the other's face as he spoke. 'I was shown a signed statement this morning by Oswald Holmcroft which claimed in so many words that the lady in the tower was an imposter. Your wife was one of the signatories.'

'Oh, *that!*'

'Oswald Holmcroft said you had the documentation. I would like to see it.'

'The documentation,' Giles repeated. 'Of course you shall see it. In view of the affidavit it's essential you see it. I'll just...'

He excused himself and returned a couple of minutes later with a large brown envelope. It contained various items, each one of which was passed across.

'My wife's. Not very helpful, as you can see.'

In fact, it was a statement from Lady Isobel affirming that

the Russian lady known as Anna Karenina could not be the person she claimed to be, etc., etc., and must be an imposter. A similar signed denunciation, in both English and Russian, had been contributed by Carew Kingston Esquire.

'This one's from that fellow Holmcroft. He had the audacity... well, you can see.'

Oswald Holmcroft had given sworn testimony before a commissioner for oaths. The prince smiled at its emphatic claims.

'And here's a chap I don't know at all, but I believe he's a young historian. Holmcroft got him to authenticate his claim.'

The document was a polite letter from Bernard Pares declaring, quite simply, that Anna Karenina was a fictional heroine. Also among the documents was a copy of the <u>TO WHOM IT MAY CONCERN</u> statement received from Oswald Holmcroft, now still lying damp on the windowsill.

'Who wrote this document?' The hand was bold and the ink of the homemade kind that the prince had used for his telegram. 'I think your daughter said she wrote it and made a copy? Is that correct?'

'Yes, she wrote it and made a copy, but she's not one of the signatories. She did it because she felt the whole thing was so silly. And that's it, my dear Dmitry. Hardly irrefutable claims about the lady's non-existence. But you have seen her, you have that horseshoe and – most important of all – you have known her longer than anyone. What is more, you are a Russian prince.'

'True.' The prince handed back all the documents. 'Apart from the elderly servants, you and I, your son and daughter-in-law and the doctor are the only people who have actually seen her – here, I mean, in Stadleigh Court in recent weeks?'

'That is correct.'

'And she has been living here as a recluse?'

'Again correct.'

He sighed deeply. 'I should like to see her again before confronting your lawyers, if that were possible. There are certain matters I wish to clarify. Forgive me if I don't detail them immediately. They are rather... rather personal. Personal doubts, if I may put it that way.'

Giles said he understood and would do his best to arrange it. He would have to speak to 'the servants', as he called Boris and his wife, and it depended naturally enough on Anna Karenina's willingness to see the prince again.

***

Giles's promise to do his best was successful. Boris bowed respectfully at the top of the curved staircase. His expression was as melancholy as his deeply creased, sallow features could make it. The tightly pursed lips caused tiny furrows of age to make his mouth resemble a pincushion and his voice, in its quavering softness, matched it.

'Your excellency, our dear mistress is... in... great... distress.'

To the prince's relief, he did not seize his hand, nor did he fall on his knees. The old man's own distress was expressed by a refusal to show his feelings other than through a dignified moistening of the eyes appropriate to his melancholy appearance and the dismal tone of his voice. He gravely corroborated what the doctor had said about 'the young master' – Sergius or Sergei or Seriozha, the lockjaw victim

– having suffered further spasms. There was apparently the need for a second opinion and another doctor was awaited. For Boris this meant that 'he is soon to be gathered up... into the bosom... of Our Lord.... Soon... Very soon, I fear, your excellency, very soon.'

His pessimism forewarned the prince that he might be received rather coolly, especially as he had to apologise for wearing a dressing-gown. The sight of Boris's massive stone toga of a frockcoat represented a formality and decorum he knew he could not match and left him so full of apprehensive foreboding that he followed the slow, elderly, cumbersome step-by-step ascent of the next flight of stairs without noticing any of the accompanying miasma, glad that it offered a momentary compensation for the near-naked honesty of his dressing-gown.

The elderly retainer tapped on the door of the sitting room, entered and announced the prince. On hearing Boris speak, the veiled figure standing by the window turned at once and held out a hand. The prince's response was to offer a somewhat agitated apology for being so inadequately dressed, only for it to dawn on him that he might well not be the first, let alone the only man to wear a dressing-gown in her sitting room. He kissed her hand while making every effort to hide what he was holding in his other hand and began to explain his reasons for wanting to see her. She laughed quietly.

'Prince Dmitry! Really! A Russian prince should never apologise for wearing a dressing-gown. Russian princes can always claim the privilege of dressing exactly as they please. And you are as smartly dressed as any! There is no need for an apology!' She dismissed Boris with a single wrist movement. 'I was admiring the view. It is a beautiful evening, isn't it?'

Standing as she had been by the closed window, one elbow resting on the back of one of her rickety gilded armchairs, she had been watching approximately the same view as he had been seeing from his bedroom, only from a higher elevation. The same sky, the meringue-shaped clouds, now seemingly no longer perilous for mortal man but white items tinted a deeper shade of pink that were like hands offering a blessing to a view of terraces and formal hedges reaching down toward the tree-lined riverbank and the distant silhouette of the battlements of the ruined castle on the other side of the valley.

The evening light was of course less intense, certainly far less intense than the bright sunlight of the morning's visit, but it had a faintly luminescent brilliance that made her veil almost transparent. So apparently thick when the prince had first seen it, there was now a fleeting instant when he felt sure he could see her features behind it, especially her eyes. The instant was only fleeting, but he caught a glimpse of her beauty, he thought, purified, it seemed, by age and ennobled by an ascetic suffering that left him feeling he was a voyeur and should be ashamed. She may have noticed this because her attitude changed. She turned back to look out of the window, no longer laughing but giving a deep and typically Russian sigh.

'Toska-a-a!'

The word was uttered dreamily. How often had he heard that word spoken by expatriates! *Toska-a-a!* The glimpse of an arc of sky, a leaf on a tree, a line of cloud and one is lost in heart-stopping nostalgia and yearning!

'Anna Arkadyevna,' he said a little sternly, unwilling to let such emotional gluttony come between them, 'I wish to talk about your enemies.'

She grew a little rigid, but this did not stop him from telling her quite candidly what he had discovered. He went on to assure her that what Oswald Holmcroft had shown him and the evidence of the 'documentation' meant nothing by comparison with what he had found on the bed of the river. That, he insisted, was tangible proof. He unwrapped what he had been holding and showed her the horseshoe, the rusty nails having been removed.

'Frou-Frou's!' she cried.

'Exactly, Frou-Frou's. Your horse.'

'Oh, my beloved horse!'

'Yes, but in a court of law it could well be argued, my dear Anna Arkadyevna, that it was no proof *you* were the rider. The horse might have been real, but were you? Do you,' he inquired as tactfully as possible, 'have any other evidence that could be offered as proof?'

If he had been able to see her face, to have had a clear view of the expression in her eyes, he might have judged more certainly, because he did not want to undermine his own certainty that she was who she was. Her demeanour, though, said it all. Her raised head, haughty but not arrogant, and the light touch of her hand on his arm left little room for doubt, but it was her tone of voice that clinched it.

'My dear Prince Dmitry, I feel sure you will protect me. I would not speak to you now if I were not sure of this. The truth is simple.' She paused a moment, gave another sigh and looked down at her fingers, now clasped tightly together. 'I came here with the help of dear Hannah. That is the truth. I came here with nothing. Dear, faithful Boris and his wife, they came later. I had been disowned, you see, literally disowned. Disowned by my husband, who would not give me a divorce or let me see my son. Disowned by... disowned by the one man I once loved, Count...' The prince was sure she *did* pronounce the name Vronskii, but almost under her breath, raising a handkerchief to her veiled mouth as she did so and turning aside for a moment. 'And he,' she emphasised more loudly, 'disowned me by declaring me dead! I mean!' Her suddenly unclasped hands offered this as an evident untruth. 'No, I was merely badly injured. Had it not been for the love shown me by Hannah, my saviour, I would have perished! Oh, it was a terrible, terrible time! And he, *he* it was, who had accused me, you know, of having an *unnatural* love for her, because I was fonder of Hannah than of my own daughter! Of course, I loved her and she loved me in return. She gave me all her love. All he did in return was disown me and give the impression...'

Perhaps at that point she noticed the other's reaction, because the prince was on the point of asserting that Count Vronskii had been deeply contrite to the point of despair. He had known that he was almost suicidal with grief. If it had not been for his death in one of the engagements below Plevna, he would very likely have lost his life by his own hand. He was about to point this out when she seemed to acknowledge it by hobbling stiffly away from the window and reclining gracefully on to the high-backed sofa. This made it harder to catch a glimpse of her features behind the veil, which he regretted because she had begun speaking quite softly in a much less aggressive, more confessional tone.

'I know I can be accused of expecting too much from him.' She adjusted her black dress round her and indicated the prince should sit where he had sat before. 'We did not have faith between us. Love needs the certainty of faith for it to put down roots and grow. You see, there was the triumph of success in him. He boasted of me. He took from me all he could and I was no use to him any more. And all the time my love kept growing more passionate and selfish, while his was waning and waning, and that's how we drifted apart. And where love ends, hate begins, you know.'

Saying this, she appeared to begin talking to herself. She mused, for instance, about the likelihood of receiving a divorce from her husband and marrying the Count. Mentioning her husband, Aleksei Alexandrovich Karenin, she painted a picture in her soft voice of his looks, the reticent, lifeless, faded expression of his eyes, the bluish veins on the backs of his hands, his way of speaking, the way he cracked his fingers, and from her words a portrait of the man sprang to life. But when she described the feeling between them, supposedly of love, she literally gave a little shudder of disgust. Her love had been for Vronskii. But could she have married him? No, her love for Vronskii had become her life, but when that love perished her life perished with it.

As she spoke, certain things became obvious. Proof in the form of something tangible or scientifically valid mattered a great deal less than the need to believe. The prince acknowledged to himself that he *believed* in her. He believed she was who she was. He also realised that by asking for proof he had inadvertently forced her to remember the misery of those final moments, above all the loathing she had felt for all the people she encountered on the way to her alleged death. That repugnance had never been completely banished from her life.

'You ask me for proof,' she said, again as if speaking to herself. 'My proof was what I heard that woman saying in the carriage: *"People are given minds in order to get rid of what bothers them."* That's all. I wanted to get rid of what bothered me. I had no faith, you see. And I had no one to believe in me or to believe in. There was only my Seriozha and he, well... I had lost him for good.'

It was on the tip of his tongue at that moment for the prince to point out the obvious with the best of intentions, which was of course that her son was no distance from her after all, but he checked himself because she dramatically raised her hand in prohibition of another word from him. Simultaneously the fragile brilliance of the evening light suddenly lessened. There was a noise, perhaps an animal from outside, perhaps the muffled yell of a sick man. The prince lacked the courage to speak. In any case, it was soon clear that, behind her veil, Anna Karenina was silently weeping.

He bit his own lip sharply enough to draw a little blood in an effort to suppress his own tears. He knew he should say something comforting or make some gesture of compassionate understanding, but he could think of nothing. She let her arm drop and inhaled deeply. Then she spoke quite loudly and very calmly.

'He will die, my dear prince. We all know it. You cannot save him now. I am resigned to the inevitable. It was a heaven-sent pleasure that he eventually came here and I loved the few weeks we had together, but I know I will lose him again. My life has been a pattern of light and dark, but through the dark there has always been the glimmer of a candle flame. That is what I have enjoyed most of all. Here in this tower, where I have been a prisoner, I have enjoyed the happiness of love, you know – a secret, immoral, shared love, unworthy perhaps, but a solace. I owe this place so much. And most of all, of course, I owe it to my dear Hannah... Her sacrifice, you see, if I may put it this way, has given me a greater happiness than anyone can imagine!'

This was a reminder of what Lady Helen had said about her brother Gerald. Oddly, it was an aspect of Anna Karenina's life that the prince found hard to come to terms with and he at once searched his conscience to know if he should mention the relationship next day, however obliquely and confidentially, when he made his statement. It might in a man-to-man sense give some degree of emotional validity to his sworn testimony on her behalf. Hard-bitten lawyers would understand, he felt, if they were given all the facts and would condone rather than condemn. Then he abandoned the idea. Anna Arkadyevna's candour had to be respected. It led him to feel greater respect for her lover as a result. Again, though, the room visibly darkened. There was need for a candle, he thought, but in leaning forward to ask him to light one, as he supposed, she began saying something excitedly in what sounded like an alarmed stage whisper: 'I think *he* is back! I heard him threaten me last night!'

'Who?'

'Vronskii! I heard him!'

'Where?'

'In my bathroom! I distinctly heard him!'

She was mad! In her bathroom! She must have seen the expression of utter disbelief on the prince's face because she drew back instantly into the deep shadow of her sofa.

'No one believes me. Perhaps I *am* mad,' she murmured. 'They say the mad hear voices.'

'He threatens you? What does he say?'

'He says he will kill me.'

'Oh, but surely…' Her claim merely fed the prince's disbelief and he said so.

'Oh, no,' she insisted, 'it is *him*, it is the Count! I'm sure of that!'

He was equally sure she was talking nonsense. He knew Count Vronskii was dead. He said he was killed below Plevna. She merely turned her head away and refused to say another word.

There appeared to be no further point in continuing the conversation. After the usual courtesies, he bowed and said goodbye. He was sure she was no imposter and would testify to that effect, but it was clear that her secluded life had left her subject to delusions and an obsessive fear of so-called "enemies".

13

The prince awoke late on the day of the soiree. Breakfast was late because Cotton spent an hour or more fetching the Rudge Explorer from the other side of the river. Then an overworked laundry maid apparently mislaid the prince's clothes. The recital of explanations and apologies left him without any choice: it had to be evening dress for morning wear. If this annoyed him, he was even more upset and annoyed by the strangeness of Anna Karenina's claims of being threatened in her own bathroom – and by Count Vronskii of all people!

'When it's all over I must get back to London as soon as can be arranged,' he admitted to Cotton.

'Yes, sir, I will see to it. I will consult the train times in Bradshaw.'

'I will have to attend the soiree, of course, but after that I imagine I will be free to leave.'

'Yes, sir, of course. Meanwhile Lord Irmingham wishes to see you, sir, as soon as possible.'

Giles, it turned out, was also puzzled and worried and annoyed by the lady in the tower when he welcomed the prince into his study. He delivered a litany of complaints as he paced up and down in his pale blue cassock to the accompaniment of a gentle hissing.

'Her son, you know. She's worried about him. So I've called for a second opinion.' The arrival of a doctor called

Simons was expected shortly. 'Gives himself airs, you know, very tiresome.' Anna Karenina had meanwhile complained of hearing more threats.

'I know she is perfectly sane. We must attribute her fears, I suppose' – Giles shook his head in a show of melodramatic despair – 'to nervousness, to her lonely life, to worrying over her son, all sorts of things. I most earnestly hope so. She will insist on speaking Russian or French and I can't always understand what she means.'

The prince understood his host's exasperation at the lack of sense, most especially the extraordinary claims about being threatened in her bathroom, but agreed she was perfectly sane. As for proof in a tangible sense, there was nothing he could add. Luckily she had apparently made a statement of her own.

'Here it is,' Giles said. 'My daughter Helen translated it earlier this morning.'

A desk drawer was unlocked and two papers were fished out, one of which, though written in a shaky hand, was in Russian and stated quite simply that Anna Arkadyevna Karenina was alive and well and living in Stadleigh Court. The other paper offered a word-for-word translation and had been written by Lady Helen Swanning, judging by the handwriting and the ink. The prince looked at both and handed them back with an assurance that the translation was accurate.

'Good, good.' A rapid batting of eyelids. 'You can probably imagine why I wanted this kept secret. It's what my father wanted and what she herself wanted. She has also since sworn an affidavit. It was in connection with her late husband's will. My lawyers will show you everything this afternoon. All I would like you to do, my dear Dmitry, is to make a similar statement confirming that she is, in your opinion, the lady whom you met in St Petersburg, entitled, you know, to be known as Anna Karenina and that you would testify to this effect in a court of law.'

The request was challenging because such testimony was easily contestable, as the prince well knew, but it was his duty to keep his promise. He agreed.

Giles was engaged in thanking him when the bald-headed Dr Simons was announced. He immediately strode into the study to offer his second opinion. With a flourish of a monocle and in a solemnly pompous tone of voice he claimed that the patient required hospital treatment which was apparently out of the question; that one overworked, young and inexperienced doctor was not enough; that the conditions under which the patient was now being treated were not hygienic and the disease was at an advanced stage. Coupled with a lack of specific remedies, the prognosis could not be favorable. He replaced his monocle, snapped shut his medical case, left his audience in no doubt that the worst should be expected, bowed and made his way out.

Giles shrugged his shoulders. 'You see?'

The strain in his face said it all. There was nothing the prince could say that would improve matters. He had lunch in his room so as to keep out of the way of all the preparations for the soiree. Once again, rather surprisingly, the organ was used, its bass notes reverberating loudly, but it was hard to be sure whether the equivalent of spring-cleaning in the Gothic hall or the rearranging needed to accommodate long trestle tables and rows of chairs produced the greater noise.

The prince spent the afternoon drafting an affidavit in the presence of the two London lawyers, a process lasting much longer and proving more exhausting than expected. Because the resultant document would have to be translated into either French or Russian at some later stage, exactitude in the correct legal wording was imperative. The experience so tired the prince that all thought of leaving for London was abandoned for the time being. Cotton was relieved.

'Yes, sir. In any case, it has begun to rain and I think it will continue raining for most of the night, by which time your bicycling clothes should be ready, sir. The laundry has promised it. And according to Bradshaw there would not be a suitable connection with the main line to Paddington until shortly before midday tomorrow. Which I think would be soon enough.'

'Good,' the prince said.

***

The soiree opened at six o'clock in the evening. In her long black dress, diamond tiara and highly powdered complexion Lady Isobel was a graceful hostess. She received everyone with welcoming smiles, handshakes and the occasional offer of a kissable cheek. The prince had been instructed to stand beside her. Introduced as 'our dear friend from Russia, Prince Dmitry Rostov, a relative of Count Tolstoy, you know,' he found himself the object of flickeringly darted looks usually reserved for radical archbishops or men with open fly-buttons.

Though she played her role to perfection, she was outshone by her stepdaughter who swept in after most of the guests. Lady Helen wore a plain moiré silk dress, perhaps of her own making, that lent her appearance a sheen of magic consciously enhanced by her brilliant eyes and pale bare shoulders. Her beautiful red hair, lustrous with raindrops, was held in place by two ornate spiral pearl clasps. Lady Isobel surveyed her, smiled politely and coldly offered a powdered cheek. It was not kissed.

'Come, prince,' she said, turning him away from the new arrival, 'I know Gerald would like to have a word with you.' She guided him imperiously towards her stepson without regard for guests who were forced to give way. 'Your man Cotton has been extremely helpful in giving Charles fishing lessons. Gerald would like to thank you for letting him.'

Buffet-style food set out on long trestle tables was already proving an attraction. Gerald, equally politely, had held back and was evidently on his own. Lady Isobel darted away – 'to see to things,' as she put it.

'Very nice chap – your man Cotton, I mean, prince, a very nice chap.' Gerald broke into a drawl. 'Not native, I suppose?'

'Native?'

'Not Russian, like...'

'No, Cotton is not Russian.'

'I thought not. The servants – oh, you know who I mean, I won't beat about the bush – they're, well, quite difficult really...'

Clumsily coded though the words might be, their meaning was crystal clear. The prince was reminded of the picture of Gerald he had noticed on Anna Karenina's occasional table. Before he could ask a question, Gerald avoided any awkwardness by quickly changing the subject.

'Charles is a very brainy boy, you know. It's a problem when you find yourself out of your depths talking to your own child. Your man Cotton seems to have had no difficulties like that. Charles couldn't talk about anything else. I am an absolute duffer myself. Apart from horses absolutely not interested in a thing. I try to keep in the peak of fitness, take regular exercise, generally do what I can – like your pedal cycling, prince. Horses, though, are my thing.'

It was an appropriate moment to mention Frou-Frou.

'Oh, yes, a beautiful filly. Lovely creature. What about her?'

The prince mentioned he had found a horseshoe belonging to her.

'Where?'

'Near the old ford.'

Gerald stretched his neck. 'Yes, that was a very nasty thing, a really terrible thing.'

'Hadn't a memorial been put there?'

'Yes, she insisted. I think a kind of headstone was fixed up there. To commemorate what happened, you know.'

'What exactly happened?'

'We were never sure what it was or why.' Gerald had lowered his drawling voice and paused. He looked as if he were chewing hard. Then he added: 'The poor woman – you must know who I mean – she was hurt very badly. She's unsure why it happened. All she could think was that a train had whistled. The horse, poor animal, had to be destroyed.'

'If the horse were real, the rider would be real, too, wouldn't she?'

'Of course.' Gerald looked incredulous and slightly puzzled. 'Why on earth not?'

'Because not everyone believes in the existence of Frou-Frou's rider. If the horse existed as the horseshoe proves it did, that must mean that its rider existed too, and probably still exists, and the sad irony of it all is...' The prince placed his lips close beside Gerald's left ear '...is that Sergius, or Seriozha, her son, very likely stepped on the horseshoe and contracted tetanus poisoning. And is now very seriously ill.'

'Come again,' said Gerald, knitting his brows.

'Tetanus poisoning,' the prince whispered.

Gerald looked at him blankly. 'I knew he was ill but I didn't know he was poisoned.'

'No, not poisoned by someone...'

At that moment the organ burst into peals of sound from the gallery at one end of the hall. The effect was so thunderous it caught everyone unawares. Most guests were still standing near tables where all manner of vegetarian food was laid ready – plates of raw vegetables, chunks of cheese, nut cutlets, stuffed eggs, fruit from the kitchen gardens and orchards, cucumber and egg sandwiches, potatoes in various resourceful combinations and so on, accompanied by the dispensing of glasses of fruit cordial and lemonade. The ensuing concentrated munching coupled with the loud music meant the end of conversation. Most people exchanged no more than significant looks and posed themselves attentively in listening mode.

The prince more or less intentionally drifted towards Lady Helen. A glance exchanged with her silently inquired if this was Carew Kingston's composition. She removed a strip of carrot from her lower lip and nodded. Next to her was Oswald Holmcroft in evening dress a shade too tight for him. He bowed rather stiffly.

'I think it gets quieter soon,' she managed to say and licked her lips.

The composition had opened in a spirit of true Russian patriotism with a fanfare celebrating the victory over Napoleon – at least that was what could be justifiably assumed. Successive loud chords illustrated the resistance and courage of the Russian people and concluded with a series of crescendos representing the Battle of Leipzig and the triumphant arrival of Russian troops in Paris in 1814.

Just when the unwary English ear might have supposed it was all over and there had been one or two tentative handclaps, the piece picked itself up off the floor and launched into a plaintive, meandering melody evocative of lakes and forests, snow-covered rowans and silver birches, icy sunsets and smoke rising into pale wintry skies. This thin musical gruel of Tchaikovsky at his most sentimental continued for a while until it suddenly transformed itself into Borodin at his loudest. Surges of wild brassy chords, causing ladies to blink rapidly and clutch their reticules, evoked happy peasants celebrating the joys of harvesting. Once again the composition sank back into whimsical snatches of melancholy folksong, not that the guests, judging by the regular jaw movements and the fixed looks, were at all aware of the music's intentions. When the whole piece concluded with a strident march clearly suggestive of sunlit uplands and the liberation of the working class, a philistine majority of the guests concluded aloud that the organ bellows needed more muscle. Higher notes had tended to end up as little more than dying whistles and some of the deeper chords had proved reedy. In short, it ended not with a bang, but a whimper, and elicited only a few desultory handclaps.

The guests knew the form and quickly settled themselves into the rows of chairs facing a small podium and lectern set up beside the enclosed stairs to the organ gallery. The lectern had a row of candles that illuminated the whole area. Giles Irmingham at once stepped forward. He raised both hands. The down-falling light from the high windows, coupled with the candlelight, emphasised the priestly authority of his cassock and his strong features. He stood there and his uplifted arms coupled with the gaze of his blue eyes quelled all attempts to make conversation.

In his sonorous voice he began by thanking everyone for coming to the soiree. It was necessary, he explained, gesticulating with the soft movements of an orchestral conductor, to set an early start to the proceedings because many guests had come a long way and were busy people who had work to contemplate in the morning and, what is more, in the name of the great Russian writer and thinker, Count Leo Tolstoy, the spiritual values of life – as celebrated, of course, by the "Russian Rhapsody", the composition of 'our remarkable jack-of-all-trades, Mr Kingston, to which we have just been listening with such rapt attention' – the spiritual values, he assured us, were uppermost. The remarks ended with an appeal to the Reverend Ellis Chalmers to make an opening statement and explain – 'far better than I can myself, I assure you all' – the true relevance of Tolstoyanism for the present age.

The Reverend Ellis Chalmers rose from his seat in the front row and strode up to the lectern. Again there were a few handclaps, but Giles gestured for quiet. The new speaker, a tall, long-faced man dressed in clerical black, adjusted his *pince-nez*, surveyed his audience and cleared his throat. His long, lean body bent forward against the lectern with the thrusting intentness of a figurehead on a ship's prow. His voice matched this stance in its Ulster brogue as thick as sea-spume.

'Ladies and gentlemen, should we not all be in awe, in deep and profound awe, of the majesty and might of the great pantocrator, after listening to such music? Despite certain what I might call minor technical defects, the spiritual effectiveness, the, ah, rich paean of heavenly praise that the music offered, must give us pause, just for a very, very brief instant in our busy lives, to consider – to consider what? – to consider, I say, the most important question we can ever ask ourselves. And that question is: 'What is our life? What is it that gives meaning to our lives? Do we really know what our lives mean?'

A hardly unexpected fidgeting passed through the audience in the pause that followed. The Reverend Ellis Chalmers dry-washed his hands and then spread them wide in front of him as if confessing to a secret.

'The great Russian writer, Count Leo Tolstoy, to whom Lord Irmingham has referred, author of such great works as *War and Peace* and *Anna Karenina*, having achieved all the fame any man can reasonably hope for, felt at the age of fifty that he was overwhelmed by a dread of the dark, by a sense of horror at the meaninglessness of his own life. He fell into deep despair, despair not just for himself but for all humanity, and it brought him to the verge of suicide. He posed to himself the ultimate question: "Is there any meaning in my life which would not be destroyed by the death that inevitably awaits me?" It is a question we should all be courageous enough to pose to ourselves. And if we are honest we have to answer it by saying, No, there is no meaning to my life that will not be destroyed by the inevitability of my approaching death. So why go on living?

'To go on living you have to love life and to love life you must have faith. "Faith," said Tolstoy, "is a knowledge of the meaning of human life as a result of which man does not destroy himself but lives." "Faith," he said, "is the power of life." The power of life itself, once a man yields to it and lets it carry him forward, brings him into an incessant search for God, since "God is life," as Tolstoy puts it. Man therefore acquires a task in life. He has to save his soul. And in order to save his soul he has to live in a way that is godly. Which means denying himself certain so-called pleasures of the flesh, such as the flesh of animals who have to be slaughtered to assuage his perverted tastes...'

'Poppycock!' cried the voice of Raymond Vernoncourt. Ripples of disgruntled and facetious murmuring spread quickly among the audience and people craned their necks to see who had spoken.

'...such as alcoholic stimulants and tobacco, such as the indulgence in sexual activity outside of marriage – and incidentally,' the Reverend Ellis Chalmers now raised his voice, 'I will not be put off by such ignorant and ni-hi-li-st-ic barracking from someone who should know better! But that is not the main thing in Tolstoyan teaching. The main thing is that goodness is outside the chain of cause and effect. If goodness has a cause, it is no longer goodness, and if it has a reward it is not goodness either. To put it very simply, it is the simplest people who have the best and fullest understanding of the meaning of goodness, and at the heart of that understanding is the simple intuition that temporal life always stands under the imminent judgment of the eternal. To be fully aware of what this means a change of heart is needed...'

'Poppycock! Pretentious poppycock!' roared Raymond Vernoncourt.

'Shut up!' a voice cried, supported vigorously by several others.

'To be fully aware of what this means a change of heart is necessary. Human beings must change. They must change in their hearts. They must recognise the central importance of Christ's teaching from the Sermon on the Mount, namely that the true good of mankind is only served by a policy of non-resistance to evil by violence. Think of that a moment! It deserves serious thought not only for its essential pacificism but also for its very grandeur. In other words, no good is served by retaliation. The evil in man is eradicated only by love, by that love of life which faith nurtures and which leads to our lives being slowly assimilated into the life of God, permeated by His love and forever transfigured by it so that our lives are no longer meaningless, no longer corrupted by despair and rotted by thoughts of suicide. That is what we mean by Tolstoyanism! Amen! Amen!'

'Amen! Amen!' echoed several voices.

Tears clearly stood in the speaker's eyes. Too moved, it seemed, to continue speaking, he took off his *pince-nez*, wiped his eyes and slowly and blindly staggered away from the lectern to increasing ripples of rather self-conscious and unsure applause. As it quickly died away, the steady, chill, obtrusive sound of heavy rain wafted into the hall from outside, accompanied by hissings from the log burning in the large marble fireplace.

'Can you resist the ideas?' Lady Helen whispered. Sitting beside her in the front row, the prince was so enchanted by her bright eyes that even a murmur of dissent would have seemed a shame, so he smiled. At that moment she leant towards Oswald Holmcroft on her other side and requested her silk shawl. The arranging of it over her bare shoulders, in which the prince assisted, occurred just as the organ bellows could be heard recharging. One pure strong chord emerged.

Absorbed as he was by Lady Helen's extraordinarily sensual, musky perfume, which he knew would hardly have met with Tolstoy's approval, he was astonished to find himself confronted at that moment by a slim, dark-haired boy of about sixteen, in well-pressed trousers and gleaming white shirt. He stood on the podium beside the lectern and began to sing unaccompanied. The song was 'Drink to me only with thine eyes.' It was sung in a voice so pure and commanding, with such range and sweetness, it seemed in its higher registers to flicker like a star throughout the resonant spaces of the hall and overpower the noise of the rainfall.

The audience exploded into applause the instant the singing stopped. The boy, at first astonished, looked round in bewilderment and then broke into a shy smile. He gave a low bow. The stately figure of Mrs Emerald Stephenson in a tea-gown of bright red silk with large gigot sleeves rose from the front seats and approached him, arms outstretched, as if recognising a long-lost child. The boy's response to her kisses and embraces was a kind of mystified squirming. He went quite red and eventually managed to escape into the shadows of the hallway.

'Why,' she exclaimed, 'that is a most wondrous experience! Who is this delightful and talented boy?'

Someone explained he was a member of the kitchen staff.

'Why, that sure is the neatest thing I ever heard!' Her strong American voice matched in its resonance the redness of her dress. 'Lord Irmingham, let me say this – if I've heard nothing truly enlightening since being here in your beautiful home as an honored guest, then right now, this very moment, I have heard the most uplifting words and the most uplifting voice of any I have ever heard in my entire life! An' I'd just like to say how I will surely treasure these last few moments until I draw my last mortal breath, I surely will...'

'Mother, please desist,' came the voice of her son.

Monty Coulsham had risen to his feet beside her. His outfit of green velvet jacket with a pink handkerchief dangling from the breast pocket and a purple kummerbund wrapped round his slender waist was sufficiently surprising to elicit a few titters from the ladies in the audience and some not very complimentary low-key remarks from the men. He had no sooner spoken than a series of loud hammer strokes came from the direction of the organ gallery.

They grew louder and turned out to be footsteps descending from the top of the enclosed gallery stairs. Julie Mayhew-Summers, Julie the Unruly, slowly emerged into view at the bottom of the stairs in a bottle-green dress, shading her eyes from the hardly very strong candlelight of the podium. She gave a little mock bow and demonstrated with a pumping movement that she had been assisting the organist. Sympathetic laughter and shouts of approval greeted her.

She spent a short while unselfconsciously putting her hair to rights. It was clear she had arrived for a purpose because Monty Coulsham handed her a small volume. He then raised a hand to insist on quiet and opened his mouth as if about to speak. In a moment utter silence reigned.

What followed was a short oration delivered in a self-confident American way. It began with a reference to the fact that Count Leo Tolstoy's teaching sought to embrace the whole personality, the whole of life. Monty Coulsham said he believed in the same thing so far as art was concerned, especially poetry, the most articulate of the arts. Symbioticism – the word was pronounced slowly syllable by syllable as if it were an incantation. Sym-bi-ot-ic-ism, the poetry of the new age, should embrace all planes of experience. It should appeal to man's religious sense in transcending the mundane and it should stimulate the natural wellsprings of charity and altruism in man by demonstrating the universally divine character of language. And it should, above all, abolish the unreal distinction between so-called fiction and so-called reality and thereby transmute the sordid reality of life as we know it into the moral ideal for which all mankind yearned.

'Mood!' he suddenly declared, sensing the beginnings of restlessness in his audience.

People sat up quickly.

'Mood!' he repeated.

His audience blinked nervously.

'Yes, mood! Just a few miles from where we are right here and now...' a raised and shaken hand brought preacherly justification to his claim '...your great English poet, William Wordsworth, felt the mood of place. There is no greater symbiosis between man and his environment than a mood of place. "O sylvan Wye!" your poet sang, "thou wanderer thro' the woods, How often has my spirit turned to thee!" "That serene and blessed mood" is what he called the experience of recollecting the Wye and its "beauteous forms" – "that serene and beauteous mood"...'

'"In which,"' broke in Julie the Unruly's soft, intense voice, *'"the affections gently lead us on, –*

> *Until the breath of this corporeal frame*
> *And even the motion of our human blood*
> *Almost suspended, we are laid asleep*
> *In body, and become a living soul:*
> *While with an eye made quiet by the power*
> *Of harmony, and the deep power of joy,*
> *We see into the life of things."'*

Julie's articulation was a little theatrical, a little high-pitched and certainly thinner than the rounded, resonant sound of Monty Coulsham's deep American voice.

'Supposing God is life,' he went on, his eyes moving to and fro over his audience as if he were watching a slow tennis rally, 'then your great poet celebrates divinity in his very singing, does he not? He is a seer as well as a celebrant. He is "a living soul" who sees into "the life of things." Most of all he encompasses that sense of the eternal forever immanent in our temporal life, a sense of divine impulse springing from the symbiosis of man and nature. In that he claims to discern "the still, sad music of humanity." We here, on the banks of the river Wye just above Tintern...'

'Why, Montgomery!' interrupted his mother. She had been seated during his oration, but now rose commandingly to her feet and addressed the audience. 'My son Montgomery will not mind me saying, ladies and gentlemen, that he is the very best symbiotical poet in the entire world. Excuse me, Montgomery, for interrupting.'

She resumed her seat.

'Thank you, mother. That sure clarifies things. Now I know my friend Miss Julie Mayhew-Summers is ready to deliver your great English poet's grandest lines. Julie, please. They express, if I may put it this way, the still, sad music of humanity as the river Wye flows ever onwards and is ever present to us, as it is right now, and enters our lives like "a motion and spirit that impels all thinking things." Julie.'

'"For I have learned,"' said Julie the Unruly at her most articulate,

> *'"To look on nature, not as in the hour*
> *Of thoughtless youth; but hearing oftentimes*
> *The still, sad music of humanity,*
> *Nor harsh, nor grating, though of ample power*
> *To chasten and subdue. And I have felt*
> *A presence that disturbs me with the joy*
> *Of elevated thoughts; a sense sublime*
> *Of something far more deeply interfused,*
> *Whose dwelling is the light of setting suns,*
> *And the round ocean and the living air,*
> *And the blue sky, and in the mind of man:*
> *A motion and a spirit that impels*
> *All thinking things, all objects of all thought,*
> *And rolls through all things."'*

The prince did not hear the appreciative applause that greeted the end of this reading. He felt suddenly assailed by an inexplicable, cold *frisson*. Someone, he felt, had just walked on his grave. The nape of his neck felt cold as if a drop of cold rainwater had fallen from the high ceiling. He automatically raised a hand to feel for it but there was nothing there.

'Oh, look, father's going to say something!' Lady Helen whispered. 'Oh, what a pity! It'll be over in a minute!'

There was something in her whispering that made the prince shiver all the more. Giles stood motionless before the lectern. The general mood in the hall had no doubt achieved a form of symbiosis in the sense that it had grown perceptibly more solemn and emotional. The steady hiss of rain persisted, though the row of candles by the lectern suddenly appeared to be struck by a gust of air. The flames all bent sideways and then recovered. Giles's sonorous, well-modulated voice filled the immediate gap of expectation to be sensed throughout the hall but it had a slight unsureness and the audience listened very attentively.

'I have come to a cross-roads in my life.'

They were the opening words. Perhaps of all those in the audience the prince was the only one who fully understood their meaning. The ensuing references to a change of circumstances and the need to make personal choices were later held against the speaker himself as evidence of Giles's complicity in what happened. Later the prince was perhaps the only one to know the truth. He could never deny the speaker's sincerity, yet he could never have anticipated the immediate reaction to the confession that followed.

'For me personally,' were the speaker's concluding words delivered solemnly but shakily, his eyes blinking in the candlelight, 'the coming of a new age must involve a literal change of heart and way of life. I intend to follow the example of Count Leo Tolstoy. I have tried for several years to spread abroad his ideas, as this and other soirees can testify. Now the time has come to follow his ideas more strictly. My friends, it is my intention to give up this way of life, to leave Stadleigh Court...'

A cry came from Lady Isobel.

'...yes, to leave Stadleigh Court, to retreat to the commune in Irmingham on the other side of the "sylvan Wye" and to lead there a strictly Tolstoyan way of life, to follow a vegetarian regime, make my own clothes and shoes, live frugally enjoying the fruits of the earth and my dear daughter's company, being a more decent human being. That, then, is the personal message I wish to leave with you tonight. God bless you all, God bless...'

'Giles! Giles! You mustn't!'

Lady Isobel screamed out these words. She had stood up. In startled amazement everyone saw how she was apparently being restrained or comforted by the bespectacled figure of Carew Kingston, who had an arm round her shoulders. He seemed to be trying to persuade her to sit down.

'No, Giles, no!' she screamed. 'You said you wouldn't! You promised me!' She burst into loud sobs.

At that very moment Lady Helen jumped up and rushed to her father. Flinging her arms round him, she kissed him vigorously on both cheeks and remained clutching him for longer than strictly necessary. Long enough, at least, for the prince to acknowledge to himself that this was an emotional climax to her own private yearnings and evidently a victory over her stepmother.

Both Giles Irmingham and Lady Helen quickly left the Gothic hall. A hysterical Lady Isobel was also led away. There was no one left to say goodbye. In a subdued mood filled with a sense of letdown very like the prince's, guests began urgently seeking out coats, capes and umbrellas offered by footmen. They were lined up by the open front door through which could be seen glistening carriage lamps and rain falling steeply in a dusky forecourt.

14

The rain was loud. The prince opened the bedroom window and in came the solid, leaden, echoing sound of rain falling vertically on sodden grass and foliage. The whole darkness seemed saturated by it. The noise gave him the momentary shivers. Like an invisible, disapproving audience, it hissed at him. He felt he had behaved shamefully in some way. Perhaps the outer darkness held him responsible for the failure of the soiree or reproved him for not believing Anna Karenina, not taking her seriously, not properly accepting her claim to be threatened by "enemies". He closed the window abruptly.

The atmosphere had certainly been subdued immediately after the soiree. Even Cotton had been affected. He had served supper in the bedroom in almost total silence, only broken by some dour and uncharacteristic predictions about the likely state of the trains the next day. It had been agreed, in any case, that they would catch the train due shortly before midday if possible. On that note Cotton had left.

The prince retired to bed once he had closed the window. The bedside candle extinguished, he could only extinguish the guilty feelings associated with the persistent, if muffled, sound of the downpour by thinking about London, Portland Place and news of his wife, Princess Alisa. Stadleigh Court, though, could not be blotted out. When sleep came it was fitful, filled with annoying, easily forgotten dreams. By first light he was fully awake.

This time he opened the window to hear nothing but the sound of a modest dawn chorus. Although he would miss such a delightful country sound once he was back in London, he was reminded by a slight headache that he had slept badly and felt a sudden renewal of the *frisson* experienced at the end of the soiree. Why he should have been reminded of this puzzled him. To steady himself and clear his mind, he felt he needed fresh air, although the view through the open window showed scarcely more than very faint sunlight gifting the early-morning mist with a sheen of gold and in the process illuminating in the immediate foreground only the gravel walk of the terrace and the stone balustrade.

The air was indeed fresh, though. It contained what felt like an invitation to warmth in anticipation of a hot, sunny day. 'Ideal for a stroll' was the thought uppermost in his mind as he studied the scene briefly. So he washed in cold water, unshaven though he was, dressed himself carefully in the newly laundered linen whites, picked up his Panama hat and cautiously opened the bedroom door. The house had about it the sort of quiet that descends on places once the party is over. It can give the first person to arise a rather grand feeling of being alone in the universe. Acknowledging the grandeur of such solitariness, he placed one foot, then the next, on the wide staircase, unable to prevent each downward pressure from erupting into a series of rippling creaks, and slowly, surreptitiously, one step at a time, descended to the hallway. His worst fear was that he would attract the attention of some inquisitive servant in the hallway or be visible to someone working in the large Gothic hall. He did not meet anyone. What is more he found the front door, though locked and bolted from the inside, could easily be opened without making too much noise. In a moment he found himself outside.

The sun had already begun to break through the mist. Glistening and chill, the morning showed evidence everywhere of heavy rain. Large pools had formed on the forecourt. The roses in the rose garden had a pathetically weighted look. Heavy raindrops still fell from the trees. He strolled the way he had gone with Lady Isobel, through the wrought-iron gates into the rose garden and then along the broad gravel walk between the balustrade and the side of the house. He had only a weird, almost underwater view of the lower terraces of the garden in which long shadows stretched like fronds from the yew hedges, while visible through the mist as through a film was a brightly sunlit silhouette of distant hills on the far side of the Wye. Parts of Stadleigh Court, the roof, the battlements and towers, were beginning to glow a mild shade of gold where they were picked out by the first rays of the sunrise.

He looked up. There was his open window catching the first gleams. His eyes followed an easterly direction towards the elevation adjacent to the huge tower where another window was open. This he recognised as the window to Anna Karenina's bathroom which she had herself opened when she showed him her 'secret place'. He recalled particularly that this had been the first time she mentioned her "enemies". It made him aware suddenly of the little echoes caused by his footsteps in the gravel. He instantly chose to make less noise by going along the soft damp grass at the edge of the walk. Here the pressure of his shoes only gave rise to a slight squelching.

He then caught sight of it. Lying directly ahead of him

and directly below the open window, it looked at first glance like a dead bird, a large raven perhaps. Of course, it couldn't be that. The earlier *frisson* returned. A rat of terror ran along the crown of his head and down his spine. He knew it couldn't be a bird. It was much bulkier. It was human, humanly proportioned, humanly curled.

He had the very odd feeling that a trick was being played on him. Assuming it might be one of the guests behaving in a deliberately eccentric way, he expected the shape any moment to uncoil and spring up like a jack-in-a-box. He cannot say why he felt this. He paused, then took one further step. He looked. Bent over, leaning as far forward as he could, he peered.

Up to midway along the crown of the head there was no hair, only a livid red indentation like a huge birthmark over a depression in the frontal part of the cranium. Grey hair grew wispily at the back of the head and along the sides. The face itself was turned away from him. He could only tell that the eyes were open, as was the mouth. The body was clothed in a black silk kimono with a bamboo motif that had fallen open to reveal the shapeliness of the white bosom. Otherwise the garment clung in a sodden embrace to the body's contours and left only the hands and the feet shining nakedly white against the grass.

***

Guilt returned. Cravenly. He did not want to touch her, be near her, be involved. His first reaction was to look sharply to left and right to see whether anyone had seen him. No one was about.

All he saw was the empty sunlit gravel walk, motionless cedars, shadows extending sharply from the balustrade. The facade of the Court was now impassive as the light fell full upon it and made windowpanes sparkle like silver.

Should he just slip away? Go? Pretend he'd not been there?

Of course he couldn't deny it! He stepped back quickly on to the gravel. Perhaps she's not dead, was his first thought, although he knew in his heart she was as dead as the many dead he had seen in the Turkish campaign. He did not even ask himself how, let alone why. He simply stooped, grabbed a handful of gravel and began throwing small stones one by one at the window of the doctor's room.

It took a while for them to have an effect. Then the window creaked open and a head of tousled fair hair emerged. Dr James Parkinson blinked down at the prince with the sun in his eyes and said nothing. A certain amount of waving and pointing led him to stretch out to see what was meant, but as soon as he did so he appeared galvanised and vanished from the window. Some couple of minutes later he came running with big strides along the broad walk dressed in heavy boots and a long tartan dressing gown.

He squatted down beside the curled shape the instant he arrived. Unwilling to admit to himself what he assumed must be the truth, the prince began explaining in a very quiet voice that he had found her just as she lay and hadn't touched anything.

The doctor nodded. Then he looked up at the open window. To all intents and purposes they both had the same thought. Had she fallen or did she throw herself? Neither seemed to make a great deal of sense because the drop from the first floor window to the ground could have caused serious injury but would not have been an inevitable cause of death. Watching the doctor bend down more closely, the prince could not help wondering if he had any reason to suspect she was so ill she would want to kill herself. For as long as a minute he watched the corpse being studied and the kimono slightly adjusted to aid inspection. The morning was silent all round except for birdsong.

The doctor said softly: 'Her son died last night. You probably didn't know that.'

'*Bozhe moi, ia ne snal!* My God!' The prince crossed himself. 'It could be, you know...'

'What?'

'Too much for her. When she heard, as I suppose she did.'

'It was all too much for him, for her son.' James Parkinson paused and shrugged. 'I did my best, you know.'

'Of course, you did your best.'

'The spasms had come back and he was so weakened.'

There was silence between them at that point. The prince found nothing to say. Could she have killed herself on hearing of her son's death? It was a question that had to be asked. On the other hand, whatever the cause, they were both standing beside someone who had died and it was only right that they should respect that fact. The prince clasped his hands and closed his eyes. He prayed quietly for the soul of Anna Arkadyevna Karenina. When he had finished, he crossed himself again. He saw the young doctor still staring down at the body and murmuring something.

'What is it?'

'The trouble is...' James Parkinson began. 'The trouble is, you see, there's some *rigor mortis*. She must've been out here for some hours... It's just that...' Then came another shrug of the shoulders.

'What?'

'I think old Boris said... Maybe I got it wrong.'

'What?'

'He said he wasn't going to tell her. Only I may be wrong. I can't always get his meaning...'

The prince acknowledged the problem with a slight grunt. 'So it's only *if* she knew, we can suppose...'

There seemed no point in pursuing it. Now was hardly the time for discussing motives. Instead, whispering very softly, James Parkinson said: 'Look at the way she's lying... Curled.'

There was no difficulty in following the direction of the doctor's eyes as he surveyed the corpse under the black kimono and then looked up. There was a pause as they both looked up at the window.

'Would a body fall and lie like that?'

'I don't know.'

'One thing is sure – that damage to the cranium is old. As for the marks...'

'What marks?'

'Look!' he pointed.

The prince leant down and looked. He could hardly fail to notice a faintly bluish tinge to the skin round the nostrils and mouth, but on the neck, when the doctor held back the garment for him to see, were purple marks. Also round the neck were two door keys attached to a cord. He averted his eyes before turning and looking more closely. His cowardice sickened him. The trouble was that her face had the same candid charm, the open eyes the same soft, triumphant look as in the portrait outside her sitting-room, except now they stared upwards unseeing in the sun's brightness.

'I don't think that's all, you know.'

'What?'

'I think she may have been... she may have been held down.'

'Held down?'

'No.' James Parkinson shook his head and went on shaking it for several seconds. 'No, no, I don't like this.'

'You don't like what?'

'I don't like what I'm seeing, sir. I think it's a matter for the police.'

From across the river, like a pin struck through the quiet birdsong of the morning, came the faint, shrill note of a locomotive whistle. The prince took off his Panama hat and ran the back of his hand across his forehead. He realised he was sweating.

'We must let Giles – Lord Irmingham – know first. There are matters...'

His own involvement and responsibilities suddenly stared him in the face. If there were foul play and Anna Karenina had been murdered, everyone could be suspected, all the secrecy would unravel and reputations, his included, could be damaged irreparably. He knew he was innocent, but he also knew he had enemies and they could blacken him as they had blackened her. Most of all, he knew he owed her something more than prayers. He realised he owed her the truth now she was dead more even than when she was alive, because he suspected no one in England was better qualified to find it than he was.

'Look,' he said, 'I'll go and find Giles. You stay here. Those keys round her neck, let me have them, will you.'

The doctor eyed him doubtfully. 'They might be evidence.'

'They won't be if they're not round her neck.'

'Then I'll have to say I gave them to you.'

He had apparently already come to the firm conclusion that Anna Karenina's death was suspicious and that, as at any scene of a crime, everything should be left undisturbed. The prince had no such qualms. His agenda was different. He repeated the request for the keys and the doctor reluctantly agreed.

'Thank you. Now, please, trust me. I will get Giles at once.'

***

The bedroom was eventually found after the prince persuaded a young maidservant to show him the way. It meant being led up the wide staircase, down the corridor past his own bedroom and then to somewhere beyond Giles Irmingham's study. The girl was garrulous. She assured him in a whisper and with a disapproving shake of the head that ''is lordship don't share with 'er ladyship, sir, you know.'

Once the bedroom was reached, an elderly valet in a loose fitting gown tied at the waist admitted him into a kind of dressing room. There was reluctance at first to wake his lordship. The prince assured him it was really urgent and found his words rewarded by the sound of Giles's authoritative voice asking what the noise was all about. Despite the valet's continuing protests, the prince entered the bedroom to find Giles already sitting on the edge of a four-poster bed thrusting his feet into slippers. He naturally looked shocked.

'What the blazes! I heard voices... Oh, Prince Dmitry, what on earth...'

The prince overlooked all niceties by telling him at once what had happened in the most confidential of whispers.

'No! You can't mean it!'

'I do.'

'She's dead, you say, possibly murdered?'

'Possibly.'

'Possibly murdered.' Giles shook his head. A moment later he summoned the valet to bring his dressing gown and said he would go outside and see for himself. But on his own, he added.

'Thank you, my dear Dmitry. But tell no one, no one at all! I absolutely insist on that!'

Politely but firmly he ordered the prince not to accompany him, pocketed keys from a bedside table and padded off down the corridor in his slippers.

Obediently the prince stayed behind. He had obviously been expected to return to his bedroom, but the absence of Giles Irmingham and the doctor gave him the chance to make use of the keys from around Anna Karenina's neck. He wanted to assure himself that she couldn't have been hearing threatening voices in her 'secret place'; and *if* she had been murdered in her bathroom, he had to see how it could have happened... and who, who... His thinking stopped there. It was essential to find out as soon as possible.

He followed Giles out of the bedroom, saw him disappear down the corridor and then had no idea which way to go. A few steps to his left was another short corridor. He went down it and found myself facing a door that looked like the door into the tower. Neither key fitted the lock and he wondered for a moment whether Anna Karenina had kept them round her neck for some other purpose. Then, to his astonishment, the door sprang open of its own accord, leaving him confronted by the bare boards of the organ gallery. An alternative way of reaching the organ, he realised, rather than the enclosed staircase from the Gothic hall. Sounds of people moving about and talking to each other rose clearly from below. The trestle tables were being dismantled.

He shut the door at once and walked quickly away. The carpet underfoot meant that he passed several doors without making a sound. The house was beginning to wake up. He knew he had little time to discover what he could before rumours began to spread. Luckily, after a turn in the corridor, he recognised the door to Giles's study, a stained-glass window, and stale cooking smells. Adjoining the corridor was the door to the tower.

He tried the larger of the keys and found himself exactly where the doctor had first led him. Flights of curved stairs led upwards and downwards, but he felt fairly sure he was on the landing where he would find Anna Karenina's bedroom and bathroom.

Morning sunlight had still not penetrated to the landing

in any strength, nor were there any sounds from the kitchen or from upstairs. He tiptoed towards the bedroom. The door was ajar, which surprised him. It also surprised him that the bed looked as if it had not been slept in. Had Boris or someone remade it or had his mistress been killed or killed herself before going to bed? She had been in a kimono, after all. Putting aside such thoughts, he found himself immersed in the clammy, unaired smell of perfume and sleep familiar from his first visit, the same mirrors repeating his presence in their silvered depths as he passed through the bedroom towards the bathroom.

It shocked him to find the bath still half-full of water. Somewhat sinisterly, looking depleted and unreal, Anna Karenina's long black garments were hanging on the bathroom door and other garments were draped over a wooden chair, underneath which, side by side, were two elaborately embroidered Chinese slippers. A considerable spillage of water had occurred just next to the bath, but near the wide-open window now filling the room with light, there were only a few drops. A large bath towel, still folded and apparently dry, was hanging on a rail fixed to the wood paneling. A gutted candle stood in a holder on a small table.

He instantly tried to interpret what he saw. Had she got out of the bath dripping wet, put on her kimono and then flung herself to her death through the open window? It could explain the mess by the bath but not the absence of wet by the window. The wood paneling beside the bath had splashes on it. There were also drips on the floor near the door and even the sign of a shoe print. It was much larger than any print from one of the Chinese slippers, but one print from the sole of a shoe could mean anything. It could have been Boris's footprint, for instance. He supposed she had heard about Seriozha and perhaps run a bath to console herself. But why had she put on a kimono before rushing to the window? It would have been raining hard and a kimono would have been no protection. Yet there she was she now lying curled on the grass below the window in a self-protective, foetal position. She had the past reputation of being someone who had tried to commit suicide, so suicide would be understandable. But what if the marks round her neck actually meant what James Parkinson had said – something about being *held down*?

Instinct told him that, despite its brightly lit sparkle, the bathroom had an atmosphere of fear. This had been her 'secret place', a bathroom specially made for her, the solace of her reclusive life. It had been violated, as her privacy and her life had been violated. Surely, though, she hadn't been threatened! Here, in this private place! She couldn't have heard threats…

The speculation ended when there was a movement behind him. Swinging round, he saw Boris approaching. He quickly re-entered the bedroom and shut the bathroom door.

'Ah, your excellency, pardon me, pardon me. I thought the mistress…'

'You thought what about the mistress, Boris?'

'I could see she was not in her bed, your excellency.'

'Her bed looks as if it hadn't been slept in.'

'She sleeps very quietly, so it is often…' The look on the old retainer's wrinkled face as he spoke was of such distilled innocence, purity and lack of guile that the prince felt he dare not break any sad news to him. 'So I supposed she would be having a bath. I thought you might be the young Master Gerald, your excellency. He is often, well... often here. In the mornings.'

Boris blinked impassively after imparting this piece of information, his arms at his sides as if pinned there by the very weight of the ancient black cloth of the frockcoat. Suddenly, to the prince's amazement, the old man's eyes filled with tears and two large teardrops rolled slowly down his cheeks.

'The young master, your excellency, Sergei Alexeevich, did you know?'

The prince nodded solemnly.

'I felt it was my duty to...'

'To what?'

'To tell the mistress, your excellency. I could not bring myself to tell her last night. Particularly as she was... well, I hardly need explain.'

Hardly need explain!

Two things were now reasonably clear. The first was that, unless she had heard the news from somebody else, Anna Karenina very probably did not know about her son's death before she died. The second was that Gerald Kempson had obviously been here the previous night.

'Boris, my friend, you saw the young master called Gerald, did you?'

An air of considerable self-importance was assumed. He gave the appearance of being asked for money or forced to donate blood in some unknown cause.

'Your excellency, I am not at liberty...'

'Forget the etiquette, forget the protocol, Boris, for heaven's sake!'

'Your excellency...'

'Was Gerald Kempson up here last night?'

The old man was shaking slightly. In a slow, dignified gesture he wiped away the two teardrops.

'Yes, excellency, I saw him.'

'Thank you. Where did you see him?'

'I was in the little kitchen. I saw him cross the landing...'

'Yes, yes.'

'...and go into the mistress's bedroom... come in here.' He gazed at the prince reproachfully as if all references to such behavior were improper. 'The mistress, your excellency, always locked the door to her bedroom. She and... and Master Gerald, they were the only ones to have keys to her bedroom. She had come in here, to her bedroom, as soon as the music started last night.'

'The organ music? During the soiree? That was the last time you saw her?'

'Yes, sir, the last time. As I say, sir, I only saw Master Gerald go into the mistress's bedroom... come in here, where we are now. When the soiree was over. Then I went upstairs to join my wife in a vigil beside the poor young master... Where is the mistress now, your excellency? Is she?' He nodded towards the bathroom. 'Her door, you see, was not locked.'

The prince did not have the heart to pretend any more. He stepped aside and let the old man peer through the bathroom door. By now his wife was calling him from the landing.

Boris shook his head in bewilderment. He followed the prince out of the bedroom, muttering, 'Where? Where?' only for his wife's commands to become more insistent. They found her and Hannah Kempson on the landing, the latter leaning on a banister rail looking down at the curved well of the staircase towards deep shadow at the foot of the tower. She faced round to the prince.

'Someone did it, you know!'

The statement was dramatic and completely unexpected.

'Your husband Gerald...' he began saying, uncertain as to whether he should make the remark a question or an accusation.

She was shaking her head even as he spoke. Boris's wife had begun a loud, grieving wail that was quickly smothered by the gruff, elderly, quavering voice of Boris himself. Though the prince thought they must have an inkling of what had happened, he was absorbed by Hannah Kempson who looked him straight in the eyes, seized him by the lapels of his jacket and whispered intently in Russian: *'You've seen her, haven't you?'*

There was no denying it.

'We loved her, you know!' Her whispering was urgent and hysterical. *'Boris loved her!'*

'But where is she?' Boris interrupted.

Hannah took no notice. *'No one could love her as I did! I loved her like a mother! I loved her because she saved my life! So I saved hers! I brought her here! I made sure she was happy here! Whatever she wanted, she should have! And when her son came, oh, she was so happy, so happy!'*

'Your husband Gerald...'

The words were repeated in an effort to discover what she meant but she was too hysterical to hear them.

'First her son, now her! Oh, my God! And if you think

poor Gerald had anything, anything to do... No! No! He would never, never!'

She broke into sobs and covered her face with her hands.

At that instant there were sounds of movement at the bottom of the curved stairs and Giles Irmingham and Dr James Parkinson came slowly upwards carrying the kimono-draped body. Bare legs and feet protruded from under Giles's armpits. The prince could not help noticing that something had happened to the pictures lining the curved wall above the dado, but all his attention was concentrated at that moment on the body being carried slowly upwards. In a matter of a few seconds, without a word spoken, Anna Karenina had been returned to the bedroom where she had not spent the night but where she was more likely to have met her death. Instantly Hannah Kempson shrieked and dashed into the bedroom behind Giles and the doctor.

Left alone, the prince felt weak at the knees. He felt not only shock but also a wave of nausea and fought hard to suppress it. Leaning on the banister to steady himself, he continued staring down at the curved staircase, aware now that the door to the garden was still open. It was the door at the foot of the tower through which Giles had brought him before taking him to his study and first telling him about Anna Karenina. Why, he kept on wondering, why had the pictures on the curved walls all been knocked sideways? Why were they like that? The body being carried up did not cause that.

He was about to take a closer look when he felt a hand on his shoulder. It was Giles, speaking in a breathy whisper: 'Dmitry, my dear chap, I must have a word.'

15

Atalanta in pursuit of the Arcadian Lion was a vivid, energetic canvas by Sir Peter Paul Rubens. Filled though it was from corner to corner with up-rearing, bright-ochre horses, snarling white hounds, muscular tree trunks and equally muscular naked men, pinkly glowing as from recent hot baths, no part of it was more exotically or erotically attractive than Atalanta herself who, bare-bosomed, appeared about to unleash with gusto a gold-tipped arrow towards a large lion. Several other maidenly persons were also revealing their pink round bosoms and the lion, to its credit, seemed to be baring its teeth more in petulant disapproval of such outrageous nudity than with any predatory malice.

'Here,' said Giles, 'we can talk in here.' He closed the door of the Rubens Room behind them. 'It is, my dear Dmitry, essential *not to involve the police*!' The words were literally hissed. 'Essential! You found her, didn't you?'

'Yes.'

'Did anyone see you or did you see anyone?'

'No.'

'You're sure?'

He assured him that there had been no one about and the only other person involved had been Dr James Parkinson.

'So there's a good chance we can keep it all quiet. I must ask you not to breathe a word about it to anyone. Will you do that?'

He sank into one of the high-backed upright chairs round a small baize-covered table in the centre of the room. He was still wearing his dressing gown and had chosen this paneled room as the safest place for their talk. He looked pale and his hands were shaking. It had obviously been an arduous and taxing experience to carry the corpse from the foot of the tower to the bedroom by way of the curved staircase. Seeing him in such a state, the prince was only too ready to respect his wishes.

'You are asking a lot...'

'I know I am. My dear Dmitry, I am asking as one gentleman to another, as an English gentleman, you understand.'

'As one gentleman to another, as an English gentleman...' The idea made the prince suddenly restless. He did not join the other in sitting down. He paced slowly about the room.

'I have had to make a hurried decision. Literally on the spur of the moment.' Giles's voice was as shaky as his hands. 'I think we must insist... must insist she died in her bed.'

'The marks on her throat, the discoloration... You overlook them?'

'Young James, Dr Parkinson, he'll, you know, he'll not emphasise them, he'll... he'll agree, I think. It *is* the only way. I'm sure of it.' The unsteady hands fluttered in support of his words. 'I mean, she was a bag of nerves. The fact of her son dying – the body's still up there, that's another thing to deal with, and young James isn't too proud of himself over that – it caused such a shock she, er, had a heart attack. Something like that. But not suicide, no. If it were suicide, there'd have to be the authorities involved, an inquest, God knows what. And in any case...'

'It would invalidate her right as beneficiary of her husband's will?'

'Something of the sort.' Giles was now a picture of gloom. 'So it all depends, you see, on you, my dear Dmitry.'

'On me?'

'On you saying you didn't see her.'

The prince felt deeply irritated by this remark. Staring angrily for a moment or so at the Rubens, he empathised with the imperilled lion. On the one hand, he would be forced to compromise, supposedly as someone English and gentlemanly. On the other, he would be dishonoring the name of the lady he had been brought here to identify. There was also the tacit implication, which he greatly resented, that, being Russian, he might be less than fastidious about the truth.

'Of course,' said Giles, 'I would have to ask how you came to be in the tower. Could it be you had used the keys which were round her neck?'

This had not been anticipated. He had not imagined that Giles Irmingham could be quite so unscrupulous. The question posed a threat. The prince countered it by assuming the profoundly injured air of one who was proud to be considered more English than the English.

'You'd hold that against me, would you? Not English really and hardly gentlemanly!'

'Needs must, my dear Dmitry, if necessary.'

'The doctor told you, I suppose?'

'Young James did, yes. He was mistaken over the lockjaw. His patient died. If he hadn't, well, who knows, we might not be in this predicament.'

'I see.'

Giles held out his hand. 'Let me have them back and no more will be said.'

After a moment's debate with himself the prince took the keys out of his pocket, the cord still attached to them, and dropped them with a slight metallic clink on the baize tabletop.

'Tell me,' he asked, 'have you seen the bathroom?'

Giles shook his head as he stretched out and took the keys, but the prince went on: 'It tells another story. What it doesn't explain is why we should have found her lying out there in a black kimono at the foot of the tower. If she died in her bed, how do we explain that? If she jumped after having had a bath, why was she in a black kimono? Why was there no sign of water on the floor by the window? Why? I have to ask these questions! Or did somebody "hold her down" as James Parkinson thinks? Judging by the marks on her neck, the discoloration of the skin... There are lots of unanswered questions. How do we explain such things?'

Giles looked away. 'Please,' he said, 'just don't! No questions, please. She died in her bed, that's all. It's unpleasant enough as it is without making things worse.'

The prince noted the way the blue eyes, still blinking rapidly, refused to meet his. Of course the need for self-delusion, the comforting lie, was essential. Equally pressing was the need for truth. The prince guessed that one name and one name only rose to the surface of both their minds at that moment. He leaned forward, placing both hands on the baize-covered table, and said in a quiet voice: 'I know it must be your duty as a father to protect your son. But I will have to ask him what he knows.'

Giles seemed to bat the thought away with a flicker of his eyelids. He paused, looked up at the picture, seemed almost indifferent to what had been said and a faint smile stole over his face.

'All my life, ever since I was a small boy, I have been fascinated by the Arcadian Lion.' he said tiredly. 'He is morally in the right, you know. My belief is that Atalanta won't shoot that arrow. Or if she does she'll miss. How could anyone kill such an obviously moral creature as that lion? I suspect he has the soul of a high church prelate before his time.'

'Or a Tolstoyan,' said the prince.

'Or a good Tolstoyan.' Giles's smile becoming a little strained. 'Except that, like a good Tolstoyan, I can mourn his likely death. I mourn *her* death and her son's, too, of course I do. As for my son Gerald, speak to him if you like. Poor boy, he does his best, you know. Whatever he says, though, you must be sure of one thing: *she died in her bed.*' He fluttered his hands again. 'And he had nothing to do with *that.*' His eyes were lowered in disgust, 'Nothing at all! All we need to know is that a Russian lady died naturally in her bed. *She died in her bed!*'

How he could be so blind to the truth, the prince did not know. Irritated by the denial and the apparent double standards, he sighed and strode out of the room.

***

Et in Arcadia ego...'

He muttered these words as he went out through the front

door on to the forecourt and into a warm summer morning of glistening, still wet, surfaces and brilliant blue cloudless sky. Again no one was about. His only companion was the voice of his conscience. Leave well alone, it urged. Let Anna Karenina die a natural death in her bed. Let it be as Giles wished it to be. Yes, let well alone... On the other hand, his conscience also urged him to seek the truth. What had caused the marks on her neck, the discoloration? If she had been murdered, who was the murderer? And if Giles refused to entertain any alternative, either because he refused to believe his son was responsible, or because he already knew something from Hannah that entirely justified his son's role, then the prince felt he had a duty to find out what that alternative might be.

Inspired by this inner debate, his pace quickened. All other considerations apart, he was glad to get right away from Stadleigh Court, more than ever aware of the need to find answers. A servant had directed him to the stables as the most likely place to find Gerald Kempson. He had to be questioned, the prince felt, if only to satisfy himself that Lord Irmingham's son and heir was very unlikely to have killed Anna Karenina.

The pleasant morning air was refreshing and invigorating as he went up the long straight driveway towards the stables. Tall trees on either side laid regular bars of shadow across the pebbled surface. The sunlight coming through the leaves was already warm enough to make him feel hot as he passed rapidly from light to shade, so much so that he pushed his Panama hat towards the back of his head in a jaunty fashion and wiped his forehead with a handkerchief. His arm still raised in the act of wiping, he saw a figure emerge from the entrance to the stables adjoining the main gates.

'Papa, I *want* to! You said I could!'

He recognised the bare legs of Master Charles. The boy had his back to him and appeared to be arguing. Holding a fishing rod with a small fisherman's wicker basket slung over one shoulder, he was shouting. The response, presumably from his father, was inaudible.

'You said I could! And it's always best when the sun's just up! Mr Cotton said so!'

The mixture of injustice and reasoned pleading gave the boy's voice a shrill edge. He then turned abruptly, blinded by the sun as he faced into it, and began running. Practically immediately he bumped into the prince.

'Oh, sorry, sir!'

His straw hat fell off. Rather shamefacedly he stooped, picked it up, shook it and began to excuse himself by mentioning that Mr Cotton had arranged it.

'You'll be going fishing with him, I imagine,' the prince conceded, utterly unaware what arrangement was, adding that he had come to see his father.

The boy clapped his straw hat back on his head and gazed up with deep blue eyes that showed a great deal more awe for the prince than for his father.

'Mr Cotton says you're really a prince. Are you really a prince, sir?'

'I am.'

'Really?'

'Really.'

'Charles!' Gerald Kempson shouted exasperatedly as he came out into the driveway. 'Come back here!'

The boy showed no sign of obeying. 'I'm going to see Mr Cotton now, sir!' he cried out, as if the presence of a real prince acted in his favour, and dashed off up the avenue, leaving his father flushed with annoyance.

'I give up! I can't control him! I'm sorry, Prince Dmitry, you've had to…'

The prince looked the speaker straight in the face and smiled understandingly. Judging by his jodhpurs and riding coat, Gerald Kempson appeared to be preparing to go riding, but it took only a moment to read the strain in his face and to note the way he used his right hand to feel the small of his back. The prince guessed something at once.

'A strained back?' he inquired pleasantly. 'You're not riding this morning?'

'No, no... I, er... How did you know?'

'I knew you probably had a strained back.'

'You did? Why?'

'What puzzled me was your motive.'

'I don't quite understand…'

'Your motive for doing what you did.'

The answering look was defensive, even a little defiant, except that it was clear enough to the prince, as it must have dawned on Gerald Kempson himself, that he would never prove a master of deception. He tried to divert attention by smiling as ingratiatingly as possible to his inquisitor.

'My dear prince, my motive for what?'

'For killing.'

'Killing?'

'If the police – the local police, I hasten to say – were to ask where you were last night, you would have to answer, wouldn't you? Knowing, if I may put it this way, what I know now.'

A guilty pink rose slowly up the handsome face as he tried to rebut the challenge.

'Knowing what?'

It was a blunt enough question that the prince rebutted in turn by simply saying: 'You were seen entering her bedroom.'

'Oh, this is ridiculous! How can you accuse me? I mean this is unspeakable, I mean I'd never have dreamt...'

'You were seen entering her bedroom.'

'No, you don't understand!'

'So presumably you were the last person to see her alive. In a court of law, given the circumstances, you'd have difficulty proving your innocence. As I say, the puzzling thing is the motive.'

'The motive?'

'The motive. You had the opportunity, of course. The motive makes no sense.'

'A bit beyond me, that. Are you accusing me of... of... No, I'm not going to say a word! Not a word!'

'I have spoken to old Boris,' the prince said quietly, 'and I believe what he says. He would not give false testimony.'

All the pinkness vanished. Gerald Kempson had gone pale. He swung on his heel and tried walking away across the cobblestones of the stable yard. Half-a-dozen horses watched from the open upper halves of their stable doors and a couple of boys were busy with besoms brushing away surplus rainwater. He had unmistakable difficulty in walking though he tried to conceal the pain in his back. The prince walked beside him, speaking quietly: 'I have been wondering. Why,

I wonder, should you have wanted to kill her? Boris told me, you see, that only you and she had keys to her bedroom. You could easily let yourself into the tower with one key and then enter her bedroom with the other. So you had the opportunity. Last night, after the soiree, that is, you went to see her, didn't you?'

'I am not saying another word!'

'You went to see her, but I don't imagine you found her in her bed. You very likely found her in the bathroom.'

They had come to a gateway into a garden. Gerald Kempsom leaned on the gate and gave the prince a look of deep dejection. Perhaps he knew he was cornered. He tried to turn away, had second thoughts, opened the gate and led him into a kind of rose bower. He flopped down on to a bench, his hand pressed to his spine.

'You've seen Hannah, have you?'

The prince nodded and sat down beside him.

Gerald Kempson looked down at the tips of his riding boots. 'Then she must've told you. I can't deny I was there, of course.'

There was no point in pressing him. Nor did the prince feel the need to admit he was guessing. He waited patiently during the pause that followed, a silence filled with the sound of a wheeled vehicle being prepared in the stable yard with a certain number of shouted commands. Hooves struck cobblestones, horses neighed.

'But I didn't do it!' He was suddenly defiant. The accusations had stung him. 'I would never, never have hurt her! Never!'

'Tell me.'

He seemed trapped and desperate. He sniffed and spoke directly to the ground.

'I was her lover. I am not going to deny it. In any case, I don't suppose it's a secret. We had a very close, loving relationship. You may think what you like, but it was what my wife wanted. She would do anything – anything, I mean it – to please Anna. Anna saved her, saved Hannah, you know. And then Hannah was able to do the same for her.'

The self-control and candour were impressive. There seemed no point in prompting him to say more. He drew in a deep, shuddering breath and continued.

'I fell under her influence. Just like Hannah. She had that kind of power. I never felt ashamed. You must believe me, it's like that... *was* like that... Can you understand what I'm saying?'

'Yes.'

'After the soiree I went to see her. She liked to hear about events at the Court and things like that. I would tell her in English. She understood most of what I said, I think, though I wouldn't always understand her. Mostly it didn't matter... Well, I let myself into her bedroom. You're right, I'm the only person who's got a key and she always locks herself in at night. Do you know the layout of the tower?'

'Yes.'

'My father had a special bathroom made for her. It used to be a separate room, but it was converted.' He licked his lips. 'Well, she didn't answer me when I called her name, but I thought I'd just glance in the bathroom. There was a light in there. I looked in. It was all steamy as if she'd just run a bath. And she was in it. She was lying there in the bath. The water was right over her face and she wasn't moving.'

The sound of a carriage rattling slowly over cobblestones and the clatter of hooves came from the stables. Gerald Kempson seemed to be roused by the noise.

'This is the truth, you've got to believe me!' He had raised his voice. 'I was shocked. I didn't know whether she was dead or not. I tried lifting her up. The water was still quite hot, but she slipped back again. I thought what the hell do I do, do I get the doctor, do I just leave and say nothing? What the hell do I do?' He clenched and unclenched his fists. 'I knew I'd probably been seen – Boris, you know, he'd probably seen me – and so I knew I'd be thought responsible. So I panicked! I couldn't help myself! I knew I had to make it seem... Oh, God, I knew I probably wouldn't be believed if I said I'd just found her like that!'

Suddenly, very quietly, he was crying. He had bent forward, his hands over his eyes, and all the prince could see was his shock of red hair and his heaving shoulders. 'I loved her, you see! How could I do something like that?'

Fully in the sun as he was, the prince began to feel hot. He took out a handkerchief and wiped his face.

'Shall I tell you what I think you did?' he asked after a short pause.

Gerald kept his hands over his eyes. His response was a slow, reluctant nod.

'You thought you must make it look like suicide, so you carried her down the curved staircase and then you...'

The hands were removed from the eyes. 'How do you know that?' he cried. 'Did Hannah tell you?'

'No. My guess is that it was more or less pitch dark. You carried her down the stairs and as you went down all the pictures on the walls were knocked sideways. First of all, though, you must have dressed her in that kimono.'

'Yes, yes, I did. I couldn't let her be found without any clothes. But I panicked. As I told Hannah, I simply didn't think! I carried her downstairs and didn't lock the bedroom door. It was raining cats and dogs. I took her outside and laid her down... That was when I did my back in... Oh, how silly, completely silly! I thought then how silly I'd been and I knew the best thing would have been... it would've been best if I'd just put her in her bed... but by then, you see, I couldn't lift her again... my back, you see... So I left her there...' He made gestures suggesting utter hopelessness and lack of sense. 'After that I came back here. This is where we live.' He pointed to a cottage at the end of the garden. 'It was raining, you see, and I was soaked to the skin.'

'So you didn't see the marks?'

'Marks?'

'Marks on her neck?'

'I didn't see any marks. It was pitch black! I couldn't see anything at all!'

'And then you came back here?'

He agreed, shaking his head as if trying to shake himself free of his own stupidity. He ran his tongue round his lips. 'It's the truth, you know. Believe it or not, it's the truth.' Then he recollected himself: 'I don't know why I'm telling you all this. What marks are you talking about?'

It was harder to answer that question than to believe his confession. The prince would be compromising himself, he realised, if he admitted seeing Anna Karenina lying where he'd found her. So he did what he knew Giles Irmingham expected him to do, like a good English gentleman.

'You don't need to worry,' he said softly. 'She died in her bed.'

The words did not sink in at once. Suddenly he found his wrist seized in a tight grip and tear-stained eyes turned fiercely on him.

'You don't believe me, do you?'

'Oh, I believe you.'

'Hannah wouldn't believe me at first. When I told her last night, I mean.' The prince's arm was shaken furiously. 'You must believe me, it's the truth!'

'I do believe you. The trouble is you mustn't.'

'I mustn't?'

'You've got to believe she died in her bed.'

'Don't talk in riddles! You're always talking in riddles! Oh, my back! Last night you said about Frou-Frou...'

The prince then explained as briefly as he could what had happened in the tower that morning and how it had been agreed that Anna Karenina had died in her bed. As he spoke the belligerence and fright gradually faded from the other's face.

'Father really told you that?'

'Yes.'

He wiped his eyes with the back of his hand. The relief was so great he stared ahead of him.

'You better know something. Father's never thought me strong enough – mentally, you know, in terms of my brain – to take over from him. I am a dunce, I know. I'm a weak person. I'm easily led. I mean, what I've just told you – I had to tell it to someone.' He blinked and looked away.

The prince cleared his throat. 'Believe me, I am not

going to tell anyone. Because there is no need for anyone to know. She died in her bed. A Russian lady died in her bed. She did not throw herself under a train and she did not commit suicide last night. She died in her bed.'

He stood up, raised his hat and walked away.

16

It rang true. Gerald Kempson could hardly have concocted it. He may have been a dunce and easily led, but he had enough foresight to know he could have explained none of it without admitting the most indiscreet secrets and making himself appear disreputable, scandalous, discredited and suspect. S o he panicked. He would divert suspicion. He would make it seem she had killed herself as she was once supposed to have killed herself. All of which his father already knew. So no one need know any different: a Russian lady had died naturally in her bed.

Vzdor! Vzdor! The prince knew this was nonsense. The marks on her neck and the discoloration were incontrovertible proof she had died *before* Gerald Kempson found her in the bath. She had been 'held down'.

The prince was so convinced of this as he walked back across the cobbled area of the stable yard that he knew he should act on it, but tiredness intervened. Maybe he should leave things as they were. He should return to London as he had planned. It seemed the most sensible thing to do. He could debate the issue of truth versus convenience as much as he liked, but he would probably in the end be none the wiser. So he gave up thinking about it and strolled back towards Stadleigh Court in the wake of two carriages that had just disappeared through the main gates.

By the time he reached the forecourt he found the carriages already drawn up outside the front door. One was being piled with luggage. Mrs Emerald Stephenson had seated herself in the other. She wore a wide-brimmed turquoise hat adorned with large yellow ribbons, a pleated frill over her ample bosom and a long-handled parasol that she was on the point of opening. Beside her was her son, Monty.

'Have you heard, prince?' she called out.

'Heard what, Mrs Stephenson?'

She beckoned for him to come close and from the shade of the now open parasol she imparted the confidential news that there had been a death. 'Did you know that, prince?'

He looked solemn. 'No. Who is it?'

'A lady.'

'A Russian lady,' added Monty in a slightly louder voice and smirked. 'Fare thee well!' he sang out to Julie the Unruly standing alone on the entrance steps at that moment and blew her a kiss.

'A Russian lady,' the prince echoed. He had to express amazement but was secretly alarmed. 'Who told you?'

'It's just...' Mrs Emerald Stephenson made a show of extreme confidentiality, moving her eyes to left and right and gesturing with her gloved free hand '...what I've been told. Did you know there was a Russian lady here at the Court?'

'No.'

The pretence of ignorance could not be sustained for long and it was a relief when she dismissed the matter.

'No, well, it's for Lord Irmingham to let you know, my dear prince, not for little old me to spread gossip.' She gave a pert smile. 'Montgomery and I are leaving, you see. It is all a mite urgent. But we are both of us more and more dedicated to your great Leo Tolstoy and his ideas, isn't that so, Montgomery?'

'Sure is! Fare thee well!' he sang out again. 'And if for ever, still for ever fare thee well!'

Julie called back something, waving a handkerchief, but her words were drowned in Mrs Emerald Stephenson's delighted exclamation: 'Oh, here's my companion, what you might call my *pro-tezh-jay*! He's such a... such a...'

Looking a great deal paler in the bright sunlight than he had done the previous evening, the kitchen boy with the beautiful voice came running through the front door. Mrs Emerald Stephenson patted the seat opposite her and he jumped breathlessly into the carriage. Giles Irmingham appeared in the doorway a moment later.

'Oh, I'm so grateful to you, Lord Irmingham! I predict a great, great future. Why, he's such a great *find*, isn't he?' She looked to the prince for confirmation. 'Don't you agree, my dear prince? I intend to promote him, let the entire world know what a remarkable voice he has! That's right, Arthur, just settle down, there's a good boy! Goodbye, Lord Irmingham! Goodbye, prince! Goodbye, Julie, my dear! You be in touch now! You be in touch!'

She gave a regal flutter of her gloved hand. Julie the Unruly waved back and then dabbed her eyes. Monty Coulsham brandished a large green handkerchief. Giles gave a hand wave and the prince doffed his Panama. All called out their goodbyes. The carriages ground their way across the forecourt and entered the driveway with the white parasol suddenly dappled by leaf-shadow and the raised handkerchief flowing out like a pennant.

'A most strong-minded woman,' Giles whispered. 'Most strong-minded. I had to tell her about the, er, unfortunate death. I thought it only polite.' Raising his voice, he mentioned he had had to fetch the kitchen boy. 'She would insist, you know. I had a job persuading the poor boy. His parents didn't object. It'll probably mean plenty of money. Will you be staying longer? Miss Mayhew-Summers is leaving very shortly, aren't you, my dear?'

Julie the Unruly wiped her eyes, blew her nose and managed a small smile. 'I shall be going with Mr Palmer, Lord Irmingham.'

She was dressed very smartly in a pink-striped mock waistcoat and high collar and simple draped skirt with a hat hanging on a ribbon down her back. The prince was tempted to compliment her but she tucked her handkerchief into her sleeve, looked at both men with red-rimmed eyes and announced sternly that she would be going to America.

'Freedom, Lord Irmingham, freedom, prince, what a joy that would be! The next century will be the American century, you know. I am just longing, longing to be off!'

She dashed away shaking back her hair, straight-backed and haughty, with a shimmer and sway of her long skirt. The effect was to produce spontaneous admiration of the elegant sway of her *derriere* and a degree of sexual interest that Giles no doubt shared.

'Yes, well...' he said.

The prince lowered his eyes and said he would probably be returning to London that afternoon.

'Yes, yes.'

The repetition of the words along with the averting of

rapidly blinking eyes left no doubt that Giles Irmingham did not want to discuss anything at that moment. They parted in the hallway and the prince went straight up to his bedroom.

Cotton had left a note in his copperplate hand containing an apology for his absence. He had promised to give a fishing lesson to Master Charles Kempson, although he gave an assurance he would be ready to leave by the midday train. Rather than annoyance, the prince felt quite happy to think of the two of them down by the river engaged in such a gentle pastime. They were probably quite unaware, he supposed, of Anna Karenina's death or all the other matters with which he had been concerned that morning. Deprived as he had been of breakfast, he felt even more deprived at that moment of sleep and admitted as much to himself by yawning, crossing himself and walking over to the bay window. There he sat down to have a rest.

The sun fell directly on the windowsill. It drew attention to the folded sheet of paper put there to dry, the testimony of Anna Karenina's "enemies". No longer sodden, the paper unfolded stiffly as he picked it up. The homemade ink of the Tolstoyan community might have been washed out in the immersion, but he need not have worried. Lady Helen's handwritten statement appeared to stand out as clearly as the names of the four signatories.

The initials were less distinct. He could make out *'B.P.'* *'O.H.'* was strong. *'C.K.'* was fainter. *'I.I.'* was almost invisible.

He stared.

Could he be staring at what he thought he was staring at?

All his tiredness vanished in a flash. He could scarcely believe his eyes.

Was it deliberate? Had someone placed the clue there deliberately?

Why hadn't he thought of that before!

He had found the clue! It had been there all the time!

He almost felt like shouting, *'Eureka!'*

The initials were the clue when placed *in that order*! It was uncanny!

He had seen the initials before, of course he had! He had never realised what they meant *in that order*!

The puzzle over its relevance suddenly brought a re-enactment of the old nightmare. The name reminded him of the Count Vronskii he had known in the war against the Turks. Suddenly the shock of the discovery brought with it a wave of tiredness that stole over him. He let his head fall back on the cushion at the chair-head. Everything had become clear and everything was far worse, everything except the old nightmare into which he now slipped.

Again he was running and running along a rocky hillside in Bulgaria, through orchards below Plevna. Again the bullets came towards him with the flutter of butterfly wings, floating like deadly snowflakes. He zigzagged and zigzagged. Again they came slowly with a little whizzing of wings through sunlit air. Suddenly drenching pain overwhelmed him and plunged him into blackness. He was floating. He felt he was floating across the surface of a river into the path of a black-canopied boat. The figure lying in it propped up under the black canopy raised a pale white hand and slowly lifted the heavy veil concealing her face. The staring eyes of the dead Anna looked at him. He found himself transfixed by them.

Then he saw the terrible, livid cavity on her forehead. She began to open her mouth to speak and suddenly it was not her lips moving, not her face he was seeing. He was seeing the face of a Turkish soldier he had killed, the stilled, yelling mouth in the boy's beardless face and the horrified eyes raised to his, peering at him, trying to outstare him with their awful reproach.

'Not you!' he screamed. *'Not you! I killed you!'*

'Sir!'

'I killed you!'

'Sir, I am Cotton!'

He opened his eyes. 'Oh, my God!'

'I'm sorry to have woken you up! You were shouting in Russian, sir!'

'Was I? Oh, I'm so sorry. Cotton, what is it?'

'Breakfast, sir.'

And it was breakfast! He had brought it up on a tray. Thank God, the prince thought, it was Cotton! And he was in England, in his bedroom in Stadleigh Court! And there was no dead Turk staring at him!

'Sir, Master Charles wants to show you something very secret. He won't even show me. After you have had breakfast, sir.'

So he did have a modest Tolstoyan breakfast, quite similar to the one at Lady Helen's, and was very grateful to Cotton for bringing it. Clearly there was some anxiety in the way Cotton hovered until the prince had drunk the last of the apple juice, telling him meanwhile of the morning's fishing. In a discreetly lowered voice he then divulged his news.

'I am to blame, sir. I took the liberty of telling young

Master Charles I had spoken to you about his interest, sir, in, er, ladies', er, bosoms, sir, and he was very excited, sir, because he's sure there's something you don't know...'

'About bosoms, Cotton?'

'Well, sir, no, sir. He was very contrite and said he wanted to make a clean breast. He said he wanted to show you...'

'A clean *breast*, Cotton!'

'Ah, sir, I see what you mean!'

'A clean bosom, perhaps.'

'Yes, sir. Exactly, sir. A clean bosom. He wants to make a clean bosom and show you his secret, sir. I said he would have to wait until you had had breakfast.'

The boy had been waiting outside the bedroom door. As soon as the prince approached, he was seized by the hand and led impatiently down the corridor. The boy did not speak. He merely pulled the prince and the latter followed without a word. They went down the corridor in the direction of Giles's study but branched off into a small passage. By now a slightly disgruntled feeling of being involved in a wild goose chase made the prince reluctant to be dragged to the end of the small passage and to a door opening into what looked like a linen cupboard with rows of shelves either side piled high with folded sheets and towels. It was dark and he hesitated to go farther but the boy insisted. At the far end was what appeared to be a paneled door. It had a door handle and a key in the lock. The boy signaled urgently for quiet as he drew the prince towards this door, drew out the key and quickly squatted down. Having apparently satisfied himself about something, he then asked the prince to do the same.

It always amused the prince how children tend to assume

adults can always squirm into the same confined spaces they can or, as in this case, squat down easily to look through a keyhole. He obediently did as he was told as best he could, since this was obviously the secret he was intended to see, and saw what at first looked like a snow-covered terrain, a rim of shadowy snow in the immediate foreground with, beyond it, what looked like brown trees but clearly could not be brown trees. And then he moved his eye slightly and just at the edge of his vision, through the pear-shaped aperture, he saw something that was unmistakable. Part of a brass tap. He realised he had been looking at the curved, white-enameled rim of a bath.

The prince was being shown a peephole into Anna Karenina's bathroom. He turned and looked into the boy's shadowy face and the eyes made doubly bright by the darkness. They shone with guilt.

'Sir, tell her I'm sorry, sir. You're Russian, sir. Tell her in Russian. Please, sir.'

This frantic whispering left the prince wondering if the boy had heard something about a Russian lady. He gave a little smile.

'Peeping Toms,' he scolded softly. 'That's what they're called, aren't they? Peeping Toms always get found out in the end. Let me have the key.'

He had naturally not supposed that something as simple as the turning of a key in a lock would do it. Nor that the turning of a doorknob would solve the mystery. But he tried the key, turned it and turned the doorknob.

At first nothing happened. A second pull and suddenly the door swung open.

It had been tight-fitting, apparently part of the paneling, with the keyhole concealed below the rim of the bath, but there, as if it were an Aladdin's cave, was Anna Karenina's bathroom, the pipework, the gleaming enamel, the wood paneling, the brown bath-towel still on its rail, the open window. The bath had been fixed across the doorway.

What a casual arrangement! the prince thought. He gave a spontaneous cry of amazement at the sight. Any of her "enemies" could have gained access to her when she was at her most vulnerable, just as Master Charles could have squinted at her curiously as she bathed.

So she *had not* been deluded! She *had* heard threats! Worse still, she could easily have been 'held down'! Speechless, both the prince and the boy stared at her 'secret place' in dawning awareness of what it meant,

'What on earth is going on in here?'

It was Lady Isobel's voice. She was behind them, standing in the corridor and peering in at what was no longer a dark linen cupboard but a length of sunlit passageway opening into a bathroom. The look on her face showed that more than one guilty secret had been uncovered. 'You knew about this, didn't you, Lady Isobel? If you told anyone, you might be an accomplice. I think you know what I mean.'

She stood uncomfortably blinking her eyes. It was as if the brightness of the erstwhile linen cupboard laid bare her complicity.

'I don't know what you mean! I... I... You, Charles, you wretched boy, go home at once!'

The boy needed no prompting. He made a dash for it. Pushing past her, he raced down the corridor as fast as he could.

The prince was preparing to confront her, because he realised she must have known of the makeshift arrangement for the bathroom, when he was distracted by the sudden appearance of Boris. He was standing on the other side of the bath. His wrinkled face and bloodshot eyes expressed such shock he instantly crossed himself.

'Did you know about this, Boris, my friend?' the prince asked.

'Your excellency, did I know?' He looked round him in bewilderment.

'Did you know this door could be opened?'

Boris flapped his arms in a sort of clockwork response. *'This was our mistress's personal... completely personal...'*

'I thought not. So you never saw this door open?'

The denial was emphatic. At that moment Boris caught sight of Lady Isobel and looked even more startled.

'What exactly are you saying?' she asked in her most authoritative English tone. 'I do wish you would speak in a language I can understand. In my own house, what's more! Who is this decrepit old man?'

It was astonishing she had not seen Boris before. The prince replied tartly that he was an elderly Russian servant who would never have harmed his mistress.

'She was murdered in this bath, Lady Isobel. Someone who knew about this door, about the access through the linen cupboard, that person probably murdered her. Who would that be, do you imagine?'

She protested at once at being asked such a thing. Her expression was one of dignified denial, though she reddened slightly at the implication of the question. 'You don't mean, prince, that I am responsible? You're surely not accusing *me*?'

'Not directly. I know where you were last night.'

'I was at the soiree.'

'Exactly. But someone else wasn't. Excuse me, I must strike while the iron is hot.'

He pushed past her as the boy had done and shortly afterwards his footsteps could be heard going rapidly down the main stairs.

'While the iron is hot!'

He told himself how despicable he was as he raced across the hall and out of the front door. To use a phrase like that – one of the first English sayings he had learned at the start of his attempt to be more English than the English – was abominable, he knew, but time was not on his side and the iron, whatever form it might take, was hot, there could be no doubt about that! He had to see Lady Helen at all costs!

17

In the hot mid-morning sun, which made him regret he had not picked up his Panama hat, he raced down the steps and went quickly from terrace to terrace of the Stadleigh Court garden. He knew it was now or never. It was a Russian matter. If he were to find the truth, it would be on the other side of the river. Irmingham held the clue. He had to see Lady Helen first of all because he was sure she must have known or at least suspected the motive.

As soon as the river came into view and he saw the reflections of overhanging willows and alders reaching like fingers into its apparently still depths, the truth seemed to be literally there, touchable, and he had only to cross the creaking footbridge to find it. In this confident mood he hurried along the riverbank and turned into the lane leading directly to the little settlement of rundown houses and rutted main street of the village known as Irmingham. Children were playing under the trees. Otherwise there was no sign of life. To his surprise, the front door of Lady Helen's cottage was wide open. He dashed up the garden path and peered in.

The hallway was cool and quiet, filled with the lived-in air of cooking smells and floor polish. On the right was Dr James Parkinson's consulting-room. The prince caught sight of him sitting with his back to the door, hunched over a table. A collarless white shirt open at the neck revealed a crimson line where the stiff collar had chafed it. The sight of the chafed skin and the bent back came as a sudden revelation of his sheer youth and inexperience. He seemed to be studying a newspaper clipping and was so deeply preoccupied he did not even look round when the prince entered after knocking softly.

'Willya nae gie a man a wee bit o'peace! Canya nae see I'm busy!'

Still he did not look up. He was so busy reading he did not pay any attention. Then his visitor introduced himself. The long back quickly straightened up and the freckled face acknowledged recognition.

'Prince!'

'Can I make a guess?'

'Guess what, sir?'

'Just a guess you'll be applying for… for somewhere else.'

'After what happened this morning I can't stay here.'

The prince took the precaution of closing the door behind him as he spoke. The gaudy wall chart of the human anatomy presided over the room like an avenging angel, so it seemed only right he should do his best to bolster the doctor's spirits.

'You only did as you were told.'

'I did it because Lord Irmingham insisted. And that's the truth. Whether or not it's for the best, I don't know. So she died in her bed!' James Parkinson shrugged. 'The sooner I'm away from here the better. I'm sorry for saying you had taken the keys – I had to, you know. If there were something not right…'

The prince offered an assurance that everything was all right. He said he merely wanted to ask a couple of questions.

'Look, I deny everything! I know nothing!'

'I'm not saying you do.' The defensive, resentful tone came as no surprise. The doctor was to be respected for that. 'Please tell me – the marks you and I saw on her neck, in your opinion, were they made by pressure, by someone holding her down?'

There was no direct answer save an apparently obdurate folding of the arms and tight closure of the eyes. The prince took this to mean that Dr James Parkinson wished to do no more than signify his agreement or disagreement by nodding or shaking his head.

'I believe she was drowned? Am I right?'

A slowly acknowledged affirmative nod.

'Could the marks on the neck have been made by the pressure of fingers?'

Another affirmative nod.

'Did you have a key to her bedroom?'

A rapid movement of denial.

'Did you ever go into the linen cupboard?'

'What?'

The doctor opened his eyes and looked at the prince in amazement.

'No, I thought you hadn't. Thank you, doctor. You have told me all I wanted to know.'

'I have told you absolutely nothing!'

Which, of course, was undeniable and made his questioner smile. All amazement, even curiosity, vanished from his face as it settled into tired contemplation of the prince's faintly amused smile. 'What linen cupboard?'

The question was put to rest by an inquiry as to where Lady Helen was.

'I think she's in the back garden, probably in the conservatory or summerhouse. Look,' added Dr James Parkinson in clipped, angry tones, 'I know only one thing. The lady died in her bed. Her son was a victim of lockjaw plus pneumonia plus... plus my incompetence, my lack of experience. And I'm looking for another post.'

'If you want a letter of recommendation or support, just let me know.'

The doctor very nearly allowed himself to laugh. The prince took a visiting card out of his waistcoat and apologised for its crumpled shape by explaining it had been drenched in the river. As he handed it across he asked where his compatriot was.

'I think he went out. Probably shooting.' The cockled if still legible card was held in James Parkinson's hand a moment, while the embossed Rostov crest and the full princely title were studied. Then it was laid down respectfully on the table. 'I feel very honoured, sir. Thank you.'

'Where did he go?'

There was a shake of the head. 'He's a strange case. No offence, prince, but for someone who complains of having painful legs and often walks with a stick it's astonishing how fleet of foot he is when he has a gun in his hands. Of course, he keeps us well supplied with fresh meat – rabbits, you know – and the people round here like him for it. I can't say where he went.'

The prince thanked him and reminded him of the promised recommendation. He said he would go in search of Lady Helen because he would be returning to London shortly.

***

As soon as he re-entered the hall he felt once again the need for urgency. He was now more than ever convinced he had to act on what he knew. On the other hand, it surprised him almost simultaneously to be beset by choices.

Turning to go out, he could not avoid seeing the sitting room and the shelves of the bookcase. The volumes were lined up as neatly as ever in correct alphabetical order with Oswald Holmcroft's book on Cromwell in pride of place on the second shelf. A couple of shelves lower were many under T for Tolstoy. Finally, on the bottom shelf, a small leather-bound volume of the poems of William Wordsworth was wedged quite tightly at the end. It had obviously not been taken from its place recently. He crept into the room and finding it empty drew the leather-bound volume carefully out.

Not theft, he consoled himself as he scrutinised the volume and thrust it in his pocket, no, not theft. It was *evidence.* Yet the reason for having such evidence and the wish to see Lady Helen posed contrary urges. Which should come first? He remembered what she had said about the local churchyard, but he also knew that what had happened during the soiree was probably more important. Against his inclination, but in the name of truth, he felt impelled to reassure himself before going to look for her. He went out through the front door and blinked in the hot sunlight of her front garden.

A horse and cart loaded with straw creaked and swayed along the main street, dogs barked and children played more noisily than ever. In short, the main street of this modest village of Irmingham seemed momentarily busy. He aimed to find the church. It took him barely five minutes to reach it and enter the churchyard by the wicket-gate. A brick-paved path led up to the church door. Although the path was reasonably free of weeds, the graves on either side were rank with thistles and tall grass and he could see why Lady Helen had been using a sickle to do her bonking, as she called it. She had said something about Carew Kingston's mother being buried in the churchyard. He wondered where.

The jumble of older graves and headstones at the front of the church among yew trees told him nothing. At the back, beside the mossy brickwork of the path, there were newer graves, newer headstones and newer inscriptions among obvious signs of clearance. This seemed a more likely place to find what he wanted. Dotted with headstones and shrubs, in part darkened by trees, the extensive churchyard resembled an overgrown garden with occasional piles of damp, yellowing grass giving off a fragrance of hay in the hot sun.

Headstone after gravestone yielded nothing, even recently carved ones, until in the shade of a yew by a relatively open area of rising ground clearly pitted with rabbit holes a fairly recent white marble headstone shone like a beacon. The name Kingston was clearly visible in a carved inscription:-

In Memoriam –
Elizaveta Ivanovna Kingston, nee Crow,
late of St Petersburg,
deceased in her fifty-fourth year.

It was simple and dignified. A bunch of recently cut hollyhocks stood rather garishly in front of it in a brown jar. It told very, very little, however: no dates, no relationship, not even whether she was interred there, but one feature puzzled the prince especially – *nee Crow*. It seemed unnecessary until the meaning suddenly came to him and he snapped his fingers.

'Voron!' he muttered. Hadn't Oswald Holmcroft called him 'Crow'? So that was it!

Things fitted together. All he had to do now was confront 'Crow' Kingston with what he knew. For this reason he searched round in his inside jacket pocket and drew out the Oswald Holmcroft document. The signatures verified all his suspicions. The four sets of initials – *B.P., O.H., C.K., I.I.* – made everything seem to fit together.

It would take too long to inform the police and would very likely be unnecessary. Giles would not alter his version of events, Dr James Parkinson would deny all knowledge, the ranks would close. He refolded the sheet of paper, thrust it back in his pocket and prepared to go back to Lady Helen's cottage

Two shots rang out in quick succession at that moment.

Lead shot ricocheted off a stone. He felt a sharp pain near his right hip as if someone had aimed a fist at the spot. He flung himself flat on the grass. Birds rose in a flock from nearby trees, rabbits dashed past.

Glancing round, he had no idea where the shots came from. All he saw was a dead rabbit a short distance away. For a full minute nothing happened. Things returned to the normality of buzzing insects.

Long grass nearby was stirred by footsteps. From behind the yew tree a peaked cap and shabby red shirt, belted at the stout waist, came into view. A disguise of sorts or a simple protection against the heat had been provided by a handkerchief tied over the mouth and nose but, silhouetted against sunlight as he broke open the twin-barreled gun, the man was obviously Carew Kingston. He stopped dead when he saw the prince.

'Ah, it's you!'

'Akh, eto vy!' The exclamation was made in Russian and sufficiently spontaneous to be genuine. The prince climbed to his feet and began brushing himself down. He found his jacket pocket had been torn away.

'You didn't expect to find me here, Mr Kingston?'

He was justifiably annoyed. It was not the first time he had been shot at, whether intentionally or unintentionally, and had his clothes messed up. But annoyance was tempered for the moment by relief at having simultaneously found both the Kingston headstone and the man himself.

'No,' was the casual answer. The gun was snapped shut and swung over Carew Kingston's shoulder. 'I had assumed you would be going back to London.' He picked up the dead rabbit and put it in a bag tied to his waist. 'Your book, I think.'

The volume of William Wordsworth's poems had slipped to the ground. The prince quickly retrieved it. The leather cover had been ripped by the force of the ricochet but no harm had come to the pages inside.

'Thanks to Mr Wordsworth, I'm still alive. No thanks to you.'

'Why should I intend to kill you, Prince Rostov? You are not my enemy, except in a class sense, and you are not an edible commodity like these rabbits. I assume you are here for some purpose. My dear mother's memorial, perhaps?'

'Not your mother, surely?'

'Why do you say that?'

'*Nee Crow*?'

'I can explain.'

'Not now, please. Now we've met I'd like to talk about this.' The prince indicated the volume of Wordsworth.

'You admire the work of William Wordsworth, do you, prince?'

'And you? Do you admire his work, Mr Kingston?'

'No, I have not read any of his poetry recently.'

'Really! And have you heard any?'

'Excuse me?'

'I asked if you had heard any of his poetry recently? For instance...' The prince flipped through the pages '...Miss Julie Mayhew-Summers who worked the bellows for your "Russian Rhapsody"...'

'She got tired.' There was a note of disgruntlement in the simple statement.

'That was a pity, of course. But during the soiree she recited lines from Mr Wordsworth, the English poet.'

Carew Kingston narrowed his eyes and gave the other a look of angry puzzlement. As if repudiating what had been insinuated, he drew the handkerchief rather roughly from his face to reveal his short, white-tipped beard.

'You don't remember them? Let me read them to you in my best English accent.' The prince cleared his throat and reverted to English. 'Here, in this churchyard, it seems very appropriate to achieve a symbiosis or, as the poet puts it:-

"...*that blessed mood*
In which the burden of the mystery...

Is lightened – that serene and blessed mood,
In which the affections gently lead us on –
Until, the breath of this corporeal frame,
And even the motion of our human blood
Almost suspended, we are laid asleep
In body, and become a living soul..."'

He looked up from the sunlit page. 'You have never heard these lines before?'

'Of course, I have heard them!' the other exclaimed peevishly, wiping his face with the handkerchief. 'I can't remember exactly when... I, er...'

'Symbiosis?'

'Excuse me? Prince, you are talking nonsense!'

'You could have heard it all quite easily from the organ gallery. Except you weren't there, were you?'

Carew Kingston had begun walking away during the reading. The prince knew he was trying to evade his guilt by walking away. They walked side-by-side round the path to the front of the church.

'Your contribution to yesterday's soiree was not only musical, it was deadly, Mr Kingston. You know her son is dead and now she is dead, don't you? Mind you, according to you, she never existed.'

The other gave a sharp little chirrup of nervous laughter. 'Of course, I know that!' He ran his handkerchief over his short beard and wiped his neck. 'Of course, she never existed! Prince Rostov, I shake my head over you, you know.' The handkerchief was tucked away.

'Oh, she existed! I am prepared to swear in a court of law

that she lived, she breathed, she loved, she feared and she died at Stadleigh Court! You know she did.' The prince's mouth was dry from an awareness of the other's menace. 'But she died in her bed. A heart attack.'

'So?'

'You can ask Dr Parkinson. You can ask Lord Irmingham.'

'I do not need to ask anyone about someone who did not exist.'

'True.' The prince even smiled a little at the bizarre logic. 'It's the motive that puzzles me.'

'The motive?'

'The motive for killing Anna Karenina.'

There followed a long silence as they confronted each other among the headstones. Surrounded for a short while by nothing but the soft churring sound of grasshoppers and insects, the prince tried hard to penetrate the thick lenses of the other's spectacles. They returned his scrutiny with a bland, almost mesmerising menace and the prince was only brought to his senses by a light breeze that suddenly stirred the pages beneath his fingers. He found he was sweating so badly the paper stuck to them. Suddenly the silence was broken by shouts.

'Ah,' cried Carew Kingston in his curiously high English accent, 'my little army!'

Three small ragged boys dashed through the wicket-gate. They ran up the brick-paved path shouting for him to give them some of his rabbits. Carew Kingston opened the bag and extracted three of them.

'Take them straight to your mothers!' he ordered. 'I am,' he explained as the three urchins ran quickly back into the main street, 'well-known for my generosity.' He grinned again, gave the prince a haughty glance and spoke once more in Russian. 'You are good at telling lies, Prince Rostov. But you have no proof. Not a scrap. Just guesses.'

'Guesses, true. But I think you planned it. Cold-bloodedly. Over a month or more. Your limping, for example.'

'Due to the organ pedals. I think I told you.'

They made their way out through the wicket-gate.

'Yes, you fooled people with that,' the prince acknowledged. 'By practising your composition on the organ during the past month or so, though, you were able to discover something else. As I discovered earlier today, there is a door giving access to the organ gallery – you probably used it many times after going up the main stairs – which also gives access to the floor where Lord Irmingham has his study and bedroom. It's not difficult to get from there to the linen cupboard if you know about it...'

Carew Kingston adjusted the gun on his shoulder. 'Linen cupboard! What would I want with a linen cupboard?'

'Lady Isobel probably told you.'

The other's lack of response confirmed it.

'Yes, I guessed as much,' the prince went on. 'I am not really concerned with how you found out about that place. I am concerned that you issued threats. Very probably over several weeks. You terrified poor Anna Karenina. She was so frightened she had a special lock fitted to her bedroom door. What she didn't know but you knew was that you could access her bathroom from that cupboard. So last evening, when all the servants and guests and the Irminghams themselves were occupied by the soiree, you knew you would be free to open the door to Anna Karenina's bathroom and you had the luck of the devil – you surprised her in her bath! All you had to do was throttle her! Of course she tried to fight you off! Of course there was a lot of water splashed about! But you held her down – and she drowned...'

'You are telling awful lies! You told me she died in her bed! I protest! You deserve to die for accusing me!'

His raised voice attracted the attention of children who were playing under the trees. They stared at the two men speaking a strange language and a couple of childish voices asked Mr Kingston for more rabbits. He brushed them aside, peering guiltily round him.

'She drowned,' the prince repeated. 'You then closed the door, I suggest, locked it again... In any case, my dear Crow – *Voron*? Am I right? – if you knew about that door, you knew who was beyond it. You knew *she* existed. And afterwards you simply went downstairs to the Gothic hall, arriving in time to comfort Lady Isobel.'

'*Voron*? What do you mean?'

For the first time Carew Kingston showed signs of losing his nerve. He quickened his pace. They went down the main street indifferent to the shouts of the children. It was only when they reached Lady Helen's cottage that he turned to the prince and asked cryptically, in a threatening whisper: 'Who told you about that?' His eyes shot towards the open front door. 'Was it...?'

'No, it wasn't Lady Helen. The name for crow is...'

'Ssshh!' Carew Kingston dumped the bag containing the rabbits in the hall. 'Upstairs, Prince Rostov, if you please!'

18

The prince was led upstairs to a spacious sitting room containing a piano, bookshelves, a large photogravure reproduction of Tolstoy's portrait by Repin and several framed photographs of groups of people uncomfortably posed on verandah steps at Tolstoy's home, Yasnaya Polyana. He knew then that he had been invited to be more than a guest. He was to be confronted, he realised, by proof of Carew Kingston's cleverness.

In the instant of being invited to sit down, he received apologies for the state of the room. A higgledy-piggledy array of books, music sheets, clothes, stale food and writing materials strewn over the main table and clothes draped here and there on chairs clearly emphasised bachelorhood and a degree of personal neglect. By contrast, and as if arranged to occupy pride of place, the top of the piano contained two pictures. One showed a photo of Carew Kingston beside a cutout illustration of Tolstoy addressing a group of peasant children.

'Proof of my discipleship,' Carew Kingston announced, proudly pointing to it.

The prince smiled courteously, more aware of flies circling above it than of the picture itself. He sat down expecting the other to sit as well, but Carew Kingston preferred to remain standing

More prominent was a photograph in a gilded frame

depicting a young couple dressed for a wedding. The faded, iconic look of the youthful faces smiling obediently on a hot day somewhere out of doors had a poignant charm. It reminded the prince that, like him, Carew Kingston was an exile. Probably as much by choice in his case, but if exile, as he had remarked ironically at their first meeting, might be good for translators, it was rarely any good for one's heart.

'I must ask you to keep your suspicions to yourself, Prince Rostov.' He spoke as if he were offering advice on personal hygiene. 'Please don't take offence. I have no objection to you personally. Think me a poor disciple of Count Leo Tolstoy and Tolstoyanism, if you like, but I can only say in all humility that I consider it my task to translate his work and spread his gospel, not necessarily to *be* like him. Much is muddled in his thinking, you see, and his doctrines have yet to be tested in the laboratory of life. But I share his love of the simple people. It is to them, like the ordinary people round here, that Tolstoy wants to appeal. Not to you, not to the privileged, not to Lord Irmingham, not even to Lady Helen, not to lords and ladies, but to ordinary people.'

The prince determined to be as polite as possible. 'You are a good Tolstoyan, I'm sure.' His mouth was dry as he spoke. 'You repudiate all his work prior to his conversion, as he has done. Very right and proper. But hardly a motive.'

'Motive? Ah, motive for your suspicions! Yes, the motive is hard to find!' Carew Kingston's tone of voice changed. He placed his gun in a cupboard which could be seen to contain an armoury of weapons. Quite confidently, even a little triumphantly, he then sat down in an armchair which had a flower-patterned cover similar to those in Lady

Helen's sitting room. 'You will surprise me, naturally, if you can find a scrap of proof, let alone a motive – apart, I mean, from your suspicions, your conjectures. What motive could there possibly be for killing someone who was thought to be dead already and, in any case, died in her bed – or so you say?'

There was fishing of a kind in the question, however direct and confident it might seem. It implied that something might have been overlooked, some clue inadvertently left behind. The prince did not take the bait. He merely muddied the water a little by asking: 'Revenge perhaps?'

'Really?'

'Your name, you see.'

'What about my name?'

'It puzzled me.'

'Why?'

'Oswald Holmcroft first used it. *Crow*. Then I learned your name was Carew and I assumed I had misheard. But I hadn't, had I?'

'So?'

'A simple rule of philology applied to that name, collapsing the two open syllables into one, would produce another name, wouldn't it? Perhaps your *real* name or the name of a lady from St Petersburg who died at the age of fifty-four. Someone you call your mother. That would produce a motive.'

The other's eyes blinked. Otherwise there was no reaction. The prince had expected instant denial, even some defiance, and was disconcerted. It was clear that he was expected to go on speaking until he either faltered or said too much.

'Yes, well,' he asserted, 'I recognise I must be held responsible to some extent. I see I was very likely a cause, a catalyst. You must have known that I had been invited to stay at Stadleigh Court for a purpose, and that purpose was, as it turned out, to identify the lady in the tower. Am I wrong?'

No, the prince thought, he's not going to answer until I get something wrong. He continued: 'So long, of course, as she was an imposter, or so you thought, there was no need for you to take her seriously. But if she were to be real, if she were entitled in law to inherit her husband's money, you could no longer pretend she did not exist. So I think you decided to scare me off. I think you waited and watched. A couple of days ago I think you probably glimpsed me coming out of the tower and followed me down to the river. You guessed I'd seen her. Then, in the burning stubble, you saw your chance. If you'd turned your head just a fraction to your left you'd have seen me lying in the ditch. But you didn't. You first saw me after returning here and making great play with a weakness in your legs that obliged you to walk with a stick. That was a pretence, wasn't it?'

Again silence.

'The most puzzling thing to me was why. Why should you want to kill Anna Karenina? Then I remembered something you'd said. You'd said she'd destroyed a noble, decent man. I assumed you were referring to her husband, but I soon realised you didn't mean him, you meant Count Vronskii. Here I ought to add that I knew Count Vronskii very briefly during the Turkish campaign. He was, as you say, a noble, decent man. He had been crushed by her suicide.'

This led his listener to spring to his feet. The name had

obviously struck a chord. Muttering something under his breath, he fished in his trouser pocket for a handkerchief, wiped his face and clumsily, in obvious agitation, thrust the handkerchief back before reaching up to the top of the piano for the faded photograph in the gilded frame. He held it up as if it were a priceless religious relic and then pressed the glass front of the photograph to his chest.

'That name!' he shrieked. 'You have no idea what it means, no idea at all!'

For several moments he stared up at the ceiling and the circling flies before slowly shaking his head.

'You accuse me of murder and in the same breath you mention the name of Count Vronskii! His life was taken from him! He sacrificed everything for that wretched woman! He was the one who really killed himself! She... she lived on!'

Holding the photograph at arms' length, he breathed deeply while gazing at it with admiring eyes. He had spoken in a series of breathy, high-pitched exclamations resembling hysterical shrieks and now tried to speak more calmly.

'I was his half-brother. My mother was a peasant girl. She died shortly after I was born. I was brought up by someone I always thought was my mother. She was a cousin of the Count, also a Vronskii. You know how it is. Many of our Russian noble families have *other* families. They are not talked about. They disappear. I disappeared into my English name.'

He paused, pursed his lips and gazed out of the window.

'The Russian name was always there, of course. My mother made a joke of it. She used to call me Crow as a boy. You must understand something – she loved him, my real father, I mean, the old Count, Vronskii's father. She married *my* father simply to escape from all the scandal. Here they are on their wedding day, Mr and Mrs Kingston. But for her, of course, and for me it was exile...'

He fixed his eyes on the photograph and seemed for several moments to lapse into a trance of recollection. Oblivious of the prince or the need to justify himself, he appeared consciously to seek out that very umbilical cord of memory, as if the past could produce a kind of rebirth for him. The prince respected this private moment by saying nothing, knowing that the mechanism of justice and retribution would shortly be at work to challenge him. Although Carew Kingston's raised head and jutting beard suggested a somewhat theatrical readiness to defy whatever the future might bring, he looked sad and what he said next, as if here were talking to himself, expressed the essence of that sadness.

'Exile is a living death. You must know that as well as I do. For a true Russian, for someone with Russia in his bones, exile is always a kind of death in life.'

Shrewd, slightly enlarged irises of light-blue eyes glanced downwards at the prince through round lenses as the words were spoken. His lined, drawn, still perspiring face had become a rigid mask. He again pressed the photograph frame to his chest.

'My mother came here because she was in exile. She insisted. I didn't know why at the time. It was long after my real father had died, long after my stepfather, her English husband, had died – oh, twenty years ago! On her deathbed...' he tapped the glass front of the photograph '...on her deathbed she made me swear. She knew, you see, that Anna Arkadyevna

Karenina was there, in the tower at Stadleigh Court. She knew *she* lived! And she made me swear on my honour as my father's son, as a Vronskii, as a descendant, that I should avenge my half-brother's death! Can you understand that, my dear prince?'

The prince said he couldn't. What was there to avenge, after all?

'My whole purpose in living.' Carew Kingston treated the question as completely irrelevant. 'Obvious, surely? But at first I really couldn't believe that the recluse over at the Court was real. Not, as you say, until you arrived. Then I knew the time had come. I knew I had to keep my promise.'

He had his head still raised, looking out of the window on to the so-called main street of Irmingham where, in the midday heat, nothing seemed to move at all and even the children had grown quiet. Try as he might to be dispassionate, the prince could only feel that here was one of those sad, entangled stories of seigneurial rights and illegitimacy which he knew only too well from the lives of relatives and acquaintances, and in their unraveling what always emerged was more sadness, more tragedy. In this case, a promise frozen into a deep permafrost of memory had been revived and acted on only through his chance arrival as the result of a bicycle accident. Its unraveling had led to death.

'I did it. Yes, it had to be done. It is why I have lived in exile so long.'

'The fulfillment of a promise can hardly justify murder.' As soon as the prince said this he knew it sounded priggish. He spoke shakily, without the assurance of genuine certainty. A quick lick of the lips and he started again. 'The pretext, if

I may put it this way, your "Russian Rhapsody", it gave you the kind of access to Stadleigh Court that must presuppose… well, must have meant at least some… some planning in advance.'

'An eye for an eye, a tooth for a tooth! The Bible says it! That's what matters!'

It was too much. Struggling to his feet in the face of this arrogance, the prince felt the righteousness of a judge rise like phlegm in his throat.

'I speak …' It took an effort to moisten his lips again '… I speak as Tolstoy would speak, I'm sure. He teaches non-opposition to evil by violence. That is the cornerstone. You committed a violent act. You killed her. She was a frightened woman and you killed her. It was murder. Premeditated murder. But, like Tolstoy, I will not judge you. You will have to be your own judge.'

For once the shell of the other's arrogant self-absorption seemed to crack. He turned his gaze on the prince. The mask-like, inexpressive features slowly became unmistakably hostile. The eyes glinted angrily. He curled his lips in an ironic grin.

'She died in her bed, my dear prince, didn't you say so? I will judge as I see fit. You may accuse me, but I will admit nothing in public. There will be no evidence against me.'

'I have guessed your real name.'

The prince's remark provoked a smile of superiority. 'My true name, yes. I am proud of that name. But what is an exile's real name? A true exile is half-dead already, as soon as his exile starts. No, my real name – there will be no connection! None! Absolutely none!'

274

He made a face. It seemed a waste of time to be angry with this man. Truth and fiction had become so intertwined it no longer mattered which prevailed. The prince knew for a fact what he knew for a fact. He took the Oswald Holmcroft document out of his jacket pocket and held it open for the other to see.

'I know she existed,' he said. 'I saw the black boat. It was no "gap in nature".'

'What?' The other looked deeply suspicious. 'What? What black boat?'

The question was waved aside. 'Look at this, it contains your real name.'

'What?'

'It's evidence. You know who wrote this?'

Carew Kingston pretended not to have seen it before.

'Lady Helen? Did she copy this out? It's her handwriting...'

The sudden change in his voice confirmed the prince's suspicion. There came a quick intake of breath and Carew Kingston looked away in an effort to hide his feelings.

'You love her, don't you?'

'Yes, yes, I'm very fond of her. She's like a daughter to me, the daughter I never had.' Suddenly, with a spurt of anger at having confessed so much, he declared: 'It's no business of yours! I consider you've disrupted our lives here, Prince Rostov! As for this document, Lady Helen copied it, did she?'

'Yes.' It would not take him long, the prince thought, to discover the betrayal implicit in it. The order of the initials would tell him. And what would he do then? Mutual hostility might become a lover's jealousy. 'She loves her father,' the prince said rather cruelly, 'more than anyone in the world. You must accept that, Mr Kingston.'

'I don't accept anything of the kind,' he sneered angrily, snatching at the document. 'Her father's an idealist, a fool! And you're a parasite, Prince Rostov! My mother's blood runs in my veins, you know, the blood of a Russian peasant, and we've always despised and hated lords and princes! As for the imposter, the lady in the tower, she didn't deserve to live! And don't tell me what I must accept or what I must do! I'm not frightened of death, I've lived it every day of my exile!'

The prince would have snatched the document back except that he knew the need to warn Lady Helen was more pressing.

'You're guilty and you know it!' were the words he shouted.

This caused an ironic, caustic, bitter laugh, which ended with Carew Kingston swaying a little, giving a sniff and then breaking into a smile. He raised his eyes to the ceiling again. There was a momentary pause.

'Clever of you,' he admitted, still looking at the ceiling, still smiling, still ready to laugh, 'clever of you – the lines from the English poet, the lines from Mr Wordsworth! You had me there! I hadn't thought of that! But then of course she died in her bed, didn't she?'

***

The prince slammed the door. The sound of the other's guffaws followed him down the stairs.

He was so upset he could not be sure what to do. It was only when he realised he was still carrying the Wordsworth volume and was on the point of returning it to its place on Lady Helen's bookshelf that he knew he had an absolute priority to warn her. The sitting room was empty. The busy, delicate ticking of the clock on the mantelpiece stitched its way through the silence and competed with hushed voices beyond the consulting-room door. Not wanting to disturb the doctor again, he decided to take it upon himself to see if she was still in the garden and crossed the Indian carpet to the open French windows.

It was baking hot outside. All damp from the rain had vanished from the lawn as he crossed it, glancing from side to side in the hope of seeing a gardener but fairly sure the heat had driven people indoors. He crunched along a cinder path running between a large greenhouse and an extensive kitchen garden but saw no one. He called out her name. No answer. Lady Helen had hidden herself away in the heat, it seemed, and the farther he went and the more he called, the less sure he was of finding her. All around, though, was abundant evidence of her success in ensuring a self-sufficiency of natural produce for the so-called commune.

In fact, the garden was a thriving smallholding, quite unlike the traditional cottage garden at the front. It turned into a wide area of lawn beyond the vegetables. Here huge trees rose like silhouetted giants and seemed to bear down on him with watchful eyes formed by shafts of bright sunlight. He felt their eyes flicker at him as he approached across the grass. Cupping his hand against his forehead in an effort to shade his eyes, he tried to discern anything even faintly visible in the deep shadows of the trees. He stared and stared. With the sun full on him he knew he must be conspicuous out in the open. He could see nothing. The trees formed what looked like an impenetrable wall. He spoke her name one last time more in desperation than hope.

'Lady Helen!'

The sound of his voice seemed to be deadened by the trees and the background noises of summer. For a few moments he felt sure there would be no reply. As he turned to go back to the house, he heard a movement quite close by. There was a distinct sound of a yawn. He was astonished to find he had stopped only a short distance away from some particularly deep shade just to his right.

'Prince! Prince!'

A woman's resonant voice filled the air round him. Dazzled though he was, the singing note in the calling voice made him feel he had entered some Calypso's isle.

'In here, prince! Come in here out of the sun! How nice of you to come!'

Why there had been no sign of the summerhouse earlier he simply did not know. It was there, a three-sided structure with a slatted roof, and he realised it was laid on sand and could probably be moved. Its interior seemed black as night for the first few moments before his eyes became accustomed to the shade. Lady Helen was reclining in a canvas deck chair.

'I must have fallen asleep! It's the heat of course. Oh, what's happened to your coat?' He had forgotten about the tear to the pocket of his jacket and at once showed her what had happened to the volume of Wordsworth's poems.

'It saved my life,' was his explanation after having apologised for taking it. 'I wanted it as evidence.'

'Evidence?'

He told her what had happened in the churchyard and added: 'You remember yesterday at the soiree – Monty Coulsham talking about symbiosis and Miss Julie the Unruly reading from Wordsworth. Mr Kingston should have heard all that, shouldn't he?'

She patted her mouth against a second yawn, swept back her luxurious hair and sat up abruptly. Because she was only half visible in the deeper shade of the summerhouse, it took him a moment to distinguish the dark-blue of her cotton dress from the highlights of her matching eyes and their expression of anxiety. She sat upright with her bare arms raised behind her head to hold back her hair.

'You don't mean he...'

It was less of a question than a half-formed thought. Her hands fell back into her lap as she spoke and the luxurious copper hair created a proscenium arch either side of her face. He had a distinct sense that she understood exactly what he meant.

'May I?' He indicated a deck chair folded in a corner of the summerhouse.

'Oh, please do. Jane brought some lemonade. Do pour yourself a glass.' On the table next to her was a cut-glass crystal jug covered in a muslin cloth with a beaded fringe. Two glasses stood on a cloth-covered tray beside it, one of which was half-full of lemonade and had attracted a couple of wasps. She waved the wasps away. 'I had one brought for Carew but he hasn't come. You mean he... What are you saying, prince?'

'I must warn you, my dear Lady Helen. He is a very

dangerous, depressed man. Very dangerous. I think he killed Anna Karenina.'

'How on earth can you say that?'

The air in the summerhouse had a hot woody smell. Thin stripes of fierce bright sunlight penetrated through the slits in the roof and one bright hairline crack fell directly across her face. Leaning forward, he picked up a parasol lying on the floor and used the steel tip to draw letters in the sand outside the summerhouse.

B and *P* appeared followed by *O* and *H*, *C* and *K* and *I* and *I*: *BPOHCKII*.

The name VRONSKII lay there as if carved out of granite in the brightness of the sun. He opened the deck chair and sat down.

'You did it deliberately, didn't you, Lady Helen?'

She saw what he had done, raised her eyebrows and looked at him anxiously. 'Yes.'

'Did you suspect?'

Her hands made vaguely explanatory movements. 'I thought it was funny how the initials – you know – made up that name. I mean she tried to commit suicide – you know – for love of him. I didn't know it could mean...'

'He's related!'

'*He* is?'

What the prince had just learned from Carew Kingston was briefly told. 'And I suspect he killed her!'

She looked disbelieving. 'James said she died in her bed. You don't mean he...'

'No,' he said, 'not in her bed. He held her down in her bath. He drowned her. I am sure of this now. And I think...'

he saw she was about to interrupt '...I think, Lady Helen, you suspected – suspected he was capable of it. Which is why, when you copied out Oswald Holmcroft's document, you put the initials and the names in that order so they would spell the name Vronskii in Russian, wouldn't they?'

She stretched across to him and clasped his hand. It was only a momentary lack of self-control. Equally quickly she withdrew her hand and stood up.

'Yes, I suspected.' She stared out into the garden and whispered: 'There has always been something frightening about him. But he was so helpful. I mean we couldn't have started our little commune... In any case, how do you know? And then there's poor Gerald, he... he was in love with her, I know that. Hannah virtually... Oh, what *are* you saying?' Her hands now fluttered in alarm. 'Why? For heaven's sake, why?'

The prince climbed to his feet as he explained.

'The motive for it was his promise to the woman he loved as his mother on her deathbed. But until I arrived he had not been sure. The lady in the tower might have been an imposter. I think he laid his plans some while back, but my arrival was the catalyst. So I am to blame, you see, because I identified her. And you are to blame for making the initials read like his real name. Without you and me, he would be perfectly safe.'

The words almost stuck in his throat as he spoke them. She said nothing. She merely crossed her bare arms and shivered.

'I have one question,' he said, glancing down at the initials in the sand. 'How many copies did you make? It was only two, wasn't it?'

'Just two. For Oswald and for father. Why?'

He did not mention he had left the Oswald Holmcroft copy in Carew Kingston's sitting room. He merely said: 'I have a feeling he'll know by now. You know he's in love with you, don't you? He loves you like a daughter.'

She appeared not to hear. She frowned and instantly started to leave.

'If you go back now he'll... Lady Helen, he'll think you've betrayed him. I know the kind of person he is. Listen a moment,' he insisted. 'A lonely man, an exile, of mixed blood, keeping a promise all his life to avenge the disgrace suffered by his brother – his half-brother, yes, but still his brother – because Anna Karenina lived on. It may not make sense to us, but to him – I can understand what it must have meant to him. And now he finds that you, someone he loved as a daughter, as a pupil, you have betrayed him by revealing his real name and exposing his motive for doing what he did. He can hate you now, can't he? Because he hates us, lords and ladies. Princes especially. He told me so just now.'

'Tolstoy preaches love, prince. And forgiveness.' She gave him a small smile, stooped and picked up the parasol. 'And non-opposition to evil by force. Isn't that true?' It was then that she gasped.

They both saw the figure approaching across the lawn, lit so brilliantly by the hot sun he might have been coming towards them on a stage, the panes of the greenhouse behind him bright as flares. He made no sound. The thick round lenses of the spectacles had the menace of anger and determination. Carew Kingston, devoid of his peaked cap, his mouth fixed in a thin line above the beard, was coming towards them at a slow walking pace, one hand behind his back, intent, deliberate, his blood-red shirt belted to his stout waist like a butcher's apron.

She took a step forward, opened her parasol and paused. The hesitation was noticed. He was close enough by then to see the initials drawn in the sand. He brought his hand round from behind his back and they could see he was holding a revolver. His eyebrows were raised as he peered down at the name BPOHCKII, studied it and shook his head several times in what might have been despair or disappointment, simultaneously releasing the revolver's safety catch. As he lifted the gun to the horizontal, his head moved back a little. The spectacle lenses caught the sun.

'You're out of your mind!' the prince shouted in Russian.

'Please, prince, speak English. For Lady Helen's sake. I am not shooting rabbits now, you see.'

'Carew,' she cried, 'did you kill her?'

The fact that she was not intimidated appeared to annoy him.

'If I did, it's only what I promised.'

'Did you?'

'She lived on, you know, while my brother's life…'

'Did you kill her?'

'My brother's life was ruined. She disgraced our name.'

'So you killed her?'

There was a pause. Her insistent questions seemed to deflate him.

'Yes, I killed her.'

'Why? Because of a name?'

'Yes. Because of the name down there in the sand.'

'And that's your real name?'

'Yes, it's my real name. And this is *his* gun, his real gun. It was brought back from Bulgaria. And it still works. I can prove it.'

He fired it upwards. The parasol was lifted out of Lady Helen's fingers and spun onto the roof of the summerhouse. There it rolled down lazily and tumbled into shadow. Birds rose in a screeching flock from the nearby trees.

She flung herself back against the prince for protection. He held her in his arms, though he tried as far as possible to place himself between her and the menace of the gun. He could sense the way the whole garden was alerted by the noise of the shot and the birds and fear broke over him in a chill gust.

Carew Kingston again shook his head, this time rather curtly. 'I am used to killing vermin. But not you, my dear Lady Helen. What you wrote – it's as if you pointed a finger at me. "Guilty!" you said.'

'You are mad!' the prince managed to shout.

It provoked a sharp response. 'No, not mad! Betraycd! Humiliated! But I was right! She did not deserve to live! It is justice!'

The words were barked out so forcefully and with such anger the prince felt Lady Helen shiver as he held her, but at that instant she released herself, to his surprise, and quite calmly exclaimed, as if it were part of an ongoing discussion: 'How can you talk such nonsense? Justice, indeed! Whose justice?'

It was too much for Carew Kingston. Her reasonableness seemed to put an end to his attempt at justification. The revolver was raised in a threatening gesture. Whether or not he intended to fire at her was unclear, but she anticipated him by defiantly dashing forward at the instant of firing and the quick movement distracted him. At a distance of little more than a couple of metres the bullet entered the prince's thigh a split second before he heard the explosion.

It was like a sunburst of pain ripping through his leg. He screamed with agony and collapsed on the sand. With both hands he clutched his thigh where the bullet had entered and it took him a moment or two to do the sensible thing and turn his grip into a kind of tourniquet. At the same time he realised Lady Helen was shouting fearlessly at Carew Kingston, shooing him away. All the prince could do was succumb to the pain as he watched the blood pump out through the cloth of his trousers and feel the return of the shock and nausea he had felt after the wounding at Plevna. A sickening coldness began creeping through his body as he gritted his teeth and tried to fend off the encroaching wave of faintness. Then Lady Helen was leaning over him. Her hair touched his cheek. She had the tray cloth in her hand and pressed it against his thigh.

'Oh, prince! Oh, my dear, my dear... Here!' He took the cloth from her. 'Go away!' she screamed at Carew Kingston who stood just behind her, his shadow falling across the prince's eyes as he looked up. For a brief moment he was certain the revolver would be used again, this time to kill him. 'Go away!' she cried.

Carew Kingston did retreat several steps. He paused and when he spoke his voice was hoarse and rather distant.

'I have one more thing to do.'

It was as if he were talking to himself. They both looked

at him. Perhaps there was a simultaneous and instinctive awareness of what he intended. The prince braced himself and even tried to stand. Lady Helen, her head turned, raised one hand in restraint.

'Don't shoot!' she cried.

'You may think I am guilty but I am not! I must simply mete out my own justice! My exile is finished now! Death is finished! There is nothing left of it!'

'What do you mean?' she whispered.

He did not hear, it seems. Slowly, with an awful dignity, he brought the revolver up to his own mouth.

'Oh, my God, no!' she shouted.

He pulled the trigger. His whole body was shot backwards by the force of the bullet and he fell supine on the grass. In the wake of the explosion and the slight jerk of the limbs as he died, Lady Helen made no sound. She gasped open-mouthed, one mechanical gasp after another, still leaning over the prince, unable, it seemed, to make a move. Then after thirty seconds she suddenly sprang to her feet.

'I'll go and get James.'

The statement was matter-of-fact and calm. She remained matter-of-fact and calm for what seemed a small eternity as she stared down at the suicide. Then she brought both hands up to her face. Seeing the blood streaming from the shattered skull, she started screaming. She went on screaming as she ran across the lawn.

The prince watched her and slowly the vision of a black-canopied boat floating across smooth water superimposed itself on the garden's greenery, on the white framework of the greenhouse, on the silvery bedazzlement of sun-reflecting panes of glass. He closed his eyes. The vision floated right up to him. He saw Anna Karenina look up at him with the same bright, vivacious smile she had given him when she first met him in St Petersburg, when she had clutched him to her in mistake for her own son and her perfume, her femininity, her sensuality had engulfed him with a quickening, enchanting sweetness. He was flying down a steep lane towards her, butterflies brushing his face like dry snowflakes and the spokes of his bicycle's wheels making a whirring sound through the long grass. The river came up towards him and her smile spread out before him as calmly as the sunlit water. He flew towards her and she clutched him to her.

Then he smelled what he had smelled before as a young officer, the smell, sweet and oily, of fresh blood. It came in little eddies through the hot perfumes of the garden and filled his nostrils. He heard Lady Helen's voice shouting out, 'James! James!' The shouts were faint and seemed part of a dream.

They were obliterated almost instantly by the shrill, sharp, explosive sound of a locomotive whistle piercing the afternoon quiet and trailing off into echo after echo after echo.

Epilogue

Months later he contentedly watched Portland Place through the tall windows of his drawing room. The lamps were lit, shedding pools of light at intervals along areas of cobble and paving. The wet evening looked beautifully serene. Hansom cabs went by in ones or twos, awakening minor staccato echoes among the tall houses and emphasising the width of the street. If the curtains were not drawn, it was because he liked to stare out at the gleam of rainy stonework and shiny wrought iron railing that fronted his own house. Beyond this static foreground, made mysterious by darkness, was the chiaroscuro of shadows as umbrellas moved under the lamps and splashes of light came from metalwork on cabs or the oil-lit interiors of passing omnibuses. All was magnified by the rain into soft, liquid, painterly streaks in keeping with his mood.

He was content because he had no reason to be otherwise. The winter season was coming to an end. Soon he would have to make plans for the annual visit to the Tula estate, along with the likelihood that his mother-in-law might be coming to stay for several months. Her health was improved after Princess Alisa's extended visit during the summer when, so it turned out, there had been a few weeks of considerable anxiety over her back pain. One doctor had even thought she might be confined to a wheelchair for life. Eventually all was well. In the meantime, though, the prince had 'kicked his heels' – a phrase he often used now in an effort to be more conspicuously English than ever – literally from one engagement to another, from one house party to another, from card game to horse race to theatre visit throughout his grass-widowhood. One thing he had not done: he had not mounted a bicycle. The hurt to his thigh had been too painful, he usually took care to explain if anyone queried his limp. He was reminded of the sharp pain of the bullet wound once again as he turned sharply away from the drawing room window.

There was a sound behind him. Momentarily all he heard was the low hiss of the gas lamps on either side of the chimneybreast, slightly louder even than the soft crackle of a coal falling in the fire. Then came soft footsteps and he knew it was Princess Alisa.

She came into the drawing room dressed for that evening's dinner in a loose but elegantly fashionable dark-blue Liberty gown that was enlivened by a choker of pearls at the neck and a tiara worn majestically in tight control of her abundant blonde hair. Turning from the window to greet her, the prince could hardly fail to notice the glass-fronted portrait above the mantelpiece containing his wife's face, younger perhaps by a couple of years, looking in mauve-eyed brilliance from below modest curves of eyebrow directly at him, only for his gaze to meet the very same eyes shining happily as she approached.

'What were you looking at, dear? In any case, the curtains ought to be drawn.'

He said he had just been watching the traffic in Portland Place. In fact, what he had been thinking about earlier, before the sheer thoughtless pleasure of contemplating the traffic had proved more attractive, was how successful he had been in erasing the whole episode of Stadleigh Court from his mind, especially as he knew his wife had her own good reasons for suspecting he had not told her the whole truth.

'Dinner will be ready in fifteen minutes, my dear.' Speaking as she looked down at the fire, she pulled the bell-pull beside the chimneybreast. 'I must just go and see that the table's properly arranged. My Nathalie'll be dining with us tonight.'

Nathalie was employed as her lady's maid but because the employment had begun in Russia they tended to regard each other as bosom friends. He heard Princess Alisa speaking to someone immediately after leaving the room and practically at once a young maid came in to draw the curtains. Rather embarrassingly he found himself nervously pulling at the starched cuffs of his dress shirt, as if they were not extending the requisite length beyond the sleeves of his velvet jacket. As he did this, a mantelpiece clock tinkled out the half-hour in discreet strokes almost in time with the sound of the runners being pulled along the curtain rails. The maid curtsied to him and left.

A little fastidiously and perhaps too automatically for his own liking he felt for his watch, flipped open the lid and checked it against the clock on the mantelpiece. The gesture reminded him – again for no clear reason – of the way he had consulted his pocket watch after his bicycling accident. He was reminded at that instant of his injury and the damage done to his clothes. Now, standing in front of the fire, dressed formally for the evening meal, he could not help smiling at how the formality surrounding the London custom of always dressing for dinner contrasted with the state of things when he had first met Lady Helen. Princess Alisa would have been shocked, he thought. He replaced his watch in the pocket of his waistcoat.

The front door bell rang on the floor below. It was a distant ringing and the sound was hardly audible. Since there was no ensuing sound of voices or hurried footsteps, the prince resumed his contemplation of the painting above the mantelpiece until he heard a faint footfall. It was Cotton. He entered almost noiselessly, bowed and approached with such an ingratiating and concerned expression that the prince inhaled quite sharply as though having suffered a very unexpected, caustic insult.

'Sir, I have taken the liberty of showing a lady into the study. She was most anxious to speak to you alone.'

'Alone? Who on earth?'

'Alone, sir, yes.'

'Why?'

'Well, sir, I think you know her. She comes from… If I mention a certain name, may I whisper it, sir?'

'Are you absolutely sure you must be so discreet?'

'I am, sir.'

Cotton leaned forward and whispered. The prince expressed his amazement by pursing his lips.

'Well, then, I think, I'd better… Yes, thank you, Cotton.'

He nodded, swallowed hard, acknowledged Cotton's tactfulness in treating the matter so delicately and followed him out of the drawing room, down the stairs and into his ground-floor study.

If he were to meet the person alluded to by Cotton, he

knew it might be hard to suppress delight at seeing her again. Equally, it would be difficult to avoid recalling what had happened. He could hardly fail to be reminded of the bullet wound to his thigh and the doctor's rapid treatment of it that had most certainly saved him from the disease of wounding. It was so fully healed by the time Princess Alisa returned from Russia that he attributed the scar to his bicycling accident. Yet it was precisely his wife about whom he now worried most, since she had unimaginably sensitive emotional antennae that would instantly perceive the undercurrents of feeling set racing by someone whose unusual beauty had set his own heart racing so fast.

At first glance, though, he could not be sure. She had her back to him and was facing towards the large wall mirror near his desk. Even when she turned on hearing the approaching footsteps and Cotton's introductory words, the hood of her cloak, still wet from the rain, concealed her face so successfully he did not recognise her immediately. It was only when he invited her to sit down that he glimpsed her features. The brilliant blue of her eyes shone out at once and dazzled him. She was clutching a bag very tightly as she sat down and kept it firmly in her lap with gloved fingers when she was seated.

They spoke simultaneously, he saying, 'I am delighted' and she saying, 'Prince, I apologise for not giving any notice…' and both laughing a little awkwardly. He drew up a chair.

The encounter had its dangers. There was so much that could not be broached, just as he had to quell the immediate impulse to acknowledge her commanding beauty by smiling too much or being too obviously appreciative. A still greater danger was the sort of embarrassing constraint that could stiffen and perhaps in the end curtail any fondness between them.

'I had so hoped,' he said, 'I might have heard something from your father about, well…though, no news is good news, I suppose…'

'My dear prince,' she announced in the hostess manner she had used when they first met, 'I haven't much time. There's a cab waiting outside. I have something for you, you see, but first of all I must apologise on my father's behalf.'

He was grateful for her forthright way of dealing with his unease. Her urgency spared him any more politeness.

'I will be brief. We owe you explanations and apologies, I know, but, you see, my father simply did not receive your Christmas greetings, I'm afraid. Isobel simply did not trouble to have anything sent across. They're no longer on speaking terms, which is all very sad. She insists on staying in the Court and my father prefers to live in what was my cottage. Oh, you can't imagine what difficulties there've been! It was only last week, you see, I learned your London address because it was only then I discovered your card. And then of course there was the difficulty over *her* will – you know who I mean – and no money was forthcoming due to a court challenge and, of course, the deaths of both beneficiaries, so the financial situation was very – well, very unsatisfactory.'

She spoke it all with the sort of concentrated urgency due not only to a waiting cab but also because it had been learned by heart and he readily imagined that she might have rehearsed it all beforehand. His immediate reaction was to leave all the 'difficulties' to one side. As if aware of this, she patted the bag she was holding in her lap.

'Yes, well,' she said, drawing in a breath, 'I won't trouble you with an account of our worries. They will, I hope, remain quite private.'

'Of course.'

She paused as if verifying his meaning. A logjam of uncertainties was slowly allowed to free itself, it seemed. She raised her chin stiffly. Things had obviously changed since he had last seen her. She had changed, he thought. Her beautiful eyes no longer scrutinised him with the intensity he remembered. They were much softer, more understanding and, strange to say, more sensitive and private in expressing the shadings of distress and disappointment of which she had just been speaking.

'You must have thought it so rude, terribly rude of us,' she began saying. 'No response, nothing…'

'I assumed your father might have been too preoccupied.'

She took in a deep breath. 'Yes, that's been the trouble. So much has been lost, you see. When it happened, things just got lost.'

'Lost?'

'Yes, lost. You didn't know, I suppose?'

'No.'

'It was my stepmother Lady Isobel who started it. She decided on fumigation.'

'Excuse me?'

'She decided to fumigate.'

His mouth dropped open in surprise. 'That means? Pardon me, I…'

'I don't really know how it began, but she apparently found someone who said that the tower had to be fumigated and in doing the fumigating the whole tower caught fire. Everything was burnt. Of course, it was dusty, smelly, full of old stuff...'

'You mean the servants were burned?'

'No, no, they'd been sent back to Russia. It happened after they'd gone. And the fire didn't just destroy the tower, it went right along that whole wing. Father's study was burnt as well. Local firemen managed to save the stairs and the hall and about half of the Court, but there isn't a lot left. My stepmother's still there. She insists on being Lady Isobel and having charge of what's left. And my father's in the cottage, as I said. He has the bedroom you slept in. You see, I'm not living there any more.'

'You're not living there.' He found himself repeating the words, quite neutrally, without any note of query or surprise.

'No, I'm not living there. I couldn't stand being there after what happened. My father's now in charge of the little commune. I got married, you see.'

The news had a shockwave impact. In a way it was more shocking than the news of the fire or the news of her parents' separation. He could understand what a tinderbox the tower might have been and how marital conflict might cause its own conflagration, but Lady Helen being married implied that an earthquake had occurred in her life.

'Congratulations,' he stammered. 'I didn't know. When did you...'

'Just before Christmas. Oswald's mother died last autumn. He couldn't think of marriage so long as his mother was alive.'

'Ah!'

'Yes, I'm a married lady. I'm Mrs Helen Holmcroft.' She gave a contented little laugh. 'And we're very happy. Oswald's up here for a conference on Cromwell. It's a happy coincidence we could come up to London together.'

He nodded. It was as if what she had just said so distanced her that she was literally carried from him like someone disappearing away into the distance on a train, obliterated now by a smoke far more dense than the smoke from the burning tower of Stadleigh Court. Yet there she was, sitting in front of him; and he nodded at his own silliness in not recognising that all along it had been Oswald Holmcroft. He also recognised she had very likely been as much an 'enemy' of the lady in the tower as Oswald himself and the others named in the document she had herself written.

Or had she? He knew it would be wrong to ask. So much had happened, as she had just told him, that to mention the name *'Karenina'* might be dangerously upsetting. Suddenly she interrupted his thinking.

'That's not really why I came, prince. No, I brought something.' She rummaged in the bag in her lap. 'I've brought something for you, something I think you should have. You see, the fire in the tower destroyed practically everything. All the wooden flooring, all the beams, everything was burned to a cinder and when all the debris was searched through about the only surviving thing was an old samovar – and this thing which father felt you should have, because I think you found it, didn't you?'

She finished her rummaging by drawing out of the bag a brightly gleaming piece of metal. She held it up much as if it was a weapon or a not very pretty object she hoped to sell at auction. He saw it was the steel horseshoe he had found on the river bottom by the old ford. The nails had gone, but the impressed mark was as clear as ever. It was the 'proof' he had shown to Giles Irmingham. He had given it to the lady in the tower.

'*Akh, slava bogu!* Of course! Thank you!'

It was supposedly the only tangible 'proof' of the disputed existence of the lady in the tower, though he knew better than anyone how little it could actually prove.

'I hope you don't mind. Father said it could be a memento.' She handed it to him and quickly snapped shut the catch on the bags in her lap. 'Now I think I ought to be going.'

He detained her a moment. The feel of the metal in his hand was like a heavy coinage, if worthless, but he weighed it briefly.

'The initials of her "enemies" in that document you wrote were just as much proof, weren't they? They were a warning to Mr Kingston that you knew his real name and his real intention, didn't you? Did you also want her dead?'

'Really, prince, I don't think...'

She naturally enough waved aside the implication of the question as if it were quite beyond the bounds of probability or reason, not to say propriety, only for the gesture to be accompanied by a sudden tapping on the study door. Cotton appeared followed almost instantly by Princess Alisa. The prince rose quickly to his feet.

'My dear, I must introduce Lady... No, forgive me, Mrs Helen Holmcroft, daughter of Lord Irmingham. You remember how I told you they kindly looked after me when I had that accident with my bicycle last summer. Mrs Holmcroft, let me introduce my wife Princess Alisa.'

'Delighted to meet you, princess.'

'Yes, Mrs, er... you can stay to dinner, can't you?' Princess Alisa said. 'We would be so pleased.'

Mrs Helen Holmcroft rose slowly when addressed, assuming at once the dignified, if rather commanding manner of a Lady Helen, and smilingly extended a gloved hand.

'It is so kind of you but, you see, I have taken up far too much of your husband's valuable time already. In any case, I have a cab waiting for me outside.'

'You met my husband on his holiday last year, didn't you?'

'Yes, princess, I did. We were talking about one or two matters relating to it.'

The vaguely formal ring of this remark immediately intrigued the princess. Her expression became one of slightly amazed curiosity.

'Was this thing one of the matters?'

She had noticed the horseshoe in the prince's hand. The prince, though, knew this was a pretext. Her bright eyes were already shrewdly surveying and weighing up the other woman's attractiveness.

'An old horseshoe, princess. A memento.'

The words were uttered very lightly through smiling, parted lips, giving the impression that any further question would be extremely impolite. Their meaning was enhanced by a seemingly deliberate intensification of the steady blue gaze with which she clearly urged caution. It was a theatrical instant. Candlelight made her copper-red hair flare beacon-like and graced her features with a magic brilliance as if Rossetti's *Monna Vanna* had suddenly sprung to life.

'Forgive me, I really must be going.' She turned to the prince. 'It was so nice meeting you again.'

A gloved hand was extended. The prince transferred the horseshoe to his left hand and gave a courteous handshake with the other, bowing a little as he did in honour of the unmistakable spell cast by her beauty. Princess Alisa followed suite, although for her the handshake was more dutiful than admiring. Mrs Holmcroft dispensed polite smiles and nods to each in turn, except that she added in a kind of hasty and embarrassed afterthought: 'It does prove, you see, that she *did* exist, doesn't it? Just a memento, then. Goodbye.'

She swept out of the study followed by Cotton. Princess Alisa looked questioningly at the prince who was still holding the memento. He placed it gingerly on the desk.

'A memento of what, Mitya dear?'

'It's quite a long story really. Really quite long. I'll have to give you the gist of it over dinner.'

Also by Richard Freeborn

Novels:

Two Ways of Life
The Emigration of Sergey Ivanovich
Russian Roulette
The Russian Crucifix
American Alice

Translations:

Ivan Turgenev, Sketches from a Hunter's Album, Rudin,
Home of the Gentry, First Love and other stories, A Month in
the Country, Fathers and Sons
F. M Dostoevsky, An Accidental Family

Academic Studies:

Turgenev: The Novelist's Novelist
A Short History of Modern Russia
The Rise of the Russian novel
The Russian Revolutionary Novel: Turgenev to Pasternak
Dostoevsky
Furious Vissarion: Belinskii's Struggle for Literature, Love
and Ideas